Praise for

THE CALLER

"The crimes in *The Caller* . . . are pranks, but they're hardly harmless. In fact, they're so fiendishly creative they eat away at their victims long after the unsettling events, and the unraveling of their peace of mind, the shattering of their false senses of security, is the real subject of this terrific new book by one of Scandinavia's great mystery writers."   —*Boston Globe*

"Ms. Fossum is a classic example of the Scandinavian literary talent for cold blood . . . [she] is adept at building toward terror while writing crisply unemotional prose."   —*Washington Times*

"There is something profoundly creepy about the idyllic setting, expressed in great detail, broken up with these moments of pure negativity, almost like a David Lynch film."   —*Daily Beast*

"I think Karin Fossum is at the top of the heap of Scandinavian detective fiction, primarily because of her willingness to experiment, and her crystalline characters, perfectly sharp in every way, their motivations cruelly dissected, their behaviors impeccably real."   —Mark Rose, Bookgasm.com

"Fossum is back on track with her eighth Sejer mystery . . . Getting into the heads of the detectives, victims, and perpetrator, she offers a chilling morality play reminiscent of Ruth Rendell or even Patricia Highsmith. Good stuff for admirers of the clever and creepy."

— *Library Journal*

"The consistent focus on all the characters involved in a crime makes Fossum's stand out among Scandinavian crime authors . . . with a focus on characters and the impacts of crime, Fossum's psychological thrillers will appeal, in particular, to fans of Anne Holt and Henning Mankell."

— *Booklist*

"Fossum manages to create menace without a high body count, and strikes a realistic note by not allowing her investigators to wrap up everything."

— *Publishers Weekly*

"As in Ruth Rendell's books as Barbara Vine, readers are invited to watch helplessly as things go from bad to much, much worse for an unlucky group of basically nice people. If that's your pleasure, you could hardly do better."

— *Kirkus*

THE CALLER

Also by Karin Fossum

Don't Look Back

He Who Fears the Wolf

When the Devil Holds the Candle

Calling Out for You

Black Seconds

Broken

The Water's Edge

Bad Intentions

Eva's Eye

The Caller

Karin Fossum

Translated from the Norwegian
by K. E. SEMMEL

Mariner Books
Houghton Mifflin Harcourt
BOSTON • NEW YORK

First Mariner Books edition 2013
Copyright © 2009 by Karin Fossum
English translation copyright © 2011 by K. E. Semmel

First published with the title *Varsleren* in 2009
by Cappelen Damm AS, Oslo
First published in Great Britain in 2011 by Harvill Secker Random House

For information about permission to reproduce selections from this
book, write to Permissions, Houghton Mifflin Harcourt Publishing
Company, 215 Park Avenue South, New York, New York 10003.

www.hmhco.com

Library of Congress Cataloging-in-Publication Data
Fossum, Karin, date.
[Varsleren. English]
The caller / Karin Fossum; translated from the Norwegian by
K. E. Semmel. — 1st ed.
p. cm.
"First published with the title Varsleren in 2009" — T.p. verso.
ISBN 978-0-547-57752-4 (hardback)   ISBN 978-0-544-00218-0 (pbk.)
I. Title.
PT8951.16.O735V3713 2012
839.82'38 — dc23   2012005736

Book design by Brian Moore

Printed in the United States of America
DOH 10 9 8 7 6 5 4 3
4500584717

It's a good thing there are lies. Lord help us if everything that was said were true.

— OLD ADAGE

THE CALLER

THE CALLER

1

THE CHILD SLEPT in a pram behind the house.

The pram was from Brio, and the child was an eight-month-old girl. She lay under a crocheted blanket, wearing a matching bonnet with a string fastened under her chin. The pram sat under the shade of a maple tree; behind the tree the forest stood like a black wall. The mother was in the kitchen. She couldn't see the pram through the window, but she wasn't concerned about her sleeping baby, not for an instant.

Pottering about thoroughly content, she was light as a ballerina on her feet, not a single worry in her heart. She had everything a woman could dream of: beauty, health and love. A husband, a child, and a home and garden with rhododendrons and lush flowers. She held life in the palm of her hand.

She looked at the three photographs hanging on the kitchen wall. In one photograph, taken under the maple, she wore a flowery dress. In another her husband, Karsten, was on the front porch. The last was a photograph of her and Karsten together on the sofa, the child between them. The girl's name was Margrete. The arrangement of the three photos made her smile. One plus one is surely three, she thought — it is truly a miracle. Now she saw that miracle everywhere. In the sunlight cascading through the windows, in the thin white curtains fluttering in the breeze.

At the worktop she energetically kneaded a smooth, lukewarm dough between her fingers. She was making a chicken and chanterelle quiche, while Margrete slept beneath the maple in her little bonnet, she, too, smooth and warm under the blanket. Her little heart pumped a modest amount of blood, and it colored her cheeks pink. Her scent was a mixture of sour milk and soap. The blanket and bonnet had been crocheted by her French grandmother.

She slept heavily, and with open hands, as only a baby can.

Lily rolled the dough on a marble slate. As she swung the rolling pin, her body swayed and her skirt billowed around her legs—like a dance by the worktop.

It was summer and warm, and she was bare-legged. She set the pastry in a pie dish, poked it with a fork and trimmed the edges. Then she put a roast chicken on the chopping board. Poor little thing, she thought, and tore its thighs off. She liked the cracking sound the cartilage made when tearing from the bone. Light and tender, the meat let go easily, and she succumbed to the temptation to stick a piece in her mouth. It's good, she thought, it has just enough seasoning, and it's lean too. She filled the pie dish and sprinkled on Cheddar cheese. Then she checked the time. She didn't worry about Margrete. If the child sneezed she would know it immediately. If she coughed or hiccupped, or began to cry, she would know. Because there was a bond between them, a bond as thick as a mooring line. Even the slightest tug would reach her like a vibration.

Margrete's in my head, she thought, in my blood and in my fingers.

Margrete's in my heart.

If anyone were to harm her, I would know. Or so she thought.

She went about her business calmly. But at the back of the house, someone crept out of the dense forest and in one bound reached the pram. He pushed the crocheted blanket to the side, and Lily didn't feel anything at all.

The quiche began to turn golden.

The cheese had melted, and bubbled like lava. She glanced out the window and saw Karsten as he pulled into the driveway in his red Honda SUV. The table was set, the china old and dignified; in each glass a white napkin opened like a fan. She switched on the lights, stepped back and tilted her head, evaluating the result. She hoped her husband would see that she'd gone out of her way, that she always went out of her way. She smoothed her skirt and ran her hands through her hair. Other couples fight, she thought, other couples divorce. But that won't happen to us; we know better. We understand that love is a plant that requires tender care. Some people spread all this rubbish about being blinded by love. But she'd never understood as much as she did now, had never had this insight. Had never had such clarity of vision, or such uncompromising values. She went into the bathroom and brushed her hair. The excitement of her husband's return, the oven's heat and the low July sunlight spilling into the room made her cheeks flush and her eyes sparkle. When he stepped into the kitchen, she was ready with a bottle of Farris mineral water and a slight, elegant tilt to her hips. He carried a stack of post, she noticed, newspapers and a few window envelopes. He set them on the worktop, then went to the oven and squatted down, peering through the glass.

"It looks delicious," he said. "Is it ready?"

"Probably," she replied. "Margrete is sleeping in the pram. She's slept quite a while. Maybe we should wake her—otherwise it'll be bad getting her to sleep tonight." She reconsidered. Cocked

3

her head and looked at her husband through full black eyelashes. "Or maybe we can wait until after dinner, so we can have a little peace while we eat. Chicken and chanterelle," she said, nodding at the oven. She slipped on a pair of oven gloves, removed the quiche and set it down on a cooling rack.

It was burning hot.

"She'll certainly forgive us," her husband said.

His voice was deep and gravelly. He stood at his full height, put his arms around her waist and escorted her across the room. They both laughed because she was wearing the oven gloves; he had that look she loved so much, that teasing look she could never resist. Now he led her into the lounge, past the dining table to the sofa.

"Karsten," she whispered. But it was a weak protest. She felt like dough between his hands; she felt kneaded and rolled and poked with a fork.

"Lily," he whispered, mimicking her voice.

They fell together onto the sofa.

They didn't hear a peep out of the child beneath the tree.

Afterward they ate in silence.

He said nothing about the meal, or about the table that had been so beautifully set, but he continued to look at her with approval. Lily, the eyes said, the things you do. He had green eyes, large and clear. Because she wanted to stay thin, she tried not to eat too much, even though the quiche was delicious. Karsten was also thin. His thighs were rock hard. A thick mane of dark hair, always a little too long in the back, made him look cheeky and attractive. She couldn't imagine him gaining weight and losing his shape, or his hair, as many men did when they approached forty. She saw it happening to others, but it didn't apply to them. Nothing could sever what they had together, neither gravity nor the test of time.

"Will you clear the table?" she asked when they had finished eating. "I'll get Margrete."

Immediately he began to collect the plates and glasses.

He was quick and a tad abrupt in his movements, clacking the porcelain between his fingers, and she held her breath; she'd inherited it from her grandmother. She went into the hallway to put on her shoes. She opened the door to the warmth of the sun, the mild, gentle breeze, and the smells from the grass and forest. Then she rounded the corner of the house and walked toward the maple.

A terrible foreboding came over her.

She had shut Margrete out of her mind.

She moved faster now, to make up for what she'd done. Something about the pram was strange, she thought. It was right where she'd put it, near the trunk of the maple, but the blanket was crumpled. There's so much activity in these little ones, she thought, as she fought her terror. Because now she saw the blood. When she pulled the blanket off, she froze. Margrete was covered in blood. Lily fell to the ground. Lay there, writhing, unable to get up. She wanted to throw up. Felt something sour force its way up her throat, and she emitted a terrifying scream.

Karsten ran round the corner. He saw her contorted on the ground, and noticed the blood, slick and nearly black. He reached the pram in four steps, grabbed Margrete and held her against his chest. Shouted at Lily to get the car.

"Go, Lily!" he shouted. "Go!"

She moaned in response. He shouted louder. He roared like a wild animal, and the roar forced her, finally, to act. She rose and ran to the garage. Realized she needed the keys. Continued into the house and found them on a hook in the hallway. Then she was behind the wheel, backing out. With Margrete in his arms, Karsten yanked open the door and got in. He examined her body, looked under the clothes.

"I think she's bleeding from the mouth," he gasped. "I can't tell. I don't know how to make it stop! Can't you drive any faster? Drive faster, Lily!"

Later, neither would remember the drive to the Central Hospital. Karsten had some vague memories of running past the reception desk and pushing open the glass doors. A wild sprint through the corridors with his daughter bleeding in his arms, searching for help. Lily remembered nothing. The world spun so fast it made her dizzy. She ran after Karsten, dashing like a hunted hare that knows the end is near.

They were stopped by two nurses. One of them took Margrete and disappeared through a door. "Stay here!" she shouted.

It was an order.

Then she was gone.

The doors were made of mottled glass, the kind you can't see through. Here, at the end of the corridor, was a small waiting area, and they sat on separate chairs. There was nothing to say. After a few minutes, Karsten walked to the water cooler by the window. He pulled a paper cup from the machine, filled it and held it out to Lily. She knocked it out of his hand with a scream.

"She was making sounds," he said. "You heard it. She was breathing, Lily. I'm absolutely sure of that." He paced the room. "They have to stop it! She'll get a blood transfusion. We made it here quickly."

Lily didn't respond. A teenager with his arm in a sling walked up and down the corridor. Clearly curious about the drama unfolding just a few meters away, he stared openly at them.

"Why is it taking so long?" Lily whispered. "What are they doing?"

It was as though she were inside a wire drum rotating at high speed. It wasn't life, and it wasn't death. Later they would both refer to these minutes as pure hell, a hell that ended when a nurse came through the glass doors with Margrete in her arms. She was wrapped in a white blanket. To his amazement, Karsten saw that she jabbed at the air with her hands.

"She's completely unharmed," the nurse said.

Karsten took her from the nurse. Felt her little body in his arms. It was warm all over.

With nervous hands he began unfolding the blanket. Margrete, wearing a disposable nappy, was otherwise naked in the blanket.

"She's completely unharmed," the nurse repeated. "It wasn't her blood. We've called the police."

2

KARSTEN AND LILY SUNDELIN were led to another room where they could wait undisturbed. Lily wanted to go home. She had no desire to talk to anyone. She wanted to go back to her house and her bedroom; she wanted to retreat into a corner. She wanted to lie in her queen-sized bed with her husband and child, and remain there. Never again would she let the child sleep in the pram under the maple tree, never again let her sleep without supervision. Never again shut her out of her mind.

But they had to wait.

"What are we going to say?" she asked anxiously. "I get so nervous."

Karsten Sundelin looked uncomprehendingly at his wife. Unlike Lily, who was filled with fear, he felt, first and foremost, a boiling rage. Any charity and understanding he'd felt for others had evaporated, and left him out of breath and hot-tempered. Though he'd never had anything to do with the police, he'd never been particularly fond of them.

To him, they were coarse and simple-minded people who trampled about in black boots and silly hats. They reminded him of stocky handymen with a cluster of tools clattering on their belts; they were young and uneducated and knew nothing about the nuances of life — the details, Karsten Sundelin thought: what makes this crime against Margrete and against us particularly heinous. They won't appreciate it; they'll think it's an act of vandalism. If they find it's a teenage punk pulling a stunt, he'll get off with a warning — because the poor kid probably hasn't had an easy life. But I'll give them a piece of my mind, he thought, and sipped the bitter coffee the nurse had brought.

Lily clutched the child with an urgency that made her tremble. She studied the pictures on the wall: one of some pastel water lilies floating in a pond, another of the Norwegian mountains and endless blue skies. On a table she saw health magazines with information about what you should avoid, what you should eat and drink — or not eat and drink — and how you should live.

If you wanted to live a long life.

Karsten paced the room, extremely impatient, like an angry bull. The police station was a couple of minutes away, but because of the bureaucracy it took a while.

"Maybe they have to write a report first," he said, with tired sarcasm in his voice. He stood in front of Lily with his feet apart, his hands on his hips.

"I'm sure they write it afterward," Lily said, stroking the child's cheeks. After all the commotion, Margrete slept soundly.

At last two men strolled down the corridor. Neither wore a uniform. One man was tall and gray-haired, perhaps sixty years old; the other man was young and curly-haired. They introduced themselves as Sejer and Skarre. Sejer looked down at the sleeping child. Then he smiled at Lily. "How are you doing?"

"We won't let her sleep in the garden anymore," Lily said.

Sejer nodded. "I understand," he said. "You know what's best."

Skarre pulled a notebook from his pocket and found a chair. He seemed bright and eager, Lily thought, like a runner at the starting block.

"We have to ask you a few questions," he said.

"I should hope so," Karsten Sundelin said. "Whoever's behind this should pay for it, even if I have to take matters into my own hands."

At this, Skarre looked up, while the older inspector raised an eyebrow. Tall and muscular, with powerful fists, Karsten's temperament was evident in his eyes and in his outraged voice. The young mother sat scrunched up in the chair, closed off to the world. In an instant, Skarre had mapped out the couple's power balance: raw power versus feminine vulnerability.

"Have you been married before?" he asked Lily affably.

She looked at him, surprised. Then she shook her head.

"Boyfriends? Live-in partners?"

Now she grew slightly embarrassed.

"I've had boyfriends," she admitted, "but I also have good sense."

Of course you do, Skarre thought, but sometimes life shocks you.

"And you," he said, turning to her husband. "Anything from a previous relationship? I'm thinking of jealousy. Or revenge."

"I've been married," Karsten said in a measured tone.

"I see."

Skarre made a note, then turned his blue-eyed gaze once more on Karsten. "Was it an amicable divorce?"

"She died. Cancer."

Without losing his composure, Skarre absorbed the information. He ran his fingers through his hair, tousled it. "Have either of you had disagreements with anyone? Recently or in the past?"

Karsten leaned against the wall. As if he maintained the upper hand. Like Inspector Sejer, he was impressively tall and broad-shouldered. He glanced down at the two people for whom he was responsible, Lily and Margrete, and something rose in him, something he'd never felt before. He liked the taste of it, the rush. It's no doubt some kid, he thought. I can't wait to get my hands on him.

"We never cross anyone," he said, raising his voice.

Someone has a short fuse, Skarre thought.

Sejer grabbed a chair and sat beside Lily. He seemed friendly, and Lily liked him. He was strong and confident—not in a cocky way, but in a reassuring way that said *I'll take care of it.* "Where do you live?" he asked.

"In Bjerketun," she said. "At the housing estate there."

"How well do you know your neighbors?"

"Pretty well," she said. "We talk to them every day. We know their children too. They play in the street. The big kids push Margrete in her pram. Back and forth along the pavement in front of the house. So I can see them from the window."

Sejer nodded. He leaned over Margrete and stroked her cheek with a finger.

"I used to have one of these," he said, looking at Lily. "Many years ago. They grow up, after all. But don't think for a second that I've forgotten what it was like."

Tears formed in Lily's eyes. She liked his deep voice, his seriousness and understanding. She was reminded that policemen were like everyone else; they lived with grief and despair. When they faced tragedy, they were forced to get involved when others could just turn away in horror.

"When you get home," Sejer said, "I want you to write down everything you remember. When the little one is asleep and you've got some peace, sit down and record everything you can think of about today. From the time you got up: what did you think about? What did you do? Did anyone drive past? Did anyone call? Did someone hang up when you answered? Did you get anything in the post? Did anyone walk slowly past the house? Did you, in one way or another, feel watched? Do you remember anything from a long time ago, a quarrel or row? Write it all down. We'll be stopping by to investigate your garden. The perpetrator may have left something behind, and if so, we'll have to find it at once."

He stood, and so did Skarre. "What's your child's name?" he asked.

"Margrete," Lily said. "Margrete Sundelin."

Sejer looked at them. Lily beneath the water lilies, Karsten beneath the blue skies. The little bundle in the nappy.

"We're taking this very seriously," he said. "This incident was very cruel. But let me remind you of one thing: Margrete doesn't know anything about it."

3

WHEN SEJER AND SKARRE were back at the station, they began reconstructing the crime—because it was obviously a crime, something much worse than a cruel joke. It was brazen, calculated and mean, like nothing they had ever seen. News of the small baby found drenched in blood had spread like wildfire through the corridors of the station, finally reaching Chief Holthemann's desk. Cane in hand, he tramped into Sejer's office and hammered on the floor to express his disgust. Why he'd begun to use a cane was a mystery to everyone at the station. One friendly person had asked him how long he would need it. I'll be dragging this cane as long as necessary, he had mumbled, and if I need support for the rest of my life, so be it.

"What's all this about a child?" Holthemann said. "Can't people just steal a car or rob a bank? One can understand that kind of thing. What about the parents? Are they strong, or are they going to be on our case all the time?"

"The husband is strong, also indignant and angry," Sejer said. "His wife is jumpy as a doe."

"It's probably someone they know," Holthemann said, rapping his cane against the floor. "People argue. They bully and terrorize and lob insults at each other. Maybe it has something to do with their past. Something they've forgotten, or didn't understand the significance of."

He scraped a chair across the floor, and then sat heavily. The chief did have a sense of drama, after all, and he was definitely in his element. Originality was always interesting, and the blood-drenched baby was certainly something to talk about.

"Do you have anything to drink in that fridge?" he asked, pointing with his cane.

Sejer took out a bottle of mineral water. Skarre unrolled a map which he hung up on a whiteboard. He made some notes with a marker. They had been to the Sundelins' and had jotted down a number of details. Bjerketun was a housing estate from the early nineties, with nice, well-maintained homes, most of which had gardens, double garages and large verandas round the back. The housing estate lay four kilometers from the center of Bjerkås, and was made up of sixty homes. Those closest to the woods had built extensions, but Lily and Karsten Sundelin hadn't; they wanted to keep the garden. There, they thought, Margrete could play when she was old enough. Maybe splash in a small pool or bounce on a trampoline. Lie on a blanket and read. Behind the Sundelins' house was a dense grove of trees; on the other side of this grove was a second, larger estate called Askeland with its seventy-four homes. An older estate, the homes at Askeland had been built in the sixties, and resembled square, faded brooding boxes. The local authority assigned a third of them to welfare recipients, and this had led to an inevitable and increasing sense of decay.

Sejer studied the map. With his index finger he followed the main road from Bjerkås, where around five thousand people lived. From there he traced to Bjerketun, and from Bjerketun to Askeland. "Obviously he must have come from here," he said, and put his finger on Askeland. "He could have followed a path through the trees, carrying a container of blood under his jacket. A bottle, or a bag. I don't know what kind or where he got it. Perhaps he stood behind a tree and kept an eye on the pram, and afterward, ran back through the grove. The lab will determine the type of blood. Perhaps it's something you can buy at an abattoir. If so, we're probably dealing with an adult. Let's hope he didn't sacrifice anything to carry out his plan, a dog or cat. What do you think?"

Deep in thought, Skarre examined the map. Those who knew him were aware that his father had been a vicar, and that he'd been raised in keeping with that. Fair, trustworthy and demanding. Yet he had maintained a boyish playfulness which drew people to him—especially women. Skarre wasn't married, and had no children—at least none that he knew of. But he had seen Margrete Sundelin and her chubby cheeks, and he'd observed how she lay in her mother's embrace.

He had recognized the smell of milk and soap.

"This was carefully planned. The perpetrator must have surveyed the house, possibly for quite some time, and taken note of the family's routines. He knew what time of day Margrete slept, and perhaps even how long she slept. He could have ducked behind a tree when Lily came out of the house, and maybe enjoyed seeing her reaction. Do you know what?" Skarre said to the inspector. "This is pure evil. I'm almost speechless."

Sejer, who had a child and grandchild himself, was in complete agreement. "Holthemann, you may be right," he said. "The Sundelins may have stepped on people's toes without knowing it. They're nice, decent people, but everyone makes mistakes. Karsten Sundelin is bullheaded and uncompromising—I could see that at once. But it's just as likely we're dealing with a mentally unstable person. A woman who lost her child in a terrible way, or something along those lines. Who saw Lily walking with Margrete. You know that mother—child joy I mean. It could be someone who's been abused out for revenge, and they're striking at random. An individual who has been tormented throughout his life will happily torment others. It's an awful but easily recognizable characteristic."

"Revenge," Skarre said. "Or jealousy. The need to mark his territory."

"In any case, he's methodical," Sejer said. "He doesn't act on impulse, he stages dramas. And Lord, what a drama!"

The department chief had been listening silently. "Well, I need you to solve this!" He thanked Sejer and disappeared out into the corridor. They heard his cane thumping into the distance, a melancholic sound which, along with Holthemann, would soon go into retirement.

Skarre pulled himself away from the map. He unscrewed the lid of a Thermos, poured himself a full cup of coffee and drank greedily. Then he stood by the window and gazed down on the square where a group of journalists had gathered, like swarming wasps.

"The press are waiting," he said. "This is juicy stuff for them. What are you going to say?"

Sejer considered. "That we're keeping all possibilities open. And just like the perpetrator, we're going to be methodical. I hope to get away with three or four sentences, bow politely and return. It's OK to be a little stingy with my words today. Otherwise the story will be blown all out of proportion."

"No doubt they'll ask whether we're expecting more attacks like this," Skarre said. "How will you answer?"

"No comment."

"What would you say, just between you and me? I mean, who do you think did this?"

"I should probably keep my mouth shut," Sejer said. "It's too early to speculate."

"I won't hold you to what you say," Skarre said. "You can draw on your experience and intuition and your knowledge of people, which—as everyone says—you have in spades. If I know you,

you've already got the perpetrator in your sights now. I'm just curious. I have my own suspicions about who the perpetrator is. What this is." He raised his hands. "I'm not writing anything down," he smiled.

"It's a man," Sejer said and sank into a chair.

"Why do you think it's a man?"

"Probability." He rolled up his sleeve and scratched at his right elbow. His psoriasis flared up whenever he became agitated, or when it was really hot. The summer was hot. "Every probability suggests the following facts," Sejer went on. "He's a man between the age of seventeen and sixty, neglected and invisible. He's shy and introverted, but his awkwardness stands out. He wants respect, but doesn't have much luck. He's creative, bitter and hateful. He has a low-level job with a meager income, or he's unemployed, maybe on the dole or getting some kind of benefits. He has no close friends. He's intelligent and intuitive, but emotionally very immature. He doesn't drink, doesn't use drugs and isn't especially interested in girls. He lives simply, in a room or a small flat, or he lives with his mother. And it's possible he keeps an animal in a cage."

"What?" Skarre said incredulously. "An animal in a cage?"

"That last was a joke." Sejer smiled. "I figured you'd get it. But I thought about a rat or something similar. You asked me to paint a picture using every detail," he said. "So I used my imagination."

Sejer looked down at the crowd of reporters clustered in the square. "They look ravenous," he said. "Should we toss them some scraps?"

Skarre stood at his side. He too sized up the journalists shuffling around with their thick woolly microphones—like a group of children who had each received a giant lollipop.

"Not surprising they're here," he said. "This case has everything, drama, originality. It's a shocker."

"Maybe we've done everything wrong," Sejer said. "Maybe society relates to crime in a completely foolish way. The newspapers blow it out of proportion, and the criminal gets all the attention he wants. Maybe we ought to kill the story with silence. Force all criminals into silence."

"But what will he do if we ignore him?" Skarre asked. "We always have to take that into consideration. Will he become more dangerous, even angrier, if he doesn't get any reaction? There's something explosive about it all. We're talking about a little baby, a soap- and milk-smelling little sugar cube weighing seven or eight kilos."

"You're right," Sejer said. "He needs an audience. But it's important that we try to be balanced. I will introduce him as a person with emotions, so he feels understood. We shouldn't step on his toes."

The inspector turned his back to the window and sat for a moment at his desk. A shy man, he didn't like the prospect of going out into the square, to the sunshine and the heat and the ravenous, sensation-hungry journalists and their curiosity. But, as inspector, it was his job to be the department's public face. To inform and report, in his calm way.

"What are you thinking about?" Skarre asked, in a low, intimate voice.

"About my grandson, actually," Sejer admitted. "You know Matteus. He's at the Opera ballet school. They've just learned that one of the pupils will get the chance to make a guest appearance on the main stage. In April."

"So he's going to audition?"

"Yes," Sejer said. "On the tenth of October. For the role of Siegfried in *Swan Lake*."

"The prince."

"Yes," Sejer said. "A lot's at stake. He really wants to get that role. But there are so many good dancers."

He looked at the desk pad, a map of the world. His daughter's eighteen-year-old son had been adopted from Somalia, and now he put his finger on this country, shown in yellow. Matteus was four when he came to Norway. Now he was a promising dancer at the ballet school, with an impressive physique and rock-hard, coffee-colored muscles.

"But do you think they'll pick a black prince?" Sejer said suddenly, a little concerned. "Certain roles never seem to come in black."

"Give me an example," Skarre said.

"Robin Hood, Peter Pan."

"You're worried about people's prejudice, but you're the one who's prejudiced."

Sejer glanced apologetically at his younger colleague. "I've been thinking about it for years, I can't shake it. It's never been easy for Matteus. At school he was a loner, and had a hard time. Now this: the prince in *Swan Lake* and plenty of stiff competition. Well, we'll see how it turns out, I guess. I won't harp on about it now."

He got ready to meet the press. Straightened his back and adjusted the knot in his tie, until it was smooth and tight.

"You're thinking about the white swan girls," Skarre teased. "In feathers and tulle. And you're afraid Matteus will stand out. But even swans come in black."

"Really?" the inspector said.

"There's a pond with black swans at the cathedral in Palma," Skarre said. "They're obviously much more attractive than the white swans, and they're rarer."

Sejer headed out to the journalists. Skarre's words made him feel a little more optimistic.

That evening Sejer sat in front of his television, in a comfortable chair by the window, with a pillow supporting his back.

Sejer's dog, a Chinese Shar-Pei called Frank, lay at his feet, and was, like most Chinese, dignified, unapproachable and patient. Frank had tiny, closed ears—and thus bad hearing—and a mass of gray, wrinkled skin that made him look like a chamois cloth. His eyes, black and intelligent but with limited vision, were set deep within the wrinkles.

The case with the baby from Bjerketun got extensive coverage. Because it was a sensation, he thought, an oddity. It terrifies people—which is no doubt what the perpetrator wants.

He remained seated in front of the television. First he saw himself in a report from TV Norway, then on *The Day in Review* at seven, and finally on the evening news at eleven. He repeated the same words from channel to channel.

We're taking this very seriously.

His name and title—Inspector—flashed at the bottom of the screen. With mixed emotions he observed his own performance, noticing how the years had altered him, how he'd grown grayer, more chiseled and thinner. His cheekbones and chin stood out clearly, the slate-gray eyes deep-set. Inevitably, his thoughts gravitated toward death, how it grew from within and slowly overtook his features one by one.

Here I come: skull and bones.

He bent down and patted Frank's head, shoving the dark thoughts away. His grandson, Matteus, came to mind. Dreamlike images from *Swan Lake,* which he'd seen a few times on television, flickered across his inner eye. The small ballerinas with feathers on their heads leaping lightly across the stage, the plaintive music. A black Siegfried. Well, he thought, if he's a good enough dancer, he'll get the part. That's how it works. There's justice in the world. In our part of the world anyway; we can afford it. But justice comes at a price. Some get what they deserve. A few years in prison if they've transgressed severely, or, if they're unusually good dancers, the role of the prince in *Swan Lake* on the Opera's main stage. And Matteus was just that. In Sejer's view, at any rate, he was a remarkably good dancer. Black, strong and exotic, full of daring, exceptional. Sejer let his head loll, his hands on the armrests. His thoughts circled back to Margrete Sundelin, the baby. Someone had planned that assault carefully, and in mere seconds created a horrifying situation for her parents. A quake they must have felt deep within, and which they will remember forever. But why Margrete? Why the Sundelins?

Near midnight, he rose and turned off all the lights. For a moment he stood in the middle of the living room, observing the outline of the heavy oak furniture. He had inherited the pieces from his parents, and they reminded him of old, patient friends who had always sat there. Sometimes, when he stood alone in the dark just like this, in his own rooms, he would fantasize something he never shared with anyone. His wife Elise sitting in the tall chair by the window and whispering: *Just go to bed, I'll be there shortly.* But it had been a long time since she'd sat in the tall chair. Elise had died of cancer; he had become a widower at a young age, and his life had turned out differently from how he'd thought. It had taken him a long time to find another path through life. But that's no different from anyone else, he thought. Frank followed him from room to room. Like Sejer, Frank was slow and deliberate, with his own elegant inaccessibility. When the entire flat was dark, he shuffled into the bedroom on his stumpy legs and plopped on his mat, where he would stay throughout the night guarding his master with an alertness that only Chinese fighting dogs possess. Sejer stood in the darkness listening, thinking he'd heard a far-off noise. It could be the lift, he thought, though it was pretty late and there wasn't much activity in the building at this hour. Then he remembered that Elna across the corridor often worked evenings. She was a cleaner down at Aker Brygge, and had long, hard days. He went into his bedroom and undid the top buttons of his shirt. Just then the doorbell rang. In a flash, Frank rushed into the hallway, sat by the front door and whined, a guard dog. His daughter Ingrid came to mind, and Matteus. Had something happened, something they needed him for? They would have called. He hesitated a few seconds, but it never occurred to him not to open the door, because someone wanted something from him, and he was always ready to serve. That was his nature. But there was no one at his door, just an empty corridor with gray brick walls, an emergency fire box with an ax, and a handrail made of cast iron. He heard the lift descend, and followed the orange light with his eyes. Then he saw something lying on his doormat—a small gray envelope. He snatched it up and went inside, hurried to the window where he stood and waited. A minute or so later he saw a figure cross the car park. Young, he thought, and very fast. Definitely a man. Slender. Under forty, probably under thirty. The figure disappeared into the darkness. That was the man, Sejer was certain, who'd left the message on his doormat. In the kitchen he snapped on the light and examined the envelope. It was made of recycled paper and was blank. He got a sharp knife from a drawer and tore open the envelope. Inside was a picture postcard of an animal: a brown-black creature with a large, shaggy tail. He held the postcard with utmost care, sniffed it and read the back:

Norwegian mammals. Wolverine. Photographer Gøran Jansson.

Then he read the short message: *Hell begins now.*

He looked down at Frank, who had followed him like a shadow. "A wolverine," he said. "Isn't that something?"

He turned off the light in the kitchen and headed back to the bedroom. The dog lumbered to his mat and fell asleep. Sejer held the postcard up to the lamp on the bedside table.

Sleepless for a long while, he stared at the wolverine. My face on the television, he thought, on three channels.

My name at the bottom of the screen.

A piece of cake to track me down.

22

I'm in the phone book.

Finally he switched off the bedside lamp. Thought of the child, Margrete, and of everything that had happened, and of everything that might happen.

Hell begins now.

4

IS MOTHER HAD been drinking heavily throughout the day and now lay sleeping on the sofa, her mouth wide open. He could see the pale, dry roof. She wore nothing but a silky bathrobe; it was black and had fallen open at the front, so he could see one of her breasts.

The brown nipple reminded him of a hard little turd.

His name was Johnny Beskow, and he cut a slight figure. But he had a distinct talent for mischief, and now he was putting it to use. His eyes were cold and clear as he studied his mother. He let his disgust flow freely because it allowed him to feel something. When he felt something he was completely alive, and his blood pumped more easily throughout his body. He stared at her as she lay on the sofa, and he loathed her; his loathing took his breath away, made his cheeks burn. He loathed everything about her: her personality, her appearance, her behavior. Her sounds, her smells. She was thin and pale and haggard. She was unkempt and pathetic, a drunk, and all he felt was disgust. The thought that he'd come from her made him feel sick; he could barely stomach it. Once, many years ago, she'd wailed and squeezed him out of her body in a long, desperate scream. Without happiness or joy or expectation.

She had long dark hair and pale skin. Her age showed in a green web of lines at her temples and on her wrists. Her feet were small and narrow, with dry, hard skin and thick gray-white crusts on her heels.

"Where does my father live?" he said. "Tell me."

She obviously didn't hear him, because she was deep inside a thick vodka haze, and there she would remain for hours. She would rise from the sofa only at nightfall, then blink a few times and look at him in surprise. As though she'd forgotten she had a seventeen-year-old son who also lived in the house.

Johnny glanced at the wall, at a black-and-white photo of his mother. It had been taken when she was young. Each time he looked at this picture he would slide his eyes toward his mother on the sofa and think: What happened to her? The smiling woman on the wall, with her radiant eyes?

As a child he'd often asked about his father. "Where is he?" he'd prodded. "Where is my father? Is he abroad?"

"Your father?" she would say, her voice full of bitterness. "Don't keep on about that. He's long gone, over the hills and far away."

Johnny imagined the hills. A man ran through the picture in his mind, across a green hill only to disappear, before materializing on the next hilltop. He continued over the landscape in the same way, from hilltop to hilltop, until he was gone.

He sat motionless in his chair, staring icily at his mother. Or, as he liked to think: I'm watching her with the eyes of a fish. I could wake you, if I wanted. One day, when I've reached my limits, I will shock you from your stupor. And you will get up from the sofa screaming, covering your face with your hands. I can boil the kettle, and throw water in your face. Or, he thought, hot fat. Hot fat is definitely more effective. Fat burns into the skin for a long time, it doesn't evaporate like water. But, it occurred to him, we probably don't have fat. He stood up and went to the kitchen, opened the fridge. In the door was a bottle of cooking oil, which would certainly do the trick on the day he finally got her up from that sofa and made his mark once and for all. Because I have my limits, and if she pushes me too far, she will pay. God knows she will pay.

He returned to the living room and leaned against the window. Looked out at the driveway and front garden. Nobody is as messy as we are, he thought. They probably talk about us in the other houses: that crazy woman and her scrawny kid live there. In the garden, plastic rubbish bags and old paint buckets were strewn about. A rusted wheelbarrow filled with rainwater, a woodpile under a black tarpaulin; bushes and weeds had eaten their way toward the house with a force only nature can summon. The neglected house was rotting. His red Suzuki Estilete was parked by the steps. He sat down again. He tried to imagine his father, the man she wouldn't tell him about. If only she would give him a clue. A name, or something that would give him an idea of who he was. Or *where* he was. And if he was dead, Johnny would like to know where he was buried. To see his name etched in stone. Did her drinking drive you out of the house? he wondered. Did you find another woman? Did you have children with her, children who are better than me and who you wanted to keep? Do you know that I'm sitting here? Are you ignoring me like a dull toothache? He leaned his head back and closed his eyes. Thought of the little baby under the tree. You're OK, he thought, they will watch you all the time now, your mum and dad. They won't lose sight of you for a second, day or night. He imagined them huddled close, the little trinity. The sacred union, isolated from the rest of the world, packed inside happiness and contentment. From now on anything could happen. Every little step involved a risk; anywhere outside the house was a danger zone. And it was he who'd given them this new perspective. He, Johnny Beskow, had shown them reality.

He remained seated for a while and reveled in these thoughts. The entire time he observed his mother with the eyes of a fish.

A week before the incident Margrete had been pictured in the local newspaper under the caption "Heartbreaker of the Week." Karsten Sundelin had taken the photograph with his old Hasselblad camera. Margrete had sat on the kitchen table, stark naked except for the white bonnet tied under her chin, her body the color of marzipan from Anthon Berg. Now Margrete lay sleeping in the middle of the double bed. She'd just been bathed and was wrapped in a soft pink blanket. Lily had added some drops of baby oil to the water, which made her skin glow and smell wonderful. She was too warm, but Lily could not bring herself to take the blanket off. The small bundle in the middle of the bed reminded her of a cocoon, and she wanted her little girl never to unfold herself, grow up and walk out.

Out of the room, out of the house, out into the world.

Karsten had taken the pram to the rubbish dump. The blood had dripped to the bottom and seeped into the mattress; it was impossible to wash away. Slick as oil, and with a disgusting, fishy smell. Besides, it was an old pram they'd inherited from a family in the neighborhood. Karsten had bought a new one. It was covered in dark red corduroy, and was Emmaljunga's most expensive pram. Only the very best for Margrete now, they thought, after everything that had happened.

"She can sleep on the veranda," Karsten proposed, "where you can see the pram from the window."

Lily stroked Margrete's cheeks. The touch made the child's eyelid quiver. "We'll see," was all she said.

They lay on either side of the child. Both had hoisted themselves up on their elbows, forming a protective barrier against the world, and she slept between them like a pea in a pod.

She breathed fast and easily.

There was no one like her.

"You know what I'll do when I get a hold of him?" Karsten said.

He talked between clenched teeth. Lily didn't want to hear it. She straightened the pink baby blanket, wanting it smooth and tight all the way round. She didn't answer her husband's question. Something evil had come out of the woods, and now something evil was growing inside the man she had married.

"I will tear his arms off," Karsten said. "And his legs. He's worth no more than an insect."

Lily rolled onto her back. She stared at the ceiling and the glass bowl which covered the light bulb; she noticed dead flies in it.

"Do you think it's something we've forgotten?" she whispered. "Something we've done, something we've said?"

Now Karsten rolled onto his back. The movement caused Margrete to sigh, and the bed creaked a little under his weight. "What's that supposed to mean? Are you asking whether we did something to deserve this?"

Lily bit her knuckle. The initial shock had abated. They were back at home. Margrete was in one piece, and healthy, and vibrantly alive. But now other thoughts appeared, thoughts she hadn't been prepared for. Why right here, in our community? Why us, and our garden, and our child?

Something so twisted could be no coincidence—that would be incomprehensible.

"Not something to deserve it," she said. "But maybe we've done something that someone noticed."

"We live our life," Karsten said. "We do the same things everyone else does. We're decent people."

Lily tried to breathe evenly and calmly. If she could control her breathing then her heart would find peace, but she couldn't manage it.

"Maybe he stood there watching us," she whispered. "Have you thought about that? Maybe he hid behind a tree as I lay on the ground. I didn't look that way at all. I didn't think that far ahead." She propped herself up on her elbow again. "Did you see anything? Hear anything?"

Karsten replayed the paralyzing seconds in his head. He lay listening to his own memories, searching for something which would put him on the right track. "Yes," he remembered, "I heard something. Something starting up in the woods. There's a trail that runs to Askeland which the loggers use. It could have been a chain saw."

"A chain saw?" she said, disappointed. "That doesn't help us at all."

Karsten reconsidered, and snapped his fingers. "Actually, no, it wasn't a chain saw. It might have been a moped."

5

THE PICTURE POSTCARD which Sejer had found on his doormat was a small, cheap card with a glossy finish. The image of the wolverine fascinated him. On his bookshelf he kept thirteen volumes of Aschehoug and Gyldendal's complete Norwegian encyclopedia from 1984, and he figured the wolverine would be listed with both an article and an illustration.

He found it on page 495.

Wolverine. *Gulo gulo*. Our largest species in the weasel family is also called, in some locations in the northern and western regions of Norway, a mountain cat. A loner, the wolverine has a short head and a tail that is 25–35 centimeters in length. Black-brown in color with a yellowish stripe along its side, it's about as tall as a gun dog and very muscular. The wolverine lives in mountainous regions, but researchers believe it was originally a forest-dweller.

The wolverine is a sly and sharp hunter. In winter it lives on reindeer; in summer it preys on sheep, in addition to smaller rodents. From time to time it will eat a hare or fox, a white grouse and a wood grouse. In February/March females produce on average a litter of two to three young. The den is often made in a snowdrift against a low mountain wall in rugged terrain. Their numbers, in 1964, were estimated at 150. In southern Norway, the wolverine is listed as an endangered species as far as South Trøndelag.

When he had finished reading, Sejer studied the color photograph with keen attention.

The wolverine looked like a cross between a dog, a marten and a cat. Is that how you want to appear? he wondered. Like a rare, endangered animal? A sly and sharp hunter? He clapped the encyclopedia shut, put it back on the shelf and sat beside the telephone to make a call. Karsten Sundelin answered immediately. He had taken the day off to be with his wife and child. They were both dizzy and confused after all that had happened.

"How are you doing?" Sejer asked.

"Hm, how do you think?" Karsten Sundelin said. His voice was bitter and sharp, like a saw. "Lily doesn't feel safe anymore, and God knows if she'll ever feel safe again. So much has been destroyed, to put it bluntly."

"And Margrete?" Sejer asked carefully.

"She'll be marked by this too," Karsten said. "In one way or another. Kids are affected by something like this, don't you think?"

Sejer thought for a moment. "Is there a bookshop out where you live?"

"No," Sundelin said. "There's no bookshop. We have to drive to the shopping center, which is close to Kirkeby. We just have a Spar down near Lake Skarve. They actually sell a little bit of everything. I mean, they have medicine, a few toys, as well as food."

Sejer wrote this in his notebook. "How do I get there?"

"You drive to Bjerkås Center. Then go right. You'll see it as soon as you reach the waterfront. They have these ridiculous flags in front of the shop."

"What about people on the Askeland housing estate?" Sejer asked. "Do they shop at Spar too?"

"They used to have a shop called Joker, but it closed, so now they use our Spar. More and more people are going to Kirkeby, though, because they have a better selection. We used to have everything here," he added. "Bakery. Hairdresser, café and bank. But they're closing down, one after another. Now we've just got a grocery and petrol station and a little bar next to the petrol station."

Sejer thanked him and hung up. It was still early morning. He took Frank with him and drove the twenty-five kilometers to Bjerkås. On the first right, just as Sundelin had told him, he saw the flags fluttering by the water. A narrow asphalt path led down to the pretty beach, but once outside the car it didn't seem so appealing. There was no sand, just hefty, sharp stones like an insurmountable barrier. Which might explain why the Spar chain of shops got permission to run a business in such a place; clearly, you couldn't swim here. Farther down he saw boats pulled up on the shore. Some lay upside down. He began to walk along the beach. Since no one else was around, he let Frank off the leash. The dog ran ahead, trotted clumsily past the large stones, then was out testing the water, but returned immediately.

"Is that so, Frank?" Sejer said. "A little too cold for you, huh?"

The lake was calm as a mirror, not a ripple. He sat on one of the overturned boats and noticed a family of ducks. Frank stood growling by the water. His ears pulled back, a wrinkle in his snout.

"Stop it," Sejer said. "Let them be. They live here."

Water rings followed in the ducks' wake.

Sejer stood and stared at the main road. Bjerkås had roughly five thousand residents. They'd once had a dairy; he had passed the old red-brick building on his way down to the water. When he looked over to the other side of the lake he saw a large, white building a short distance up the ridge. An old cloister. The cloister had a little chapel where they arranged concerts and readings. He called Frank and walked him back to the car. Then he went into the shop; the delicatessen smelled of something warm and freshly cooked and, like a hungry dog, he moved in that direction. After thinking it over, he bought two meatballs.

Then he wandered around carrying the warm aluminium bag. When he got to the checkout, he found what he was looking for: a rack of postcards. There were pictures of kittens and puppies and horses, and there were small packs with thank-you notes and birthday cards. One instantly caught his attention. He picked it off the rack and read the back: *Norwegian mammals. Lynx. Photographer Gøran Jansson.*

With this discovery Sejer looked around with new eyes. He has been here, he thought. He lives here in Bjerkås, or perhaps in Askeland. It's even possible he shops at this Spar. Sejer put his bag on the conveyor belt. He grabbed three newspapers and nodded at the girl behind the till. "Do you have more of these cards? With other animals?"

She glanced at the picture of the lynx and shook her head, then pushed a streak of bleached-white hair away from her forehead, so that her little eyebrow piercing came into view.

"No idea," she said. "I don't keep track of those cards."

"So you don't remember one with a wolverine?"

"A wolverine?"

She hesitated. Apparently she didn't know about wolverines. She was very young, Sejer thought. Her green Spar uniform had a name tag which said her name was Britt. She keyed in his items. He paid seven kroner, sixty øre for the lynx. When he got back to the car, he gave one of the meatballs to Frank, then thumbed quickly through the newspapers.

BLOOD-SOAKED BABY FOUND IN GARDEN.

GROTESQUE JOKE IN BJERKETUN.

SLEEPING BABY BATHED IN BLOOD.

Our friend likes to be in the spotlight, Sejer thought. Now he's getting his moment.

He chewed small bites of his meatball as he stared across the water. Lake Skarve lay before him like a mirror. The ducks rocked gently on the water, undisturbed.

"That was a damn fine meatball, Frank." He pulled his mobile out of his pocket and found Skarre's number. "There will be more attacks," he said. "We're dealing with a beast of prey."

34

6

JOHNNY BESKOW TOOK off on his Suzuki.

He shifted gears and sped away, relaxed and free as a bird. He wore his red helmet, lined with small yellow wings on either side. On his belt he had a Swiss army knife. With the knife he could stab and cut, open a bottle of cola or, if he had a mind to, slice the tongue from his mother's mouth. He never went anywhere without it. It was a relief to get away from the house, to leave behind the smell, the disarray and his mother's pointless babbling. He loved riding his moped, loved driving at high speeds and feeling the rush of wind on his face. While he drove, he imagined people's faces as they read about the incident in Bjerketun: the collective gasp of horror and fright and indignation. Angry men, upset women, furious old people. The thought made him smile as he zoomed along. He almost wanted to clap his hands, but he thought it best to keep them on the handlebars. No one should take life for granted, he thought. They shouldn't take anything for granted.

Everyone dies.

I'll show them, damn it.

He parked at the Shell station down in Bjerkås and bought newspapers. Next to the station was a small bar with Formica tables and slot machines where he liked to drink a cola. It felt good to walk around freely, without people knowing who he was, be the talk of the town but anonymous at the same time. He settled on a bench outside the station and quickly scanned the papers. Karsten Sundelin from Bjerketun was interviewed by *VG*, and he made it clear that whoever had done this to his family shouldn't feel safe for a single second.

"What do you mean by that?" *VG*'s reporter asked.

"It's not fit to print," Sundelin answered.

Johnny folded the newspapers and put them in the storage compartment under the seat of the moped, started the motor and drove on. Not fit to print. Ha! he thought. Boy, I'm really scared now. After a few minutes he reached the Sparbo Dam. He turned right and drove the last stretch down a narrow forest path, got off the moped and leaned it against the trunk of a spruce. Then he walked to the water. In the middle of the dam was a sluice where the water flowed into a black pipe. You could hear the force of it like a strong, continual thrum. Rumor had it that, once, a boy had balanced on the dam—probably in May during exams—to capture another badge on his graduation cap, and he fell off the edge and was swallowed up by the pipe. They found his body a few kilometers down the valley. Johnny stayed at the bank a little while and observed the landscape, the glimmering water, the silent forest. He took a few careful steps on the wall, which was forty centimeters wide; you could easily keep your balance on it for a while, but if you walked out too far—like all the way to the sluice in the middle—it got serious. The sluice was enclosed in a cage, and the cage was always locked. Only those who maintained the dam had the key. But it was entirely possible to climb over the cage and cross to the other side. That is, if you could bear the sound of the gushing water without losing your composure. Johnny stared down into the dark water, elated at what he'd put in motion. I may be small, he thought—just a skinny seventeen-year-old—but I have hidden talents. How good it felt to shock people.

He sat on the dam wall and looked across the water, which thundered through the sluice into the pipe. After about fifteen minutes, he maneuvered his way back to solid ground. The Sparbo Dam, he knew, was a freshwater source for thousands of people, and what gushed into the black pipe ended up in people's taps.

So he urinated in the water before he sped off.

Johnny Beskow had a grandfather who lived in Bjørnstad.

His name was Henry Beskow, and he lived on a cul-de-sac called Rolandsgata. Near his grandfather's house, which was the very last house on the street, and also the oldest, there was a small rocky knoll from which a girl watched Johnny as he droned past on his moped. He had seen her many times before—she sat there often—and she was rude to everyone who passed. It was her street, her territory. She was thin and pale and freckled, and maybe around ten years old. The most striking thing about her was the fiery red plait of hair that extended down her back. She sneered at him; her incisors were the size of sugar cubes.

"Lingonberry head!" she shouted.

She meant the red helmet. Johnny braked. He narrowed his eyes and focused his gaze in a threatening, concentrated ray. But she didn't seem to be afraid of anything. That's because you don't know any better, he thought. I'll be back for you, you freckled little shit. Ignoring her, he drove the last stretch to his grandfather's, parked and hung his helmet on the handlebars. He wiped his shoes on the mat and went inside. The old man, who had bad legs, was sitting in a wing chair near the window. He was wrapped up in a woolen blanket, his feet on a footstool. Arthritis had twisted his fingers into stiff claws.

Johnny Beskow sat down on the footstool. "Hi, Grandpa," he said.

Henry turned. His eyes had a tendency to water, and some blood vessels had burst. "Hello, my boy. Good to see you."

"Have you had anything to eat?"

Henry nodded. "Mai was here this morning," he said.

Johnny tried to find a good position on the soft faux-leather footstool. "How is she treating you? Does she do a good job? Is she nice?"

"Mai is an angel, that's for sure," Henry Beskow said. "She is rather dark-skinned, and her Norwegian is quite poor because she's from Thailand. But the Thai people, you know, are always so friendly; everything they do, they do with a smile. I couldn't get anyone better than Mai. I worry I'll lose her," he said, becoming instantly concerned. "You can't count on the people in social services. They reorganize all the time, making cuts to save money."

"Did you take your medicine?"

"Yes," the old man said, "I did. I'm like an obedient dog, you know. I don't have the strength to argue. When you're dependent on others you grow pious as a lamb."

His crooked hands moved about his blanket, pulling at its tassels.

"Would you like me to read the newspaper for you?" Johnny asked and nodded toward the local paper on the table.

"That would be nice."

Johnny scooped up the newspaper and got comfortable. In a clear voice he read article after article, shooting quick glances at the old man to make sure he was following along. First, Johnny read a story about a horse that had gone wild during a race; when they tried to get it under control it bit one of its handlers on the arm. Next was a long article about Polish immigrants and their poor working conditions, and another that he skipped because it was about the mishandling of dead bodies at the Central Hospital. Some had been left for a month before being sent for cremation. He read the weather forecast. The heat would continue, and there was a risk of forest fires across the eastern regions of the country. He listed the television programs scheduled for that evening, which he thought the old man might want to see. Finally he read the piece about the baby in the pram. While he read, he peeked at his grandfather, but he couldn't tell what the old man was thinking.

At last he folded the newspaper and put it on the table.

For a moment it was quiet in the room.

"You haven't had it easy," Henry said, "that's for sure. But at least you know how to treat other people. The halfwit who did that should be whipped. Don't you agree, Johnny?"

"Of course, Grandpa," he answered piously. "And to make sure he understands, we could break both his little fingers."

"We could," Henry said. "How are things at home now? You can tell me the truth. Don't lie to spare me."

"Not good. All she does is lie on the sofa. It's the vodka. Is there anything you need from the shop? I can go right now."

"I'll write a list for you," Henry said. "Get a pencil and paper. They're in a drawer in the kitchen."

"Don't need paper, Grandpa. I'll use my mobile phone."

"That's beyond me," said the old man, and nodded gratefully. He sat completely motionless in his wing chair while Johnny tapped in the shopping list. The girl with the red plait was still on the knoll as he drove past. "Wobblewheels!" she called out.

When he got back, he organized the goods in the pantry—a little room off the kitchen where his grandfather kept all sorts of things. Much of the food was old, he noticed, the jars of jam crusted with

39

mold. He cleaned for a while, tidied up a bit, throwing out what needed to be tossed and wiping the shelves with a wet cloth. Then everything looked nice and neat. A red box, temptingly tucked in a corner, caught his attention. He inspected it, thinking it was some kind of breakfast cereal, but discovered it was a box of rat poison. He opened it and examined the pink grains inside. Though they were lethal, the grains looked quite appealing, and the fact that the grains were deadly fascinated him. He lifted the box to his nose; the grains had no scent. Obviously he couldn't imagine how they tasted. Probably like sweets. He read the ingredients and instructions carefully.

"When the rats go to sleep," it said on the box, "they will never wake up again."

Well, what do you know, Johnny Beskow thought.

After giving it some thought, he went outside and hid the box under the seat of his Suzuki. The rat poison could be useful, and he liked having something up his sleeve. Then he went back to his grandfather. Henry was asleep in the chair. Johnny sat on the footstool and waited patiently for him to wake up, which he did some twenty minutes later.

"Would you like me to make you a Thermos of coffee?"

"Please. You can put a little sugar in it, but don't screw the cap on too tight—you know how it is."

Johnny went to the kitchen and prepared everything. Boiled the kettle, poured the water through a coffee filter, added some spoonfuls of sugar. Got a mug from the cupboard, the one his grandfather always drank from: a blue cup with handles on each side. He set it on the table, then went to the window. He said, "Who's the girl with the red hair?"

Henry cleared his throat and coughed. Dust had lodged in his esophagus. "It's Meiner's youngest, I think. Her name is Else. They live in the yellow house down the road. You see the old cars in the front yard? They've been there for fifteen years. Meiner has probably meant to fix them and sell them on, but he never has."

"She's not nice, that girl," Johnny said with his mouth to the window. His breath created a small patch of condensation on the glass and with his finger he drew a skull.

"Do you mean Else? Actually, she is nice. She's like a little guard dog. She watches everyone who drives into Rolandsgata. Finds out what they're doing here. Then she'll bark at them when they drive off. Let me tell you: if someone comes to my house with bad intentions, Else Meiner will warn me instantly. She has eyes like a falcon, and screams like a magpie."

Johnny sat back down on the footstool.

Henry was silent for a long time.

"I'm sorry I'm so old," he said finally with a heavy sigh. "I'm sorry I'm so slow and useless and don't understand anything. It won't get any better, either."

"Stop talking like that," Johnny said sternly.

"I'm not afraid of dying."

"I know."

"Are you afraid of going to sleep? It's no worse than that. We lie down, we sail away."

He lifted a crooked hand and pushed tufts of hair from his forehead. His lips were narrow and colorless, as if life was leaking slowly from his body and taking with it color and glow.

"You won't die for a long time," Johnny said confidently.

The very thought anguished him, because he liked the old man, and he had nowhere else to go. No one waited for him; no one needed him to do anything. Henry was nodding off again. Johnny clutched one of his grandfather's arthritic hands.

"Grandpa," he whispered, "would you like me to open a window before I go? It's so hot in here. You'll be sluggish."

The old man opened one eye. "Wasps might get in."

"Do you have rats in the cellar?"

"Not anymore. Mai took care of them."

Johnny released Henry's hand. He rose and smoothed the blanket. "Grandpa, when did my mother start drinking?"

"Just before you were born. It wasn't so easy, you understand. Bad things happened."

"She won't talk about my father," Johnny complained. "I don't know anything about him."

"Let it go," Henry said, turning his face away and closing his eyes. "It's not always best to know the truth. Trust me."

7

LILY SUNDELIN PUSHED Margrete in the pram, and Karsten walked quietly beside them. She held on to the pram, and he held on to her arm; they couldn't get any closer to each other. It was mid-afternoon and the sun was burning the backs of their heads. Margrete wore a dress with red-and-white stripes, and looked like a little lollipop.

They left the Bjerketun housing estate and walked to the main road. Stopped as a car sped past.

"Do you know what occurred to me today?" Lily said. "Right when I got up? It hit me like a bolt of lightning."

"What?" He squeezed her arm.

"Her smock," she said. "It was gone. The pink smock." She leaned forward and patted Margrete's cheek.

"Are you sure?"

"Yes. For some reason he took the smock with him. Don't you think that's a bit twisted? I mean, who steals a smock? I don't understand it."

Karsten didn't have an answer. She saw him purse his lips. The incident had changed him, and while she partly liked the change, this sudden rage frightened her. His voice was coarse now; she noticed it whenever he answered the telephone. He was always on guard, always on the offensive, in case something should happen.

43

She had never seen this side of him, and she wanted him to let it go; they had to go on with their lives. Yet she was also touched, because he'd risen up and tried to protect them. He had never been so big and broad as now, his voice never so gruff.

"Do you think he's keeping an eye on us?" she asked.

Karsten looked around the road, and at the houses. "No, don't be silly. It's possible he thinks about us, proud of what he's done. Maybe he's planning new attacks. Move onto the shoulder, Lily, a car's coming. Christ, the way he drives."

They stood still as the car sped past.

"Schillinger," Karsten said.

"Who?"

"Bjørn Schillinger. You know, the man with the huskies. He lives on Sagatoppen. Did you see his car, the Land Cruiser? When we trade in our Honda, we'll exchange it for a Land Cruiser."

"Why?"

"It's bigger and more powerful, tougher. Eight cylinders. Two hundred and eighty-six horsepower. How far do you want to walk? It's really hot, and Margrete is as red as a boiled lobster."

Lily considered. The child was sleeping, and she herself had good shoes.

"We'll walk to Saga," she said. "We'll turn round on the bridge."

They reached the bridge twenty minutes later.

Just then a bus whizzed by, and they had to move closer to the railing. Lily's dress fanned around her legs. Because of the rushing water, she held on tightly to the pram, a reflex. She bent over the railing and stared down. The water was rust-brown, with yellow foam. On a shelf of rock she saw the remains of a bonfire; an empty beer can clacked against the rock wall. Karsten put an arm around her shoulder, and she leaned into his broad chest.

44

"There's a lot of power down there," he said. "Listen. It hums like a motor. In the old days, people got by with the sun and the water. Now we're destroying the earth."

"Is that why you want a Land Cruiser?" Lily teased.

He grunted something unintelligible in response, and Lily grew serious again. She noticed that his chest heaved and sank, and she had a strange feeling. After what had happened, she was vulnerable in a new way. She couldn't get over it, couldn't forget what had been done to her Margrete. Something horrible had spotted them, had pointed at them with a quivering finger, and shattered everything. It had something to do with the light, perhaps even with the rhythm of life; everything was out of sync. She looked at the round, smooth rocks at the bottom of the river. Then she saw something that looked like a tire.

She squeezed Karsten's arm. "Is that a tricycle?" she said, distraught.

Karsten strained to see. He saw something red. A handlebar of some kind. A tire. Black rubber. "The tire is too big for that."

"A pram?" she said anxiously. "Good God. Is it a pram, Karsten?"

Karsten Sundelin leaned over the railing. The thing in the water was something he'd seen many times before, but he didn't know how it had ended up in the river. Look at that," he said. "It's a Zimmer frame."

"A Zimmer frame? How did it get in the water?"

"Come on," he said, "we're going home."

"You don't think there's a person down there? Has someone fallen off the bridge?"

"No, of course not. Have you lost your mind?"

He turned the pram round and began walking home, now taking long strides. Lily hurried after him. Margrete awoke and looked up at them with her dark blue eyes. Then she began to whimper. Lily couldn't bear the whimpering; it hurt her like salt in an open wound. Quickly she patted Margrete's cheeks with her hand.

"There's always something at the bottom of that river," Karsten said. "Bicycles. Shopping trolleys. Someone probably nicked it from a driveway, and just threw it in the water. People do all sorts of odd things to amuse themselves."

8

JOHNNY SAT ON the edge of his bed listening to the sounds in the kitchen.

His mother, up and dressed, was roaming about and pawing through cupboards and drawers. Sometimes she managed to pull herself together and prepare a hot meal.

A guy can hope, Johnny Beskow thought. He wasn't used to attention of any kind. Then he heard her steps on the floor. Suddenly she opened his door and stared at him.

"You had a bag with you when you came home today," she said. "What did you buy?"

"A couple of films," he said, "from the video shop."

"Oh, did you have money for that?"

"Grandpa gave me some."

"God help me but don't you always have money," she complained. "You've got it easy."

She spotted the bag on the bedside table. She snatched it, removed the two DVDs and read the back covers. "Rubbish no doubt," she said.

"Uh-huh," he said. "Rubbish. But entertaining rubbish."

She left. For good measure, she slammed the door extra hard. That was how she marked her presence: *I'm still here. Don't you forget it.*

Before long he recognized the smell of pizza, and it struck him that he was hungry, almost lethargic; sometimes he forgot to eat—especially if his head was filled, as now, with plans. While he waited, he darted into the living room and grabbed the newspaper, hurried back to his room and rifled through it. He studied the photographs and concocted elaborate yet incomplete schemes. He was patient, and his plans were clear. People lose their jobs, he thought. They get into car accidents, they drown, they fight and steal and cause trouble, and they kill each other. They marry and have children. They celebrate birthdays, fifty and sixty and seventy. It's all in the newspaper because people have an incredible desire to communicate. He read carefully, and at length settled on an announcement. Read it many times, tore it out and put it in the drawer of his bedside table, next to the pink smock. For later. Then he crossed the room to the guinea pig's cage under the window. He lifted out the small animal and lay on the bed. Bleeding Heart was the guinea pig's name. It scurried over his chest and belly on tiny feet, and after a few rounds back and forth, grew calm in the hollow of his neck. The woman in the kitchen, he thought, wouldn't it be nice to mess with her? What do you think about that? Should we go down to Lake Skarve and fish for pike? We'll carry the fish home in a bucket of water, and shove it down her throat while it's still flopping about. That will shut her mouth. Can you imagine that?

He put the guinea pig against his cheek, and Bleeding Heart nipped him on the ear with its sharp teeth. A number of pleasant images filled his head: his mother with a fat pike sticking out of her mouth; his mother down on her knees, writhing about on the floor and gasping for air. With a finger he stroked the guinea pig's head. He liked the smell of the furry little creature, and the eyes which shone like black pearls.

His mother stuck her head in again. "Get that rat back in the cage," she said. "The pizza's ready."

She was dressed and sober.

He knew it wouldn't last. For brief moments, she came up for air and behaved as if she wanted to show him she was in charge. When she was sober, it was as though she noticed him and wanted to make a point.

He hated her drinking, hated that she slept on the sofa, snoring like a saw. When she was sober he lost control over her, and she went after him with overpowering force. But the pizza was good. He watched her snap her teeth into it; her pointed, gray tongue worked hard at the pepperoni. Even though she was sober, even though she sat straight in her chair, he could see how she longed for the poison she'd become addicted to—an addiction which tore at her, and made her hands restless and shaky.

"You need to get a job," she said. "I can't provide for you forever, Johnny. Why do you loaf around? You're young and able."

You get a job, he thought, but he didn't say it. She was on disability, and had been for years. Four thousand and twenty kroner. Plus eighteen hundred for him. And some subsidized housing on top of that. They had to share this miserable welfare money. We are poor, Johnny thought gloomily as he chewed his pizza. But the prospect of getting a job hardly cheered him up; it would mean that other people could order him around. And he couldn't stand that—he got goose bumps at the very idea. He wanted to be his own master, wanted to ride the Suzuki and be free. Besides, he was only seventeen. He couldn't work behind a till, couldn't drive a car. No one wants me, he reckoned, and was content.

His mother helped herself to another slice. When she yanked at the threads of cheese with her long, white fingers, he noticed dirt beneath her nails.

"When I gave birth to you," she said, looking at him across the table, "that's when I lost my figure. I couldn't sleep or talk to other people. When you have children they're with you all the time, every hour of the day. God help me."

"I'll be moving out soon," he said tentatively.

"Ha!" She opened her mouth wide and laughed. "And where would you move to? What would you eat? How would you pay for it?"

Johnny had a slice of hot pizza in his hand. It burned his fingers but he didn't care. He knew she was afraid of being alone. If he followed through on his threat, if he packed his things in a bag and left home, she would sit in her chair with a bottle in her hands and stare emptily at the wall. No one to wait for, no one to complain to, no one to yell at. No sounds in the house, just her own shrill thoughts.

"I'll move to Grandpa's."

She put her slice down and looked at him. Clearly, the thought troubled her.

"Grandpa has an empty room," he said.

"Why would you move to his place? He can't do anything. He's got people coming over morning, noon and night, and all he does is sit there with his feet up letting others take care of him. You'd just be in the way."

"Mai's there for an hour each morning. An evening nurse gives him his medicine, and that only takes five minutes. That's all the care he gets."

She planted her elbows on the table, and looked grim. "Well, it's considerably more than what I get."

"But you don't have arthritis. *You* are healthy."

He didn't dare look at her when he said it, because he knew it would make her angry.

"Healthy?" she snapped. "What do you know about that? You think I'm healthy? You think I lie on the sofa because I like to?"

It was best, he'd discovered, to keep his trap shut. But he clenched a fist under the table and let his contempt fill him: it made him furious, made his eyes gleam.

"All the same, when he dies we'll get our inheritance," she said suddenly. "He has some money." She munched on her food. The thought of money brought a little color to her cheeks. "I don't know exactly how much, but he saves quite a bit. Doesn't shop, you know. We'll benefit. Just you wait and see."

Johnny looked at her, aghast. He liked the old, listless man with crooked fingers. He couldn't imagine life without his refuge in Rolandsgata, the small house which was always so hot, or the conversations with his grandfather: about life and current affairs.

His mother leaned over the table as if confidentially. Greed lit up her bleary eyes. "You go there all the time," she said. "Can't you can find out how much we're talking about? How much money he's got in that savings account?"

She had lowered both her voice and her heavy eyelids.

Johnny shook his head. Her talk of inheritance disturbed him. His stomach was also full; he rose and went to his room. Hanging on his door was a metal sign which he'd bought in a secondhand shop for 250 kroner. It was a white, enameled square with blue type: *Silence Is Security*.

"Well, thanks for the pizza!" his mother shouted after him.

He closed the door and sat on his bed. Opened the bedside-table drawer and found the small notice he'd torn from the newspaper.

Erik and Ellinor Mørk from Kirkeby send a warm greeting to their mother, Gunilla Mørk, on her seventieth birthday. We look forward to celebrating the day with you. Thanks for all the many happy years, and all the best to you in the years ahead.

He scanned the front page of the newspaper and checked the date. Then he read the notice once more. Later, when he peeked into the living room, he saw that his mother was watching television with a pack of beer; and later in the evening, when she was back on the sofa, he sneaked out to his Suzuki and grabbed the box of rat poison from under the seat.

9

CHIEF HOLTHEMANN HAD years of police experience, and he was astute and analytical. Since he administered the budget, he oversaw the distribution of the department's modest funds.

"The person who did this to the Sundelins," he said. "Do you think he's dangerous? Will he act again? Should we make him a priority?"

"It's clear he's damaged goods," Sejer said. "He threatens all hell, and likes to play with fire. If he gets anywhere near explosives he might be dangerous."

"Why are you talking about explosives?"

"Karsten Sundelin. He's about to blow up."

Holthemann removed his glasses and put them on the table. An austere and unsentimental man, he lacked Sejer's warmth. As an administrator he was unmatched. But around people, whether criminal or victim, he came up short. "Where will you start?" he said. "We've got to nail this joker, quickly."

Then he recounted a story from his childhood. He told Sejer about a crime that had occurred when he was eight and living up north.

"A man went around people's gardens at night, with hefty shears, cutting up ladies' underwear hanging on clotheslines. A modest crime, but he managed to create a great deal of fear with those shears, you see. The women in the neighborhood were beside themselves."

"Was he ever caught?"

"Oh yes. He was caught. And it turned out he was just a harmless nitwit who could explain neither his actions nor his motivations. What about this Bjerketun case? Do you believe we're dealing with the same kind of nitwit?"

"No," Sejer said. "This person is probably smarter than that. At least, I think so. As my grandmother would have said, after a few Tuborg beers and a dram, he's probably a clever little devil."

He riffled through his file and pulled out a sheet of paper covered with handwriting, Lily Sundelin's exhaustively detailed description of the fateful day. He waved the sheet.

"The girl's smock was taken," he said. "Isn't that lovely? Talk about a trophy."

"Show me the postcard again," Holthemann said.

Sejer found the wolverine in his desk drawer, and Holthemann studied the image and the terse message.

"This is so bloody well planned," he said. "Also rather brash, putting this on your doormat the way he did. You saw him out the window, I heard. How much did you see?"

"That he was young and fast. He lives in Bjerkås, I think, and probably bought the card at the Spar near Lake Skarve. I mean, it's a possibility."

"Don't let the news of the wolverine card slip out to the press," Holthemann ordered. "Don't give him that satisfaction. They'll start calling him 'The Beast from Bjerkås' or something worse, and that's the last thing we want. Have you scrutinized the Sundelins? Have they made enemies?"

"No," Sejer said matter-of-factly. "There's no reason to think so."

Holthemann thanked him and left his office. The door closed

behind him, and his cane thumped monotonously down the corridor. Sejer settled in to read Lily Sundelin's report again. She had accounted for the entire day, and he jotted notes as he read. He noted, among other things, that her husband Karsten had heard the sound of something that could have been a moped. The sound had come from the grove of trees behind their house, where there was a trail to Askeland. Sejer decided to drive there alone.

The Beast from Bjerkås, he thought.

You'd like that name.

He drove straight to Askeland.

But the trail that led to Bjerketun wasn't easy to find. After he'd searched for some time, he walked on to a small pitch where some boys were playing football.

"I'm from the police," he said. "I'm investigating the incident with the baby in Bjerketun. You've heard about that, right?"

The boys rushed to his side. A few of them were dark-skinned, like Matteus, the rest were fair-haired, and they were all around eight or nine years old. They led him behind an old, barracks-like building, which served as a clubhouse, to a narrow path into the forest.

"You'll reach the logging road in a few minutes," they told him. "And if you're going to Bjerketun, you've got to keep left. It's about a half-hour walk."

"Is the trail good enough that you can drive a moped on it?"

"Easily," they said. "But it's even better to ride motocross. It's great for that. People come all the way from Kirkeby to do it. But it's actually not allowed."

"Because of the noise?"

"Yeah, it's pretty noisy. And they tear up the track."

He thanked them and began walking. There were deciduous trees at the beginning of the path. But as he moved on to the logging road, the deciduous trees were replaced with massive spruce;

for as far as he could see, the spruce stood in straight rows. The path was dry and pleasant, and smelled of needles. After a few minutes he noticed a rickety tree house that was apparently no longer used. At one time it'd been a secret meeting place, and it awakened some old memories from when he was a little boy.

He, the perpetrator, may have walked this trail, Sejer thought, on his way to Bjerketun and to Karsten and Lily's house. With his nefarious plan he had come quietly, his heart probably racing and hot with excitement. He'd listened, he'd observed, and maybe he'd thought highly of himself and his position, as criminals often do. They are unique, they think, and the usual rules don't apply to them. They are the brightest, who can do as they please and who, in the end, survive.

Half an hour later he saw rooftops shining red between the trunks of trees. He considered a moment then turned left, and soon found himself looking directly at the Sundelins' house, the garden and the big maple with its massive canopy where the pram had stood. He imagined the rush it must have been to catch sight of the pram. Maybe he'd seen movement under the blanket, the tiny baby feet kicking.

Sejer observed the house for a few minutes.

Sundelin's red SUV was parked in the driveway.

The air was hot and drowsy and silent.

As if the small wounded family had huddled together inside, in a corner.

He stared at the house until he began to feel like a peeping Tom, then turned and headed back. As he walked, he examined the trail, studying it closely, and found nothing but spruce cones. When he reached the clubhouse, he stopped. The boys were still playing football, and he suddenly wanted to join the game. He was in good shape, and it wouldn't be difficult. Besides, he was almost two meters tall, and his legs were long. Almost immediately, to the boys' jubilation, he scored a goal. Now they guarded him like a swarm of buzzing bees. After they finished, the players sat on the grass and chatted, clustered in a horseshoe around Sejer.

"All the criminals on the loose," one of the boys said, "the bad guys you don't manage to catch. Does it make you really cross?"

Sejer had to admit it often made him cross. The man who'd been in the Sundelins' garden, they would have to catch him.

"Do you have any leads?" they wanted to know.

"Nothing good," he admitted. "Not yet. But sooner or later, criminals make mistakes, especially when they've been at it for a while. They usually get careless."

"But the case with the baby, that was just a prank," said a little black child. "Does he have to go to jail for that?"

"It's not a prank," Sejer corrected. "Let me tell you something." He looked hard at each of them. "It's a form of theft. The parents' security has been stolen from them, and that's very serious. Without security, life is terribly difficult."

The boys thought carefully about what he'd said. When he left, they followed him to the car, flocking around him and waving.

"Keep to the straight and narrow, boys," Sejer ordered and drove away.

10

O NE NIGHT, A FEW weeks after the attack against
Margrete, Karsten Sundelin woke at three thirty in the
morning. He lay in bed listening. A dark blue curtain
kept the light out, but instantly he could tell that Lily wasn't
beside him. He switched on the bedside lamp. Margrete's cot,
which they'd brought into the bedroom, was also empty. He sat
up and rubbed his eyes. He knew that Lily was having difficulty
sleeping. When he thought about everything that had happened, and about how much they'd lost, he clenched his hands
into fists. Something had entered the house, something unfamil-
iar. At times he could sense it like a tension between them, almost as if someone else were listening to them and meddling
in their lives—but without words, just something shadow-like
and vague. He crawled from the bed and went to the lounge,
where he found them on the sofa. Lily sat with Margrete in her
lap. At first he thought she was asleep, but then she sensed him
and opened her eyes. He sat heavily in an armchair. Lily hadn't
turned on any lights. There was only a thin, gray glow in the
room. Margrete was asleep. For a long time he observed them on
the sofa. Some sort of fear had been planted in Lily, he knew,
and it had grown and stolen her peace of mind. Everything

they once had taken for granted. He gripped the armrests of the chair.

"We can't live like this," he said.

He heard a heavy sigh from the sofa. Margrete moved a hand, but otherwise slept peacefully.

"Well, how should we live?" Lily said wearily. She rocked Margrete softly on her lap.

"Like we did before."

"We can't do that. You must realize that."

He held back a protest. He switched on the steel lamp beside his chair.

Lily had pulled on a dressing gown, and draped a blanket across her knees. Right now you can protect Margrete, he thought, but you can't sit like this forever. We've got to sleep. We've got to work. Margrete will grow up. He didn't say any of this out loud, but instead rose and walked into the kitchen, calling out that he was making tea and would she like a cup?

"No, I don't want anything."

She sounded like a bitter old woman. Karsten leaned against the worktop. He made a fist, and cursed under his breath. Then he filled the kettle.

While he waited for the water to boil, he went back to the lounge. He wanted to say something encouraging, something to make her feel better.

"Sooner or later they'll get him," he said. "And justice will be served. Everything will be back to normal. Don't you think?"

Her response was to give him a hurt look which instantly turned to one of reluctance, as if the corner she'd located, on the sofa, with a blanket over her knees and Margrete on her lap, was a place she would never again leave. There was something unsettling about it all. She was somewhere he couldn't reach anymore. It didn't matter what he said or did, because there was no longer any energy between them; she had pushed him away.

He heard the water boiling in the kitchen.

"I mean," he said softly, "some lose their children for good. Have you thought about that?"

He knew he shouldn't speak these words, but he couldn't help himself. Because Margrete lay in Lily's lap, and she was healthy and fine and lovely. Lily looked up quickly. She made a strange sound, the kind an injured cat makes when it snarls. The kettle whistled and he stood. But when he reached the kitchen, he left the kettle and opened the fridge instead. He returned with a bottle of beer in his hand. Lily looked at him wide-eyed.

"You're going to have a beer now?"

He put the bottle to his lips. He felt very gloomy.

"What if you have to drive?" she snapped.

He drained half the bottle before putting it down with a bang. "Why would I have to drive?"

"If something happens," she said, rocking Margrete.

"What would happen now?" He glanced at his watch. "It's four in the morning."

She pulled the blanket tighter around her, as if to demonstrate her vulnerability. "Anything can happen," she said. "Haven't you realized that yet?"

He finished his beer. She's spooked out of her wits, he thought. And I'm angry. She's sulking like a child, and I'm growling like a dog. This can't be happening. We've got to sleep. We've got to put Margrete to bed. We've got to move on. There are so many things we want to do.

"If you don't start sleeping soon, maybe we can get our hands on some sleeping pills."

"Sleeping pills?" She rolled her eyes at this offensive suggestion. "Then I couldn't be alert."

"But I'm right beside you. I'll wake at even the faintest sound. I'll take care of you two."

"He came while we were eating," she reminded him, "and we didn't hear a thing."

Karsten leaned across the table and looked at her. "Yes, Lily. He did. But he's not coming back. Can't we agree on that? Come, let's go back to bed. I know you're suffering. You're probably in shock. But you need to pull yourself together."

Finally she pushed the blanket away and got up. He turned off the lamp and followed her into the bedroom. She put Margrete between them in the bed, and did so with a glance that thwarted any protest. Then she flicked on the lamp that was on her side of the bed.

"I'm going to read for a bit," she said, "but you can go to sleep. If you're so tired."

She seemed to imply that he should be ashamed of himself. Because he was so tired. Karsten felt the urge to lash out at what had happened to them. What had happened to Margrete was certainly terrible—he was the first to say it. What he'd seen when he came out to the garden, Lily on the ground screaming, the child under the blanket, bloody as slaughter, he would never forget it, never. But what about the rest of our lives? he thought. We've got to find some kind of order. He closed his eyes and tried to sleep, but the light bothered him. And each time she flipped a page the riffling of paper was like a clap of thunder to him. The sound rumbled through his head. Maybe we'll end up raving mad, he thought. Maybe that was what he wanted, the one who'd come from the forest.

Gunilla Mørk had celebrated her seventieth birthday with her children and friends and neighbors, and now she was glad it was over. The platter she'd ordered from the café was quite excellent, so too the cake table to which she had contributed a delicious marzipan ring. Will I make it to eighty? she wondered, looking out of the kitchen window. Many don't live that long, and it's not a given that I will either. As active, agile and clearheaded as I am.

The sky was bright blue, and the sun was rising. God has given us another gorgeous day, she thought. I must make the most of it. It is our duty as human beings: we must appreciate the good things. And if we don't, we'd better have a good reason. This was Gunilla Mørk's philosophy of life. But because she'd turned seventy, she had also begun thinking of death. It hung over her like a dark cloud, and wouldn't give her peace. Sometimes, in the middle of the night, this darkness came to her and disturbed her thoughts. She pulled the curtains aside and looked at the lawn. As she thought about death, she saw her own hand—it was no longer young and smooth, but dry and wrinkled. For a few moments, the sight terrified her. She raised her hand and examined it carefully, brought it close to her cheek. Of course it was warm and able, as always. So why these silly thoughts? Sometimes it seemed as though the moment cracked open and let in a dose of hard reality.

I don't have much time left.

It was early morning. She heard a little thump out front, the sound of her local newspaper being dropped into her mailbox. The postman had already moved on to the next house. He rode a bicycle with a small trailer hitched to it, and with strength she was no longer capable of mustering, he pedaled up the hill in his red uniform. Out in the garden she turned her face toward the sky and felt the sunlight. It glows the same way it did when I was sixteen, she thought, just as rich and golden. Just as invigorating. The wind is mild and the grass is overwhelmingly green and lush. I could get on my knees and eat it, just like cows do. She headed to the mailbox and fetched her paper. On the first page she saw a picture of a man with his arms around a sheep, and she read the headline.

THE MYTH OF THE NORWEGIAN SHEEP FARMER

She went inside and set the newspaper on the kitchen table. She would certainly read that article, because she had her opinions about sheep farmers. But first she wanted to brew coffee and butter a piece of bread. Everything had to be done just so, and at the right pace. Why should she hurry? After all, there was only one direction. Now I'm complaining too much, thought Gunilla Mørk, but God expects no more of a person than is given him. The food tasted good. The jam was made from berries grown in her garden, and she hadn't ruined it with too much sugar.

She started reading about the sheep farmer.

The myth of the Norwegian sheep farmer and the love he feels toward his animals lives on, but it is overblown. The image of the devastated farmer kneeling by the body of one of his sheep following a bear attack is not about grief; rather, it's about economic impact. When they want to get on the good side of public opinion, when they want to obtain larger subsidies from the state, they become first-rate actors.

This claim was made by a professor she had never heard of.

The man in the photograph, a man called Sverre Skarning, claimed that he loved all his sheep, even the black ones. She studied the farmer and the sheep. She tried to form an opinion, but didn't know what to think. They probably are fond of their sheep, she thought. And she liked the photograph. A man and a sheep in close contact put her in quite a good mood. She flipped to the next page. In between she drank her coffee, which energized her, strong and hot as it was. I'll get some things done today, she thought. Maybe I'll stain the garden furniture; it's got terribly dry during the summer. She concentrated her reading on the ongoing tragedies unfolding in the poorer parts of the world — cyclones, earthquakes, war and more war — then raised her head and looked out at the quiet garden, at the flowers and trees, and thought it marvelous that she of all people had been granted this peaceful spot on earth where nothing bad ever happened.

She came to the obituaries.

These she always read carefully, because sometimes she knew someone. She also made a note of the year of their birth, recognizing that her own was drawing near with alarming haste; those who'd now used up their allotted time had been born around 1930. Gunilla, she thought, you've got to stop. You're sitting here in the kitchen, and you are alive and well. Sunlight falls through the window, the coffee is strong. At that very moment she gasped in shock, staring directly at her own name. Gunilla Mørk, she read, was dead; she had died in her sleep. She let go of the newspaper and put a hand to her heart. She could hardly breathe. No, it was a mistake. If it wasn't a mistake, there must be others called Gunilla Mørk. She glanced around the kitchen to reassure herself that everything was in order — that she wasn't caught in some form of madness.

But all she saw was the good old kitchen, with cups and bowls. She reread the notice. Everything was correct, the birth date, the year.

OUR KIND AND CARING MOTHER, MOTHER-IN-LAW AND
SISTER, GUNILLA MØRK, BORN 17 JULY 1939, PASSED
AWAY QUIETLY IN HER SLEEP TODAY, 25 JULY.

IT'S GOOD TO REST
WHEN YOUR STRENGTH FAILS YOU
AFTER YEARS OF TOIL AND STRUGGLE

AT SOME POINT
THE HOLY NIGHT COMES
AND THE MUSES OF ETERNITY
CHANGE THE BITTEREST SORROW
YOU'VE HAD
TO A HUNDRED FIDDLES

ERIK AND ELLINOR, FRIENDS AND OTHER RELATIVES.
FUNERAL SERVICE TO BE HELD AT EASTERN CREMATORIUM,
SMALL CHAPEL, I AUGUST, 10:30 A.M.

Gunilla Mørk put her head down on the table.

She knocked over her coffee cup.

The newspaper said she was dead.

Erik and Ellinor—her children. And that stupid poem. Erik and Ellinor would never have chosen something so pompous, something so ridiculous and distasteful. And Eastern Crematorium, good Lord. What did it mean?

Who had done this inexplicable thing? Could the newspaper have made a mistake? Of course they couldn't have; if they had, the world had become unhinged. She shot up from the chair and paced around the room. Stood in front of the mirror over the sink. An old woman stared back at her with a face she had never seen. It was unsettling. Everyone I know will read the announcement, she thought. I have to call them. I have to call Erik and Ellinor. She returned to the chair and slumped in it, gripping the edge of the table. Maybe I nodded off and dreamed it, she thought, but that was obviously silly. Again she read her own obituary. She sat motionless, growing cold all over, because someone had picked her out. From the mass of people they had found her and hatched their hideous plans. She wanted to grab the telephone; she wanted to dial her son Erik's number at once. Then she would know what had happened. But it took some time for her to get up.

And when she was finally on her feet, the phone in her hand, she began to cry.

Johnny Beskow sneaked into the hallway.

Because it was important to be prepared, he stood there listening. Apparently, his mother was not at the stove. There was no smell of food, just the familiar stench of coats, dust and mold. She must be on the sofa, he thought, and looked at the clock. It was eleven in the morning, and it wasn't uncommon for her to be drunk at this hour. Once he'd found her at seven in the morning, drinking vodka in big gulps while clinging to the armrest with her free hand. She'd done this for an hour before going off to lie down, under the duvet. In this manner she moved from the chair to the bed, to the sofa, and to the chair again. And to the grave, he thought, can't you move to the grave? I'll dig the hole. Then you can just roll over the edge. He slipped into the lounge to see. Yep, she was lying on the sofa under a blanket. So he shuffled off to his room and closed the door. He lifted Bleeding Heart from the cage and fell on the bed with the guinea pig at his neck. People believe what I tell them, he thought with satisfaction. I can call whomever I want and claim whatever I want, or demand whatever I want, and people do what I say. They are polite and friendly, and they are happy to help. It's pure magic. The possibilities are endless. I can disrupt an entire community, it occurred to him, an entire city. All I have to do is pick up the phone or write a letter. I hold this power. He could feel the power in his head, the power rushing through his veins, and it made him warm and strong, even though he was, strictly speaking, a weakling. Or as they'd called him at school: the wimp from Askeland.

After a while he put the guinea pig back in the cage. The cage was filled with wood chips and cotton rags, some colorful plastic toys. He'd got the money to buy it from his grandfather, same as the moped—it had been a gift for his confirmation, which hadn't amounted to anything. His mother couldn't stay sober long enough to plan a party, and anyway there was no one to invite.

Hungry, he went to the kitchen. There was nothing on the hob, so he looked for milk in the fridge. Sat at the kitchen table and ate cereal while staring out the window. Because she was drunk, his mother wouldn't stir until evening. Then she'd scuttle to the bathroom, drag a brush through her hair, wobble back to the lounge and suddenly see him sitting in front of the television. From that point until he went to bed, she would play her role as parent. She'd ask where he had been and what he had done. What he had eaten. Whether he was going to get a job, something to bring more money to the household. Then she would complain about her headache, say it had been a little worse today so she had needed to lie down. It's actually a little better now, she would say. To justify that she'd been in a drunken stupor half the day.

He finished eating. He rinsed his plate and returned to the lounge, fell into a chair. His mother was flat on her back with a blanket under her chin; her skin seemed clammy, as if she had a fever; her eyelids had glided halfway up. I wish you were dead, he thought, I wish you would stop breathing right now. When you die I will clap my hands in joy, and in the middle of your funeral service I will sing and dance. And when you're finally in the ground, I'll visit you every night to piss on your grave.

He sent his thoughts to her in a steady, wicked stream. He liked to imagine they reached her somehow. That the hate he felt for her quietly broke her down, like a slow-working poison. He touched the army knife which hung on his belt, felt the warm metal in his hands. I will slice your eyeballs, he thought, and your eardrums. I'll hoist you into a wheelbarrow and haul you to the woods so the foxes find you. And the badgers, and the cats.

He stood up and returned to the kitchen; he had something to take care of. Looked in the drawers and cupboards. After searching for a while, he found an old pizza box under the worktop, and a pair of scissors and a marker in a drawer. With these simple tools he shuffled back to his bedroom to make a sign.

11

ERIK AND ELLINOR went to the police station together, on behalf of their mother, Gunilla. Erik Mørk was the elder of the two, already gray at the temples; his fair-haired sister was a good deal younger. You could tell there was a bond between them, a connection that had grown tight during their lives. And now that this awful thing had happened, they appeared as one furious entity. They had brought the local newspaper with their mother's obituary.

Sejer read it.

"She's seventy," Erik Mørk said. "She just turned seventy, and she's always been quite healthy. Now she's very upset. You've got to find out what the hell is going on, right now, because this is offensive, I'm sure you'll agree."

He had worked himself up quite a bit.

"I do agree," Sejer said. He reread Gunilla Mørk's obituary, then looked hard at the two siblings. "If you think about her friends and acquaintances, or the rest of the family, is there anyone you would suspect? Someone who feels slighted and wants to be noticed?"

Ellinor shook her head decisively. "We don't know anyone like that," she said. "Nor will you find any among her neighbors. Only decent people."

"Where does she live?"

"In Kirkeby," Erik Mørk said. "At Konvalveien. She's a widow, and she's been alone for many years. She's never been the nervous type, but at this point she's tied in knots. She doesn't know what to make of it, this thing that's happened to her. I mean, what do they want?"

"The only way to reassure her is to find the person responsible," Ellinor Mørk added, "so we can get an explanation of why they did this to her. Because that's what she doesn't understand. We don't either. She keeps to herself, and she doesn't draw attention to herself. She goes to the shop every day, works in her garden. That type of thing."

"Have you contacted the newspaper?" Sejer asked. "The obituary department?"

"No," Erik Mørk said. "I assumed you would do that."

Sejer began to trace the edges of something unpleasant. A carefully designed plan, a soundless form of terror.

"I'll talk to her," he said. "I'll talk to her today. First I'll stop by the newspaper. If I find anything, I'll let you know."

Erik Mørk put his finger on the obituary. "Have you ever heard of this happening before?"

"No," Sejer said. "This is really a new and very serious kind of prank. I've never seen anything like it. What about the little poem?" he asked. "Does it sound familiar?"

Ellinor Mørk rolled her eyes. "That poem is unbelievably ridiculous," she said. "Our mother has never been ill. This is insane. Our phone is ringing off the hook. People are so shocked when they read that she's dead. When we tell them it's just a prank, they're even more confused. It's what he wants. Assuming it's a man. Do you think he wants us to be confused?"

"What should we say to Mother?" Erik asked. "Somehow we've got to calm her down."

Sejer thought about it for a minute. "Tell her she was selected at random for a practical joke which has neither meaning nor purpose. Tell her it's a game."

"So that's what you believe it is? A game?"

"Not necessarily. But that's what you should tell your mother."

He found Jacob Skarre.

He looked quizzically at his younger colleague. "If you saw your own obituary in the paper, how would you react?"

Skarre had already heard about the fake obituary. He opened his mouth to respond, but, because he needed to think it through, changed his mind and kept quiet. What would he have thought if he'd seen these words in the paper some morning while eating breakfast? *Our dear Jacob Skarre passed from us today, thirty-nine years old.* Or a variation, like this: *Our dear Jacob Skarre was suddenly taken from us today.* Or: *Jacob Skarre died today, after a long illness.*

"I'd have reacted with horror, dread and bewilderment," he said. "I probably would have laughed hysterically for a while. Then I would have thought about everyone I know who also would've read the notice and thought it was true." He turned to the inspector. "I presume it's the Wolverine that's been on the prowl?"

"Yes," Sejer agreed, "the Wolverine. The Beast from Bjerkås, you can be sure of that. Talk about originality."

"What do you think his goal is?"

"To make things happen," Sejer said. "He's probably inadequate in many ways, deprived of experience and companionship. Perhaps his motive is fairly modest, and it's all about a need every human being shares. He just wants attention."

When she showed them into her kitchen, Gunilla Mørk seemed embarrassed.

"I don't like to be a bother," she apologized. "But Erik and Ellinor wanted me to report it. It's rather trivial when I think about what you normally have to deal with. It's only a silly newspaper obituary. I'd like to laugh it off, but the laughter doesn't get past my throat."

She paced uncertainly. She didn't know quite how she should behave, with two strange men in her kitchen.

"I thought I had some good years ahead of me," she said, "but when I saw the obituary in the paper, my whole world shook. I'm no longer certain of anything.

"I suppose all security is false security," she said with a faint smile. "Or so I've often thought. Because anything can happen, and it can just as well be today, and to me. I understand that rather well. We are masters of repression, but now it's as if I can't really do that anymore. I've lost something. That obituary," she sighed, "it's like a bad omen."

Finally she ceased her restless pacing of the kitchen floor.

Sejer and Skarre observed her pluck a few withered leaves from a plant on the table. Her hair was silver-gray and cut short, and she had tiny gold studs in her ears. She actually looked quite youthful.

"We've talked to the obituary department," Sejer said. "Normally the obituaries are received by post from the funeral home, and are checked by several people. But in this case there was a lapse in the procedure. Due to the summer holidays, there are many inexperienced temps at the paper, and one of them made a mistake. Someone who was overeager."

"I see," Gunilla Mørk said. "I've now been in the paper twice in little more than a week. That's quite a feat."

"What do you mean twice?" Sejer asked.

She plucked more leaves from the potted plant and gathered them up.

"I just turned seventy. Erik and Ellinor placed a nice announcement for me. I was very touched by the gesture."

"Do you still have it?" Skarre asked.

She disappeared into the living room. Pawed through a basket and quickly returned with the paper. Skarre read the short birthday notice and nodded.

"That was probably how he found you," he said. "He saw this notice, saw that you lived here in Kirkeby and saw your date of birth and your children's names. He had everything he needed right here. This is good news, I have to say."

"Why?" she said.

"It means that you were selected totally at random," Skarre explained. "He's not after you for any special reason. He just found you in the newspaper."

"Are you sure?" she asked anxiously. "Because I jump every time the doorbell rings."

"Absolutely certain," Skarre said.

Chosen at random, she thought. Nothing personal—that was a relief. She returned to the plant one last time, removed a few more dry leaves.

"There is misery in everyone's life," she said, "and young people have to pass the time somehow. I suppose it's as simple as that." Suddenly she looked at them in alarm. "I just thought of that baby out in Bjerketun. Is this connected in some way?"

"We don't know," Sejer said.

"But it's a little strange," she said, "the similarities. Perhaps some prankster has decided to frighten us all."

"We can't draw those conclusions," Sejer said. "It's too early."

She opened the cupboard under the sink, then let the dry leaves fall into the rubbish bin. "I draw my own conclusions," she said. "It was an omen of death."

"Has anything else happened in the last few days that you can tell us about?" Sejer asked. "Has anyone called? Has anyone knocked on your door? Does anything out of the ordinary come to mind?"

She thought about it then shrugged. "Nothing out of the ordinary," she said. "Ellinor is here often. And a friend of mine visits twice a week. We have lunch together. From time to time a salesman stops by. Just today there was a young boy on my doorstep; he was out looking for a job. A Polish student, he said, who needed to make some money. But I was so upset about the obituary in the paper that I sent him away. I was quite bad-tempered. I regret it now, because he was probably a good person. He spoke very bad English," she added, "so he'd made an introduction for himself on an old pizza box."

12

PEOPLE HAD BEGUN to give him nicknames.

Both among the editorial staff and among the general public he was called all sorts of audacious things, each name more inventive than the next. The beloved child has many names, Johnny Beskow thought, as he heard other people talking about him. He had finally made something of himself, and people were forced to acknowledge him. He was delighted at what he'd set in motion. I'll play this game for a long time, he thought.

Just wait and see.

He rode around on his red Suzuki moped, and he studied people with the fascination of a researcher, as if they were exotic animals. They were strange. It was late summer, and people were out in their gardens. He saw small children on trampolines, women weeding flower beds, men in driveways washing cars. A man squatted down to paint his fence, a woman yanked clean clothes from the washing line. Johnny liked all that he saw. He liked this teeming life, the chalk-white clothes snapping in the wind, the smell of paint. He liked it, and he wanted to destroy it. Everyone lives on an edge, he thought, and I will push them over.

After he'd driven around the residential streets for a while, he set course for the shopping center in Kirkeby. He parked and took the lift to the second floor, found his way to the toy shop. He wandered between the rows, picking up this and that toy and inspecting it. Then the boy in him came out for real: the simple pleasure in a fine toy, a neat material, a quirky function. He admired a red sports car. A set of plastic African animals, boxes of Lego and Playmobil. After he'd walked around for several minutes, he found what he'd been looking for—various types of masks. He picked them up one at a time and inspected them closely. A gorilla mask, a Donald Duck mask and a pig mask. The latex masks were soft and well made. He held the gorilla mask up to his face, peered through the narrow eye slits. A gorilla, he thought. That would make an impression on anyone. On another rack he found a selection of stuffed animals. Most were teddy bears, but he also found a pig and a bunny. He pulled the bunny down. It was made of white plush, and had a pink snout with long, fine whiskers—the kind of thing little girls would fall in love with and cuddle at night. He knew it would come in handy in some way or other. It's important to think long-term, Johnny, he said to himself, just follow your instincts and buy the cute bunny. He headed to the till and paid out a considerable chunk of his savings. After he'd put the gorilla mask and the bunny under the seat of his moped, he rode toward Bjørnstad and his grandfather's house. Just as he swung into Rolandsgata, the girl with the red plait turned up. She wasn't sitting on the knoll this time, but on a blue bicycle, a Nakamura. She wore a Hauger School Band pullover. Well, he thought, that's useful to know.

"Codface," she yelled.

Though it cost him considerable exertion to keep his anger in check, he chose to ignore her. Don't add fuel to this fire, he thought. Not yet. I'm special. I'm patient. Obviously I'll get that snotty brat when the time's right; so help me God, she'll get what she deserves. He rode to his grandfather's house and parked the Suzuki. Stopped at the mailbox before going in. The old man sat with his legs on the footstool. The small room was as hot as an oven.

"Hi, Grandpa," he shouted. "Here's your post!"

Henry raised his hand in greeting. His forehead was covered with pearls of sweat. He had tried, in his clumsy way, to shrug out of his knitted cardigan, but without any luck.

"We've got to air this place," Johnny said. "It's too hot in here."

Henry shook his head. "The wasps will get in. They're really poisonous this time of year."

"Then we need to find a solution," Johnny said. "Because you can't sit in this heat, it'll make you sluggish. Look, here's your bank statement. Do you want to go through it?"

He tore the envelope open with his index finger and held out the statement.

There were very few transactions in Henry's account. His monthly savings had grown over the years into a substantial sum.

"Nine hundred and seventy-three thousand, Grandpa. Wow, how you've saved."

With squinting eyes, Henry stared at the numbers. Suddenly he looked concerned. "It's all well and good that I can leave some money behind," he said, "but I'm afraid your mother will spend it all on vodka, and that the money wouldn't benefit you. You can drink an awful lot of vodka for nine hundred thousand kroner." He held the statement. A deep furrow ran across his brow. "How can we make sure she's disinherited, Johnny? Have you got any ideas?"

Johnny Beskow thought long and hard. "She won't be disinherited before she croaks," he said dejectedly. He folded the statement and put it back in the envelope, pondering. "By the way, the little twit shouted at me again today, that Else Meiner. She called me a codface."

Henry smiled broadly, so that his yellow teeth were visible. "Well, have you seen yourself in the mirror lately?"

"In the mirror? Why?"

"The question is, do you look like a cod?"

"Of course not."

"Right. So why do you get so upset? If you know it's not true?"

"She plays in the Hauger School Band," Johnny said.

"I know. I can hear her trumpet from here. Sometimes she practices at night. I've heard both 'Bravura' and the 'Entry March of the Boyars.' She's quite good, I'll have you know."

"Do they practice at the school? At Hauger School?"

"I would imagine so. On Thursdays, I think. I've seen her on her bicycle with the trumpet case on her rack, and she's gone for a few hours. She's like you. She goes everywhere on that blue bike. There's something buzzing in here," he said. "Can you see if it's a wasp? I know that sound."

Johnny got up and walked around the steamy living room, examining every nook and cranny, looking under the curtains, lifting the cushions of the sofa. "It's a bluebottle," he reported, "and it's as big as a house. I'll kill it for you. They're full of disease. I wouldn't give five kroner for your immune system."

"I wouldn't either," Henry said.

Johnny found an old issue of the church bulletin, rolled it into a tube and smacked the bluebottle. When he had taken care of it, he returned to the footstool to read the newspaper. But he skipped the story about the fake obituary, which was well covered across the whole back page. Afterward, he went to the kitchen and buttered some bread for them. He put sausage and cucumbers on the slices of bread, filled a jug with squash and added ice cubes. Then he sneaked over to open the kitchen window so a little fresh air could find its way inside. They ate in silence.

Henry's dentures clacked while he chewed. "I'll give you some pocket money," he said. "So you'll have petrol."

"Thanks, Grandpa."

"When you're older you can move. And live your own life."

"Have to get a job first," Johnny said.

After a while the old man fell asleep, his mouth agape and his chest littered with bread crumbs. Johnny rose from the footstool, wandered round the room and looked at the photos on the wall. There were many of himself as a little boy, with short trousers and blond hair, and tiny trainers with red laces. I guess I was an all right kid, he thought, I can't remember being difficult. Or maybe I was without knowing it. He dug around for good memories, but all that came to him was the sound of doors being slammed. And some images of his mother. She always stood with her back to him, bent over the worktop, always in despair over something. Her steps were hard and decisive, and she banged cupboards and drawers: an eternal storm raging from room to room. Then he examined the picture of his grandmother. She had died young, and he had never known her. But she seemed nice in the picture. Where did all the malice come from? When did it begin to grow? At length he saw a picture of himself sitting on the red moped, his helmet under his arm. In a small cabinet with glass doors his grandfather had several trophies he had won playing bridge. On top of the bookshelf was a mounted grouse that gazed at him with black glass eyes. As a boy he'd often been scared it would swoop down and get him, peck at him with its sharp beak. He returned to the footstool, reached out and took Henry's hand, squeezing it gently. The old man opened his eyes.

"Well, what do you know," he said. "I'm still here. That's not too bad."

"Did you dream?" Johnny wanted to know.

Henry considered. "No, not a thing."

"Tell me what it's like to be old," Johnny said.

Henry Beskow gave a dismissive wave with one hand, made a discontented miserable grunt. "It's difficult. It's like swimming in salt water."

"Why are you so allergic to wasps, Grandpa?"

"I don't know. It's just a weakness I have."

"How allergic are you? Are we talking about fatally allergic?"

"Yes. Ha ha. We're talking about deathly allergic."

"But why would you die from it? What happens?"

"My throat swells up, no matter where the wasps sting me. I can't breathe. Close the kitchen window before you go," he added. "I know you opened it. And take a couple of hundred kroner from the jar on the fridge, so you can buy petrol and whatever things you boys need."

Johnny patted him on his dry, wrinkled cheeks.

He didn't see Else Meiner when he rode up the street.

13

L ILY SUNDELIN BROWSED the newspaper.

She also had her eye on Margrete, who was sitting in a baby bouncer at her feet. Now and then she lifted her foot and carefully gave the bouncer a little nudge; the chubby child smiled with her toothless gums. Karsten, at the table with a crossword puzzle, observed them on the sly. So much has happened, he thought, and Lily is a completely changed person. She has another voice now, another look in her eyes.

A different sensitivity.

Lily looked up at him and pointed to the newspaper. "Have you read about the fake obituary?"

Karsten put his pen down and nodded.

"Why didn't you say anything?" she said.

"Why should I say anything? You can read about it yourself."

She folded the newspaper and put it on the table. Her gestures betrayed her irritation. Then she leaned over the bouncer and stroked Margrete's cheek. "It could be the same man. It has to be the same man."

Karsten Sundelin picked up his pen again and wrote a word in the puzzle. "Exactly," he said. "No one's talking about anything else. But talking doesn't help."

Once more he was overcome with a strange feeling: a force that rose from deep within and made it hard for him to breathe. As if a new Karsten Sundelin had begun to grow inside him, a Karsten which had lain in slumber and now wanted to escape.

He who doesn't seek revenge, he thought, sets nothing to rights. It was an old adage. Why do we not live by it anymore? Why should the authorities have to avenge them? Why did criminals have so many rights? Why were they entitled to respect and understanding? Had they not acted so unlawfully that these rights should be stripped from them?

"Something terrible must have happened in his life for him to do these things," Lily said.

"Something happens in everyone's life," Karsten said.

He stood up and went to the bouncer, lifted the child and held her close. He felt her wet mouth at the hollow of his neck, and her scent reached his nostrils. Sometimes he came close to tears because Margrete was a miracle. Margrete was his future, his old age; she was hope and light. She was the last cipher in the code to the vault of his innermost self, and he had finally gained access to the truth about himself.

He had found a warrior.

He returned Margrete carefully to the bouncer and went back to his crossword puzzle.

"Revenge is sweet," Lily said suddenly.

"That's what they say," Karsten said. "I've never avenged myself on anyone, but it's certainly true."

"But why sweet?" she said. "Isn't it a strange thing to say?"

"It must have something to do with the rush of endorphins you get when you finally do it. Something like that, I don't know. I don't really understand it." He put his hands behind his head and stretched out his long legs.

Lily could tell he was thinking of something; his green eyes narrowed. Do I love him? she wondered abruptly. The thought ran through her head, and she was quite horrified. I guess I have to love him, it's just us two. For eternity.

"When you discipline a dog," Karsten said, "you do it immediately. The dog steals a meatball from the table, and you smack its snout. You have to do it right away. If the dog's not punished in the span of three seconds it will never see the connection between the meatball and the hand that strikes."

"Why are you talking about dogs?"

He paused. Thought carefully about his words. "Our system may be just, but it's too cumbersome. And what is too cumbersome surely cannot be effective. Some fool commits a crime. After a while he's arrested and put in jail, and there he awaits his trial for months. Then there's the trial, and the fool is finally sentenced. But of course he'll appeal, and if he's sentenced again, he'll appeal again. Then he'll be sentenced again. Then he'll be given a tag because there are no vacant cells. How is that idiot supposed to see a connection?" Karsten gesticulated wildly. "Put the guy in handcuffs on Monday, sentence him on Tuesday and throw him in his cell on Wednesday. Then he'll stop stealing meatballs."

To show how serious he was, he hammered his clenched fist on the table.

"That doesn't work," Lily said. "We don't live in that kind of ideal society. We're not dogs either," she added with a sideways glance at her husband. She lifted Margrete and put her on her lap. "Criminals must have a certain mental capacity, and it's clear they see a connection. The most important thing is the consequence of their action. Besides, they'll carry it with them the rest of their lives. It will go on their record. They'll basically go through life tarnished," she said dramatically.

"Mental capacity?" Karsten snorted. "Do you think the idiot who was in our garden has any mental capacity?"

"Yes," Lily said. "I do. Perhaps he's very intelligent. And that's the reason I'm so afraid. Precisely because he is so cunning."

"But you shouldn't be afraid," Karsten cried out. "You should be livid!"

Again he pounded his fist on the table.

Lily closed her eyes. Never in her life had she been livid at anything. She couldn't summon the feeling. Something could fester inside her, but the minute it rose to the surface it was converted into helpless tears. There was something hopeless about it all, something that attached itself to her whole being; she couldn't scream and fight, couldn't get angry as others grew angry when they'd been violated. She just curled into a ball in the corner and licked her wounds. I'm a victim, she thought. I'd go to the slaughterhouse of my own volition, if anyone asked me to.

"Yes, well," she said aloud, "everyone is entitled to their opinion. The most important thing is that we're better people than he is. That we demonstrate the fact by letting the authorities handle it."

"But they only go so far." He looked at her with narrow eyes. "What should we do if they don't catch him?"

Lily cradled Margrete in her arms. "There's nothing we can do about it," she said.

14

HANNES AND WILMA BOSCH had lived in Norway for fifteen years, and they had built a large log cabin on the road to Saga. At the front of the house was a porch, and on the porch was a hammock with floral cushions. Little Theo rocked in the hammock. Theodor Bosch had just turned eight. One of his biggest heroes was the Transformer Optimus Prime, a robot which, through some quick hand movements, turned into a truck. The other hero in his life was the explorer Lars Monsen. Theo had Lars Monsen on DVD, on a poster above his bed, on his bookshelf and on the brain. In his room he even had a thick, life-size cardboard cutout of Lars Monsen. At the bookshop in Kirkeby he had begged for it, and he had carried it all by himself down the long escalator to the car. That figure of the well-known explorer was the first thing Theo saw when he opened his eyes in the morning. Lars Monsen with the crazy hair and the narrow eyes. At night he dreamed he had the same fishing rod as Lars Monsen, the same tent and same canoe. He dreamed he paddled across the waters and down the stream with a rifle over his shoulder and a knife on his belt. Dreamed he trekked across icy lakes, warmed his hands by a fire and cooked trout over the flames. Tore the fish from the bones with sharp, savage teeth.

But Theo was a thin eight-year-old, and it would be many years before he'd be an adult and could take up the life of the wilderness. Daydreaming, though, he was good at daydreaming. His imagination knew no boundaries, and sometimes it took him to remote and strange places while the rest of him was safe among the hammock's pillows. He swung and swung. He wore khaki shorts; his knees were round and white, like freshly scrubbed potatoes. His mother, Wilma, prepared a meal in the kitchen. Her body was strong and hefty and seemed infinitely safe. She was as solid as the big oak cabinet in the living room, the wooden bench in the kitchen, the nails in the wall.

So her husband, Hannes Bosch, thought.

He stood in the doorway and looked at her now, and when he turned he saw his tow-headed son in the hammock. The afternoon sun baked the cabin walls. He liked the rustling in the big woods, the broad, blonde woman at the stove, and his thin-legged son. He relished this fresh, pure ground on which they lived, the evergreens. Here is where Theo will grow up. He'll wander in the big woods, swim in the cold waters and breathe the clean air into his lungs. The lumberjacks felled big logs and built this house for them at some distance from other people.

They felt as though they had their own small country. Behind the house the stumps were lined up in a row, like soldiers at their posts.

Theo sat twisting a lock of hair between his fingers. The sun was low, the hammock swung gently. In the kitchen, Wilma Bosch opened the oven and lifted out a dish containing fish gratin. The entire house smelled of nutmeg.

"Call Theo," she commanded. "And set the table."

Hannes went to the cabinet. He removed three blue plates from the top shelf and cutlery from the drawer. Then he stuck his head out onto the porch.

"Are you sleeping? It's time for dinner. We'll go to the woods afterward, you and me."

Theo wheeled round. "You and me," he repeated, "and Optimus Prime."

Because the radio was playing "Kristina from Wilhelmina," Hannes began to sing while setting the table. "Will you be mine?" he bellowed. "My heart is burning." Wilma turned her back to him. Glass clinked in the kitchen, meaning that she'd opened two beers and a Fanta for Theo. Then they sat down.

A golden crust of bread crumbs covered the gratin.

"To Snellevann?" Theo asked hopefully.

"If you can walk that far," Hannes said.

They ate dinner in uninterrupted quiet. Afterward, they helped Wilma clear the table.

"We boys are going for a walk," Hannes said. They wore hiking outfits. Theo danced on the spot in anticipation. On his back Hannes carried a rucksack with a patch from Kvikklunsj chocolate bars.

"Watch out for adders," Wilma called out.

First they had to walk along the main road. There was lots of logging traffic on this stretch, and the road was narrow and winding, so Hannes made sure Theo was closest to the shoulder. After fifteen minutes they came to a trail called Glenna. Shortly after that they reached the metal barrier. Three cars were parked in an uneven row in the little car park.

"Now we'll take it easy," Hannes said, "because our stomachs are full. Look around, you heard what your mother said. There might be adders nearby. What do you have on your feet? Sandals, I see. Well, sandals aren't the smartest thing to wear. Lars Monsen wouldn't approve. Do you think Lars Monsen walks across Canada in sandals? But let's go. The sun will set soon, and if we're lucky the moose will come out."

With his clear blue eyes Theo looked up at his father. "The

87

moose," he repeated. "I bet he runs when he sees us." He laughed loudly and looked at his father for reassurance.

"Of course he'll run," Hannes said confidently. "He's probably hiding behind the trees watching us right now. After all, we're in his territory. That's how he views it anyway, wouldn't you say? So we should be on our best behavior, not scream and yell. We must respect nature. Everyone who walks on Glenna should be humble and tread lightly."

Suddenly he veered off the trail and took a few steps into the woods. Theo followed cautiously, glancing around before each step. He thought he heard a rattling sound. Sitting on a fallen tree, he watched as his father pulled the knife from his belt.

"Anyone who enters the woods needs a walking stick," he said. "A big one for me and a little one for you. To support us. And so we have something to fence with should we run into any mad cows. You shouldn't underestimate cows. They're very stupid, but they weigh a ton."

He snapped a branch from a tree and began tearing off leaves and twigs. When he was done, the stick had a chalk-white tip.

"You can spear perch with this when we reach the water," he said. He thrust the stick at Theo.

Theo sniffed it and found that it smelled good.

"Everything we need is in the woods," Hannes said. "Do you realize that? Food and water. Sun and warmth. We could live and work here, hunt, fell trees. Build a house. That's what people did in the olden days. What a great life it must have been, Theo. Wake at dawn, sleep at nightfall. All the bird calls and animal sounds."

Theo nodded. His father's words transported him to a magical place.

Then Hannes made a walking stick for himself, one that was longer and thicker. They returned to the trail, like two goatherds at work. Theo couldn't restrain himself; he hopped and danced, his blue eyes fastened on his father's broad back. After fifteen minutes they came to a crossroads where there was a sign with several maps and a request from the county.

THE FOREST IS A PASTURE FOR ANIMALS.

IT IS A WORKPLACE FOR LOGGERS,
HUNTERS AND FISHERMEN.
THE FOREST IS FOR RECREATION AND PLEASURE.

PLEASE BE CONSIDERATE OF OTHERS.

Theo read the request with a clear and cheerful voice. Father and son nodded at each other, then walked on. In a short while they passed St. Olav's Spring, and both drank gulps of the fresh water. From there it took forty minutes to get to Snellevann. They sat on a rock near the water and looked across.

Hannes put an arm on Theo's shoulder and pulled him close. "We're lucky, you and me."

Theo was in complete agreement. He could feel the strength in his father's body, could hear the whisper from the big woods and the life all around them.

"I brought us drinks," Hannes said. "Let's see." He dug around in his small rucksack. "You can choose between Solo and Sprite."

Theo chose Solo. He put the bottle to his mouth and drank. The fizz made his eyes water.

Hannes rummaged in his rucksack once more, searching for binoculars. He put them up to his eyes, moving the binoculars slowly back and forth across the water, then to the ridges beyond.

"Do you see anything?" Theo asked.

"Sheep," Hannes reported. "Up in the fields. Do you want to see?"

He handed the binoculars to Theo, and Theo tried to find the sheep, but it took a while. The image swayed before his eyes, and almost made him dizzy. At first he just saw some bushes and a stone dyke; because he couldn't hold the binoculars steady, the dyke floated up and down. Suddenly, it was as if the sheep tumbled into his field of vision.

"Is the image sharp?" Hannes asked. "Can you see them clearly?"

Theo nodded. "They're grazing."

"Like cows, they eat all day. What a life. Some live like kings."

Theo's arms grew tired from holding the binoculars, but he didn't want to let them go. He didn't want to head home again, either; he wanted to sit here with his father forever, on the warm rock near Snellevann, with the binoculars at his eyes.

"Mama must be done with the dishes by now," Hannes said.

"And she's in the hammock," Theo said.

"And she's snoring so the birds are flying off in fright."

For a moment they chuckled at Wilma whom they loved so much. Theo raised the binoculars again. The sheep lay like white specks on the green hillside. He caught sight of a ramshackle old barn, and far to the right, a few red cows.

"There's something's odd about one of the sheep," he reported.

Hannes waited for further explanation.

"It's different."

"Is it black?"

Theo shook his head. "No. It's more orange."

"C'mon. Orange. You watch too many films."

Hannes grabbed the binoculars. Through the lens he saw an orange-colored sheep among the white ones. It moved around comfortably, apparently without knowing of its glaring peculiarity. The sight was so unusual that Hannes stayed put, staring.

"I can't believe it," he said. "What on earth have they done with that sheep? He looks like an orange on four legs."

Hannes's laughter rang out over Snellevann. For quite some time they scrutinized the orange-colored sheep. The binoculars passed between them, and each time it was Theo's turn, he was transfixed by the unusual sight. Then he leapt from the rock and ran around, waving his arms enthusiastically. Hannes worried about the binoculars. They were from Zeiss, the most expensive kind you could buy, and he didn't want to see them smashed on the rocks.

"Sit down," he ordered. "Careful with the equipment."

Theo sat obediently and handed the binoculars back to his father.

"Someone's attacked the poor thing with spray paint," Hannes confirmed. "Maybe a sheep tagger?"

He looked once more at the sheep, couldn't get enough of it. Lifted the binoculars, lowered them again. Shook his heavy, Dutch head. "Isn't that the color they use in the Highway Department?" he said. "When they measure and mark the road? The kind of color that glows in the dark. I'm just wondering."

"The other sheep don't seem to care," Theo commented. "They just keep eating as if it was nothing."

"That's because sheep are pretty stupid. They have brains the size of coffee beans."

To get a better look, Hannes scrambled to his feet, and Theo stood up too. They observed the unusual sheep. Then Hannes searched in his pocket for his mobile. He wanted to call the local newspaper and tell them about the strange discovery. While his father made the call, Theo put the bottle of Solo to his lips and drank. He was happy.

"My name is Bosch," said the father. "Hannes Bosch. We're in the woods down by Snellevann, my son and I, and we've found something incredible. Send a reporter. Bring a photographer—with color film. Otherwise you'll miss the point."

He listened a moment, nodded several times, and winked at Theo.

"Really quite amusing," he said. "You won't believe it until you see it."

Theo drank more of the sweet carbonated liquid. He picked up his walking stick again, sat and waved it as his father talked with the newspaper reporter.

"You should probably contact the sheep farmer and ask him to bring shears," Hannes said. "He's going to have to trim right to the skin. But take a picture first, for goodness' sake. Ha ha . . . No, I don't know who owns the flock, but as I said, they're out on the hillside above Snellevann . . . Fifty or so . . . It could be Sverre Skarning's. You could start with him. One of the ewes has a yellow-and-blue tag. If it means anything to you. Or if he asks. Yellow and blue."

Theo put the empty bottle of Solo in the rucksack.

"We can meet where the paths cross," Hannes said. "At the sign there. We'll be there in forty minutes. Can I tell my boy that he'll get his picture in the newspaper? . . . Brilliant. He'll be proud. Here's a working title for you." He laughed. "Sheep shocker by Snellevann!"

Hannes put his mobile in his pocket.

They started back. Theo hopped about, waving his walking stick.

"Mama won't believe us," he said.

"We might as well say we saw a Bengal tiger," Hannes said. He drove his stick into the hill, spraying sand.

Theo stared between the tree trunks, into the dark foliage. He thought he could hear shaking and stirring everywhere.

"Are there bears in here, Papa?"

Hannes rumpled his son's hair. "There aren't any bears this far south, just orange-colored sheep."

They walked to the crossroads, and stood there waiting. Theo sat by a ditch, while Hannes paced back and forth, like a guard on patrol.

"You'll be in the paper, Theo. It'll be great. Mama will be surprised."

Theo nodded. He asked his father to get Optimus Prime out of the rucksack so he could play with it while they waited for the reporter. Hannes handed it to him. Then he stretched his arms like wings and started running back and forth along the trail.

"What are you doing?" Theo called out.

"I'm the Flying Dutchman," Hannes shouted. "An outlaw without kin."

Then he landed at his son's side.

"But who dyed the sheep?" Theo wanted to know.

"Some prankster," Hannes said, "who likes to have fun with people. Maybe the madman who's behind all that stuff in the newspaper."

"Is he in the woods now?" Theo asked, looking around.

"Oh no, you're safe," he assured him. "Norway is a peaceful country. We don't have much to worry about. No war, famine or deprivation. The safest place of all, Theo, is here, in the woods."

The journalist appeared in the bend, and it was Theo who told the story. In the end he was asked to stand against the trunk of a spruce, the Zeiss binoculars around his neck, to be photographed in true newspaper fashion. Later, he sat with his mother on the sofa and told her about the day's events.

15

A SHORT, STOUT MAN, Sverre Skarning wore big boots and had a plug of tobacco in his mouth. The fact that the police bothered to stop by because of some sheep was, to him, pretty funny. Like so many farmers, he seemed healthy and strong. He had apple-red cheeks and his trousers—held up by braces—appeared to be homemade.

They were in the vicinity, Sejer explained to him, and stopped by for their own amusement. Just in case there was any connection with other bizarre events that had occurred recently.

"Well," Skarning laughed softly, "at least the meat isn't spoiled—that's always a comfort."

"How's the sheep doing?" Sejer asked with a smile.

Skarning shook his head in resignation. "It's in the barn. They used some damn chemicals, some poisonous stuff from a spray can, so it's got runny eyes. I suppose you'll figure out what. I've saved the wool. Got it in a plastic bag. You can send it to the lab for analysis." He laughed again.

He started walking across the farmyard. Because he was quite a few pounds overweight, his gait was heavy and swaying, like a goose.

"But that one sheep wasn't the biggest problem. The bugger left all the gates open. I had sheep wandering about everywhere.

Had to take the trailer to round them up. A neighbor helped. It's dangerous when sheep are on the road. Accidents, you know. Clearly that idiot doesn't think too far ahead."

They ambled slowly toward the sheep barn. Much of the farm machinery was parked alongside the walls. At the side of the house sat a blue Chevrolet. They went into the barn, heads bent, eyes blinking in the weak light. As soon as they were inside, the smell of animals and wool and manure hit them. The sheep, now completely shorn, was in a stall at the back of the barn. But the tail and ears were still orange. Skarre erupted with laughter.

"Not even a wolf would want that one," Skarning said. "If we had wolves here. It's not pretty, eh? It looks like something knitted by old women in a mental hospital."

The sheep grew uneasy at the sound of the laughter ringing in the barn. Skarning stepped into the stall. He pulled on the sheep's ears and then examined his fingers. "The color has to wear off eventually." He looked at Sejer and Skarre. "You need to have a sense of humor about it. Worse things can happen. But one thing is certain: a real rascal did this." He patted the sheep on the rump, exited the stall and closed the gate.

When they came out into the farmyard, the sun hit them in the eyes.

"We'll have us a nip of coffee," Skarning said. "Do you have time? I'll get the wife. Don't say no. It's not every day the police visit."

He went back to the house in the steady manner of a farmer, a little hunched over with his hands clasped behind his back. His large fists resembled root vegetables. He had lost most of his hair, and his shiny bald dome was tanned from the sun. He left his wellingtons on the steps and led the men into an impressive kitchen. All around them were polished copper pots, rustic furniture with floral motifs and old handwoven rugs in splendid colors. A cat slept in a corner, fat and striped like a mackerel.

"Sit down," Skarning said.

A girl entered the room, quietly, in bare feet. Or perhaps it was a woman. It was difficult to tell how old she was; her hair was covered by a headscarf, and she was petite with smooth skin. She wore a light summer dress, and her right hand was bandaged. She stopped when she saw the men, nodded and mumbled her name, something exotic which they didn't catch.

"Coffee?" Skarning said hopefully.

The petite girl moved to the worktop. Under the windowsill sat a large, sleek espresso machine. In this farmer's kitchen it was just as exotic as the girl herself. Her hair was hidden under the scarf, but she had dark eyes, with thin, fine brows. With competent hands she manipulated the espresso machine; the bandaged right hand wasn't completely useless. Skarning lifted his pipe from the ashtray and lit it. He puffed out small clouds of sweet, white smoke.

"I've got me a veiled little farmer's girl," he grinned. "Not bad, eh? She's good with the machine. The coffee is the best I've tasted. Forget that sludge they make in the cafés in town." He nodded at the hostess at the worktop. "From time to time, when she gets too demanding, I have to show her who's boss. I put her hand in the hot waffle iron. I press the lid down and count slowly to ten. Then she settles down."

He blew out more white smoke clouds, watching them billow toward the ceiling, where they became streaks wrapped around an impressive cast-iron lamp.

Sejer stared at the bandaged hand.

The hostess poured water into the machine. Her back was narrow and girlish.

"She'll never learn Norwegian either," Skarning went on, "but it doesn't matter. I didn't get her so she could walk around the house saying whatever she pleases, whenever she pleases. I'll grant she can have ideas. I just don't need to hear them all the time." He inhaled from his pipe. Puff, puff. "She cleans," he said, "and makes me coffee."

The hostess let go of whatever it was she held in her hands. She turned round and looked at the men through dark, almond-shaped eyes. Then she stood behind her husband and bent down and kissed his bald, sunburned scalp.

"Don't frighten the guests," she said. "They're city people. They don't understand country folk. They might not get your sense of humor, you old farmer."

She kissed him again. Then she gave a trilling laugh, and gestured with the bandaged hand. "I had to go to the shopping center to return a DVD. The shop was closed, so I had to slide the film through the slot in the door. My hand got stuck. Do you take sugar in your espresso?"

Sejer and Skarre nodded in unison.

She nudged her husband. "You shouldn't sit there baaing," she said. "You spend too much time with your sheep. Soon you'll be growing wool."

Skarning gave his wife a broad, loving smile. "Come and sit now. Bring teaspoons so we can stir our coffee, all of us. Really we should have a snifter," he added, "but I reckon you're on duty. Ha ha. Policemen are always on duty."

The hostess sat at the table. The china clinked as they stirred their coffee.

"I was here with a customer who was buying eggs when they came from the local paper," she said. "Sverre had taken the trailer to collect the orange sheep and all the others that had wandered out onto the roads."

"A customer buying eggs?"

"We have some hens," she explained. "So we sell the surplus. Don't tell anyone. We don't declare the few kroner we earn—no one out here does. But a man was here and he bought a whole tray. We talked for a while. In another half-hour, Sverre returned. When I saw what he had on his trailer, I almost fainted."

She tidied her headscarf. It was dark red with a few yellow flowers.

"Who uses the forest path here?" Sejer asked.

"Everyone who lives in Bjerkås," Skarning said. He slurped his hot espresso and made a contented smacking sound.

"People also come from Kirkeby, to ride their bicycles. Some come to fish down at Snellevann. In autumn the area swarms with Poles picking berries. So there's quite a lot of activity. Those who drive here park at the barrier. So what do you think? Is it the same rascal? He wants to show us he's got a sense of humor?"

"It's too early to tell," Sejer said.

"What's the punishment for spray-painting a sheep?" the hostess wondered.

Sejer couldn't answer.

"Get some planks of wood from the barn," Skarning suggested. "I'll build stocks to put him in."

On the way back, Sejer and Skarre drove by Lake Skarve and went into the Spar for something to drink. They wandered around the aisles, each picking up a few things.

"She looked like a teenager," Sejer said. He meant the hostess.

Skarre shook his head. "You're way off, Konrad. She was at least thirty. Why don't you wear your glasses? You're so shortsighted." They stood by the freezer. Skarre picked up packages, examined them and put them back again.

"You should get contact lenses, or you could have laser surgery—then you'd have the eyes of an eagle. It costs thirty thousand kroner, and you can afford it."

From the freezer he pulled out a heavy, frozen square. It was wrapped in plastic, and was almost black in color. He felt its weight in his hands.

"Good God, look what I've found." He read the label and checked the price. "Do you realize what this is?"

"No," Sejer said. "I'm shortsighted. You just said so yourself."

"'One point two kilos,'" Skarre read. "'Price: thirty-two kroner. Best before October '09.' It's blood. It's frozen blood. Can you believe it?"

"Thirty-two kroner," Sejer said drily. He took the frozen square from Skarre's hands and studied it closely. "They sell blood," he said in wonder. "Who buys such a thing?"

Skarre shrugged. "Farmers' wives, maybe. They probably make blood pudding and the like, don't they?"

Sejer walked toward the fresh-meat counter carrying the square of blood. There he addressed a stocky man in a white apron. "We found this in the freezer, and I have a question about it. Do you sell a lot of this stuff during the course of a year?"

The man shook his head. "Nope, very little. I ordered ten liters in the spring. We've sold two, maybe. But it's part of our selection here. Say what you like, but blood is really healthy. It tastes good, too, believe it or not.

"People just don't dare try it. Preconceived notions," he added smugly.

"Who buys it?"

"You'll have to ask the cashiers. I don't have a clue about that end of the shop."

"Is it ox blood?"

"Yes."

Sejer walked between the aisles and up to the cashiers. He put the package of frozen blood on the conveyor belt; he recognized Britt with the little piercing in her eyebrow.

"Don't scan it," he said quickly. "I just want to ask you something. Can you remember selling a package like this recently?"

She read the label. Saw that it was blood and shook her head.

"Is there anyone else who works the till?" Skarre asked. "Who else works here?" He looked around the shop.

"No one else today," she replied. "But there are three of us in all: Gunn, Ella Marit and myself. We work different shifts. I'm all alone today. Don't even get to eat," she said, a little put out. She pushed a lock of dyed hair off her forehead.

Skarre took his card out of his pocket and put it on the conveyor belt for her. "Talk to the others," he said. "Ask if they remember anyone who bought ox blood here. Then call me immediately with all the details."

Britt nodded eagerly. She picked up the card, held it a moment and dropped it in the pocket of her green Spar uniform. Then she rang up their items, a mineral water, a Coke and two newspapers.

"Do you notice what people buy?" Skarre wanted to know.

She cocked her head, pressed her lips together and bided her time. "Sometimes. We get to know people. We know what they eat and so on."

"Give me some examples," Skarre said. "Of what you notice."

She hesitated. Perhaps it was difficult for her to admit that she had a voyeur's sensibility. Debating with herself and her good reputation, she threw quick, inquisitive glances at Skarre.

"If people buy chopped lungs," she admitted, "I notice. Because I just don't understand why people want to eat lungs. They look so gray and disgusting. Like a fungus. So I stare a little longer at them."

"I don't get it either," Skarre conceded. "Who buys chopped lungs?"

"Old people," she said. "And I know who drinks, who comes here to buy beer. And I know all the players." She pointed at a rack of condoms by the counter, Profil and Nøkken. Ribbed, colored and flavored. "Then there's the lady who buys painkillers every week. She must be in a lot of pain. Her hands shake terribly. I notice those kinds of things, and if anyone bought blood, I would have remembered. I didn't even know we sell it. Goodness. It's more than a liter."

Suddenly she understood the connection to the baby at Bjerketun, and her face took on an expression of alarm.

Skarre put his items in a bag, and noted her name tag.

"You'll ring then, Britt." He smiled.

She pulled his card from her uniform pocket and examined it more closely.

"Definitely, Jacob." She smiled too. "I'll call."

Later, on the way home, Sejer stopped by his daughter's house.

He parked his Rover by the curb and walked up the steps, turned to make sure his parking was perfect, and put his finger on the doorbell.

Ingrid patted his cheek and pulled him inside. When he was sitting comfortably, she stood before him, arms crossed.

"Guess what happened," she said dramatically. "Matteus pulled a muscle in his thigh."

"What?" Sejer said, startled. "Is it serious? When? Did he fall?"

"Yesterday," she said. "During rehearsal. Doing the splits."

"Where is he now?"

"He's gone to get a massage. My nerves are truly frazzled because of that boy. It's one thing after another. That's how it is with ballet. Erik has told me that straight out—it's unhealthy."

Erik, her husband, was a doctor and knew about such things.

She sat opposite him and rested her hands on the table. Sejer put his hands on hers, like a lid. When she was a girl, they played a game in which her hands were tiny birds he kept caged so they couldn't fly away. Then he let them go, and she shrieked in delight as he tried to catch them. Maybe she also remembered this, because she smiled at him across the table. She grew serious again.

"There's always something with that body of his," she said.

"How it functions and performs. Its muscles, its flexibility and strength. Its weaknesses. That body's a constant headache."

Her fingers moved under his palms as she talked. It tickled him a little.

"Not to mention all the supplements he needs, vitamins and minerals, to stay in top condition. Or all the things he can't eat. Or drink. Or do. There's a lot he can't do."

Sejer gave her hands a squeeze. "He plays that card when it suits him, Ingrid. You know how he is. We were at Roy's recently. He gobbled down a big cheeseburger with chips and mayonnaise."

She blinked, confused, and laughed nervously. "A cheeseburger? Really?"

Sejer nodded.

"I see," Ingrid said. "During the week I do what he asks, making the meals he says he needs. And he eats junk food with you?" She pouted like a child. "Well, what do you know. He's a traitor—and so are you, by the way."

"It's a grandfather's privilege"—Sejer smiled—"to be exempt from strict rules."

"Sometimes I wish he would fall and break his leg."

Sejer opened his eyes wide.

"Then he'd be forced to sit quietly and rest. For weeks."

He shook his head. "You won't get Matteus to sit still."

She sighed, as mothers do when they worry over trifles.

"Think about what you've done," Sejer reminded her. "You left Norway to go off to a civil war in a foreign country. You left comfort and convenience and everything that was safe behind. I don't even know what you did down there, perhaps I don't want to know. But you found Matteus and brought him home. He doesn't care about comfort and convenience either. He subjects himself to relentless training, discomfort and pain. But he's happy. Isn't he happy, Ingrid?"

"Have you seen his feet?"

"No."

"Don't ask to see them," she said. "I wouldn't wish that sight on anyone. People don't know what ballet is. They just see dancers gliding around the stage, and it looks so easy. So pure and fine and beautiful. But there are injuries and constant hard work."

"Oh, Ingrid."

She stood at the sink filling a water jug.

"Are you afraid he won't get the role in *Swan Lake*?"

She shrugged. "I suppose so."

"That makes two of us," he said. "Come and sit now. Much of the world is at war. We can't sit here and complain."

She poured water for them. Then she smiled at herself and her concerns. "And you, Dad. How are you doing?"

He drank the water.

"Be honest. Do you think about Mum?"

He set the glass on the table with a clink. "I don't think about her that much," he admitted. "But she's there all the time, like background noise. Images of things we did together when we were young. Memories of her dying. All the pain she went through. It's a little like living by a waterfall," he said. "The years go by and I'm worn down by the continuous roar. Which I can never shut off. But it was the card I drew in this life."

"A home by the waterfall," she said.

He nodded. "And you? How often do you think of your mum? Be honest," he mimicked.

She pushed her chair back and stood up. She wore a purple knitted jacket. She had good posture like her mother. He made a new discovery: gray strands in her blonde hair. Instantly he felt sad. Ingrid, his daughter, his little girl, had gray hair.

"I don't think so much about Mum," Ingrid conceded. "I was so young."

He didn't respond.

"From the moment she died I was focused on you. Where you

were. How you were. I went around listening all the time, for your steps, your voice. Whether you were alive. Does that make sense?"

She looked at him and it seemed as if she ached for something more than the words she spoke. Then she sat down again. Planted her elbows on the table. "Do you know why I'm so afraid of death?"

He didn't know where she was going with this, but he waited for her to continue.

"We think we're irreplaceable, but we're not. New people replace us all the time. Many are better than us. Nicer than us. Stronger than us. Have you thought of that?"

"You're suggesting I should have remarried."

"Maybe." She smiled. "You settle for so little."

He shook his head in protest. He didn't think he lacked anything at all. When I come home I take a walk with Frank, he thought, then I sit in my chair at the window. I drink a whisky. I smoke a cigarette, slowly, savoring every last drag. Maybe play an album by Monica Zetterlund. Or Laila Dalseth. Then I go to bed and sleep well.

What more could a man ask for?

Ingrid nodded at the window. She grew serious again. "I was standing over there when you pulled up. I recognized your car, and I kept my eye on you the whole time. The whole time, Dad. Every single second."

He nodded and smiled. But actually he was nervous at what he knew she would say.

"When you got out of the car, I saw you lose your balance."

He tried to find something to say, something to downplay it. "I have low blood pressure."

"Low blood pressure?" She gave a little snort.

"I've always had low blood pressure," he said. "When I sit in the car for a long time, then get up too quickly—"

"Sit in the car for a long time? Didn't you drive here from the police station? It's a three-minute trip."

"I was just a little dizzy," he mumbled. "It can happen to the best of us."

"Have you been to the doctor's?"

"I can't bother a doctor just because I'm a little dizzy now and then."

"Yes, you can," she said. "Are you afraid of doctors?"

"It's so much trouble, Ingrid, with tests and all the rest. I mean, spending half the day in a waiting room. I don't have the time."

She gave up, slumped forward. Her father was intelligent and kind and generous, but he was also, when it came to himself, unapproachable. "You're shy," she said. "You don't like the thought of getting undressed in front of someone else. Lying on a doctor's examination table. Answering questions about how you live."

"I live well."

"I know. You don't need to be embarrassed, because you're actually in quite good shape. But it's not right that you get dizzy every time you stand up."

"Not every time, Ingrid. Just now and then."

She leaned closer and tapped his nose. "If I ask you to stay for a while, or for dinner, you'll say no, because you've got to head home to Frank."

"He's been alone since seven this morning." He rose and pushed his chair into place. "When you were small," he reminded her, "you threw a tantrum to get what you wanted."

"And it worked every single time." She smiled.

The door banged open in the hallway. Matteus tumbled in.

Sejer noticed he was limping.

Ingrid didn't mention the cheeseburger.

16

JOHNNY BESKOW DIDN'T own much.

His mother never shared anything, and never gave him anything. He had his Suzuki Estilete, a helmet and a pair of top-quality biking gloves with red skulls. Two pairs of jeans, some faded T-shirts, a hooded jumper and trainers which he wore year round.

He stood in the doorway to his room, and instantly he knew something was missing.

Bleeding Heart was gone.

The empty cage confused him. He examined it carefully, putting his hand inside and lifting the little plastic maze. But no guinea pig emerged. He got down on all fours and searched under his bed. He hunted behind the curtains, under his desk and pillows, and the rubbish bin in the corner. He turned and walked, soundlessly, into the living room. His mother sat in a chair with a stack of bills. She glanced up.

"What have you done with him?!" he shouted. "Tell me now!"

She looked at him indifferently, then put her finger on a stack of yellow payment forms and made a tired face. "They'll cut the electricity soon," she mumbled.

"Where's Bleeding Heart?"

She rolled her eyes. "Do you mean the little rat? He got loose.

I can't have rats running around the house. He chewed on the cords and all kinds of things, and that can cause a short circuit and burn the whole house down. But I guess you'd probably like that."

Johnny began to tremble from head to toe. After years of bullying and neglect, he'd grown rather thick-skinned. But this was too much for him.

"He didn't get loose," he screamed. "He can't get out of the cage on his own. There's a latch on the door. You just went and took him, that's what you did. You took him. You need to tell me where he is, now!"

She gathered her payment forms, got up and shoved them in a drawer. Then she looked at him over her shoulder. "Well, what should we do with a dead rat? What do you think, Johnny?"

He knew what she'd done. Standing a few meters away, his fists clenched, he understood that she'd killed the most precious thing he owned. Somehow. And it made him angry. He got so angry that his thoughts ran to horrible places. I'll put the army knife into your spine, he thought, so you'll be paralyzed in both legs and you'll have to crawl on your elbows while I sit in a chair and tell you how you're going to die. He wondered exactly where in the back he'd have to stab her to slice the right nerve.

"I put it in an empty milk carton," she said suddenly.

He breathed deeply. Moved a few steps closer, opening and closing his fists. "And where's the milk carton? Is it in the rubbish? Are you telling me Bleeding Heart is in the rubbish?"

"Yes," she confessed. "In the bin for food waste. I won't have rats here," she repeated. "It smells of them. It smells of piss from that cage, Johnny!"

Quietly Johnny Beskow made his way out of the house. Went down to the gate where the rubbish bins stood. He opened the bin and looked inside, and immediately he recognized the milk carton. She had folded it tight, and his hands trembled when he opened it. Bleeding Heart, sticky wet, was curled into a ball. She had drowned him. Maybe in the bathroom sink.

For a long time he held the wet fur ball. I can deal with almost anything, he thought. Year after year I've held my tongue. But the day is coming when I will get up and take my gruesome revenge. She doesn't know it, but that day is very close. I just need the right moment. To hell with the consequences—life is a drag, and so is death. When I get my revenge people can do what they want and think what they want, I won't care. That's why I'm better than them.

He pulled himself away and strode to the back of the house, where he found an old rusty spade. He put the guinea pig on the grass and began to dig. Extremely focused, he dug a deep grave, laid the small animal inside and covered it with dirt. Then he found a stone and put it on top of the grave, like a heavy lid. I hope it's deep enough, he thought, so the badgers don't get you. He stood tall and wiped the sweat from his forehead. He was beaten, but he didn't intend to stay down. He marched over to his moped, put on his helmet and drove onto the road.

Twenty minutes later he arrived at the shopping center in Kirkeby. Because he liked breaking rules, he parked in a disabled space. Whenever Johnny could break a rule, he did so, and now he wished for nothing more than to be insufferable. After everything that had happened. He took the escalator up to the second floor and trudged into the pet shop. A girl behind the counter followed him with her eyes; she fingered some papers, stared at him for a moment and kept him under surveillance. First, Johnny went to the aquarium and admired the catfish. Then the girl strolled slowly toward him, long and stooped and swaying; she had large, heavy eyelids and long lashes. Her lower lip was very full, making him think of a camel.

"Are you interested in fish?"

"No," Johnny said. "I want a guinea pig. One with three colors, black, brown and white. A male. I don't care how much it costs."

"We don't have any guinea pigs," she said.

"What? Not a single one?"

He wasn't sure he had heard right. He was in a pet shop, and they didn't have a guinea pig.

The camel headed toward a row of cages against the wall, pointed and showed him what she had to offer, which was a little bit of everything.

"We have dwarf rabbits," she said temptingly, "and polecats and brown rats. And we have a large chinchilla, but it's sort of boring—sleeps all day."

Johnny Beskow hesitated. He didn't want to go home without a new pet. So he studied the furry creatures with considerable interest.

"And we have a hamster," she remembered. "It's all by itself now. Its siblings have been sold." She opened one of the cages and lifted out a small champagne-colored fur ball. "The hamster is great. It's much smarter than a guinea pig. And really tame."

He took the animal, and held it up to his cheek. "I see," he said, setting it back in its cage. He didn't want to be hasty. He took his time. The rats were strong; they smelled like cloves, and were fast as lightning. One was an albino and had red eyes, like rubies. The chinchilla seemed aloof, didn't even bother to blink, and the dwarf rabbits were for girls. He picked up the animals one by one, weighed them in his hands and held them up to his cheek. Thought long and hard.

"The hamster," he said decisively and walked to the counter.

The camel followed with the little animal in her hand.

"You'll also need a number of things," she explained eagerly. "Cage. Toys. Food bowl and water bowl. You should get this vitamin supplement which you drip into the drinking water. And they like to make a nest for themselves. You can buy cotton rags at the petrol station next door, they don't cost much." She held a little bottle with a dropper out to him. "Here are the vitamins. We also have a powder here, with minerals and such, which you sprinkle over his food every morning. For his bones. You shouldn't be careless about such things."

"No!" he objected. "Leave me alone. I already have a cage. I have everything I need, and I don't have the money for all that stuff. Jesus, it's only a hamster. I'm not running a hotel!"

She put the hamster in a box with holes. Squeezed her lips into a thin line and was affronted because he'd rejected her expertise.

But Johnny was content. He paid 250 kroner for the little devil, and left the shop with his new friend under his arm. If she drowns this one, I'll bring a spider home, he thought.

Or a snake.

When he got home, his mother was wearing a dress.

It happened very rarely, so he stood staring into the kitchen. The dress was dark blue with a white ruche at the hem and, to be honest, resembled something from a bygone era. But it was a change, perhaps even an improvement. For in this outfit she acted completely differently. She wore high-heeled shoes with ankle straps, the heels resembling spools: narrow in the middle and fatter above and below. She had brushed her dark hair, and, at first glance, she could've passed for a woman with her life under control, a woman with a certain level of self-discipline, will and decisiveness. But her suffering was just as visible. The affliction, the alcoholism, could be seen in the fierce line of her mouth, the wronged look in her eyes, the trembling in her hands and un-steadiness of her gait. It was obvious she was hardened. She'd been unjustly treated and wasn't responsible for her own situation; her alcoholism had been out of her control, just as people who are struck by lightning cannot control the lightning. She couldn't have defended herself against it. She was a victim. She didn't have a choice; she listened to her body, and her body wrenched her whenever the intoxication began to ebb. The discomfort, she couldn't bear it. She couldn't follow through, couldn't please, couldn't serve, couldn't participate. She was a shipwreck, and she was sinking. But now she had put on a dress and was stone-cold sober, or at least that's what it seemed to him. She had raised her sails. The goal, he thought as he observed her, is money. She tottered around in her high heels, and he held his breath when he saw how her ankles struggled to hold her weight, to keep her upright.

But so far, it was working.

She held her head high. Smoothing her dress, she didn't see him. He pressed himself against the door frame, holding the box behind his back. The hamster scratched and clawed inside the box, but she didn't notice it. She looked out of the window, noted the clouds, and grabbed a coat from a wall hook. The coat was ancient, a thin, faux fur, gray-brown with some darker spots.

She put it on before the mirror in the hallway.

Yes, she's looking for money, Johnny thought. She must have discovered some form of public assistance she might be entitled to. Maybe there was something in the newspaper about new welfare regulations—after all, the government has promised to help the poor. If she looked presentable, if her heels carried her, if people just noticed the ruche on the hem of her dress. Silently he leaned against the wall and listened to her footsteps, the sharp clap. The heels spoke their own language. It is my right, the heels said decisively. It's not too much to ask for.

Finally she grabbed her bag and left. He ran straight to the window and watched her stalk toward the bus stop. She's probably going into the city, he thought, to some office or other, where she'll wipe away tears in her theatrical way. She wobbled slightly in her heels. His cheeks began to burn, because he realized everyone could see her: the neighbors and anyone driving past. The spotted coat made her look like a hyena, and now she was out hunting for carrion. Without wanting to, he felt pity for her. She looked so vulnerable in the harsh light. It tormented and confused him. The empathy weighed him down, made him heavy and sad and despondent. So he tried to muster some anger instead. His anger gave him the energy to act. When she was finally out of sight, he went to his room to get a closer look at the hamster. He decided to call it Butch. Or, put in another way, the Butcher from Askeland. It was doing well. He put it in the cage, and it seemed happy in its new home. After he had eaten a bowl of cereal, he went out and started up his moped again. He put his helmet on and drove onto the road, throwing a glance toward the bus stop.

The hyena was gone.

He checked his fuel gauge and accelerated. He wore his thin riding gloves with the skulls. Speed gave him a feeling of superiority. He felt invincible, faster and smarter than everyone else. Here comes Johnny Beskow, he thought. You can build all you want, but I will tear down your towers. That's how powerful I am.

The road cut through a landscape of yellow fields, passed the church and Lake Skarve, Bjerkås town center, headed toward Kirkeby and finally went eastward to Sandberg. Out here people had more money. You could see it in the houses, which were bigger and better kept than they were at Askeland. Swiss-style houses. Double garages. Big gardens. Small, silly fountains, solar-powered lights along the driveways. He neared the center of Sandberg. To the left was a grassy slope bordering a playing field, and to the right an enormous house. He was on Sandbergveien. When he passed house number 15, something caught his attention. He eased up on the throttle. A couple were sitting outside in the sun, at a table. The man stood out for several reasons.

He was older than the woman.

He was emaciated, his body hunched.

He was in a wheelchair.

Johnny pulled off the road and laid the moped on the slope. Then he squatted down in the grass and stared at the couple. Sensing his presence, they looked at him. So he took out his mobile, pretended to punch in a number and put it to his ear. Then they turned their attention back to each other.

Johnny observed them on the sly. The man in the wheelchair wore shorts; he had bare, bluish-white legs that wouldn't support him. His hair was thin and matted, and his hands, resting on the wheels, also seemed to be unusable. There must be something more going on than paralysis in his legs, Johnny thought, because as he studied the man he noticed the thick plastic tube in his neck. That meant he needed help breathing. It meant that his illness had spread and reached the muscles around his lungs. The woman scurried about and tended to him, poured drinks, held the cup to his mouth. Wiped his chin and cheek with a napkin, fluffed a pillow behind his back. Aimlessly she rearranged a dish on the table, but neither of them touched the food.

After staring for a long time at the couple in the garden, Johnny wandered a few steps down the road. He stopped at their mailbox, read the name and address, and returned to the slope and sat. The Landmarks. Astrid and Helge Landmark, Sandbergveien 15. He found their number through directory inquiries, and dialed.

The woman heard the telephone ringing through the open patio door, and she disappeared into the house to answer.

The man was now alone in the garden. Helpless in his wheelchair with his ruined legs. He tried to work out where the woman, his helper, the one he was dependent on, had gone. If he needed something, he would have to shout. If he was able to shout. He hardly had the strength to communicate the unrest in his doughy body.

Johnny turned off his mobile. Seconds later the woman returned, a little confused because someone had fooled her into leaving. She was back quickly, stroking the man's arm. Johnny hopped onto his moped and rode off. The man's helplessness and the woman's anxiety had put him in a different mood.

On the way home, he stopped at the Sparbo Dam.

He pushed the moped the final stretch through the woods and leaned it against the trunk of a spruce. He had begun walking to the dam when he caught sight of something between the trees. Someone had beaten him there. Whoever it was had gone out onto the wall of the dam where he liked to sit. He was so furious that he wanted to scream, because that was his spot, his secret place at the water, and he had never seen anyone else there. Then he saw a blue bicycle lying in the heather to his right. He hid behind a tree, and stared with stinging eyes. The bicycle was a Nakamura. It was Else Meiner, that nasty little girl, the one with the big mouth. She was reading a book, and didn't realize he was watching her. He glared at her red plait. The sun made it shine like a thick copper wire. A little shove, he thought, and you'd fall face first into the water. I'll come back for you, he thought. I'll find the right moment, and you'll get it. He stayed a few minutes longer observing her narrow back, and then carefully returned through the heather. He pulled his army knife from his belt and slashed up both of her tires. The sun had warmed the rubber, and the knife sliced easily. He rolled his moped onto the road and walked a good while before finally starting the engine. With the wind in his face, tears formed in his eyes and exultation in his heart!

His mother was still out when he got home.

He went straight to his room, opened the door to the cage and carried Butch over to his bed. He was smaller than Bleeding Heart, his body fatter, but just as lively as the guinea pig had been. He let the hamster crawl across the duvet, and before he knew it, it had dropped some tiny turds. They were dry and hard, and easy to pick up. Maybe I should keep them, he thought, so I can mix them with the hyena's food. Later he sneaked into his mother's bedroom, and stared at her mess. The hyena lives here, he thought, this is her lair. I should get a fox trap, and I should put it outside her door. So she'll head right into the trap when she gets up to go into the hall. Then she'll have to stagger around with that trap until the iron rusts and her foot rots.

People will hear her howling throughout the entire Askeland housing estate.

He closed the door and headed into the living room. After deciding to watch a film, he riffled through the selections and finally chose a horror film called *The Living and the Dead*. He got comfortable on the sofa. The film had a promising subtitle.

"A nightmarish descent into hell."

17

H ER NAME WAS Astrid Landmark. She had recently turned fifty-three. At fifty-nine her husband, Helge, seemed much older sitting in his wheelchair. She had wheeled him in front of the television, but he couldn't follow the program; he just sat there dozing, in the blue flicker of the screen. The light made him morbidly pale.

Astrid stood with her back to him. She held clothes that needed ironing. Because the paralysis rose in his body relentlessly, like tidewater, it was difficult to look him in the eye. Soon he wouldn't be able to swallow, or talk or breathe. They understood this; they knew what to expect down to the smallest detail. The fear of death had sunk its claws in him, but he didn't have the strength to fight back. She couldn't stand it. She didn't know where to look, what to say. Almost everything was taboo, almost nothing could be discussed. Phrases like *until spring,* or *next Christmas,* or *another time* had become impossible to utter; there wouldn't be another time. They ought to discuss many things, important things about death and burial. And the cabin at Blefjell which he'd named El Dorado because it was such a money pit. Should she keep it? What about the house? Would she be able to maintain it? Would she be able to start the lawn mower? Manage the snowblower in the winter? Who would stain the house—it was already dry—or prune the fruit trees? Standing there with the iron, she was boiling hot. Strictly speaking, it wasn't necessary to iron at all, because the shirts had gone into the dryer, and they were soft and smooth. But she preferred this kind of pottering, because it made her feel busy. As long as she stayed busy, he was quiet, and the truth, the awful truth, could be kept at bay. Now, with her back to him, he wouldn't disturb her, she felt safe. Afterward, she would have to make another trip to the cellar to load the washing machine again. She'd made plans to knead bread dough, wash the front-door window and sweep the kitchen floor. All while he sat in his wheelchair. As the fear crawled through him like ants. When she finally settled in beside him, on a recliner, he felt her despair, and he couldn't bear it. When he asked her for help to lie down, she got an hour's reprieve in the semidarkness. There he lay crying against the wall of the bedroom as she watched television, sobbing.

She hung the newly ironed shirts on hangers. She heard him hawk and clear his throat — mucus in his airway — but he didn't have the energy to cough. So it remained there gurgling in his throat. She was distracted by the gurgling; it was horrible. You would think he was a hundred years old instead of fifty-nine. She gripped the ironing board. She had to be strong and encouraging. She was supposed to stand by his side until he died, indefatigable, gentle and patient. She was supposed to help him die with dignity. But she couldn't. Parts of herself she didn't know existed had risen to the surface like poison. She cursed God and life, she cursed herself and her shortcomings, and she cursed death. But worst of all, in the blackest hours, she also cursed her husband, who was succumbing to this illness, to this miserable decline. It wasn't part of the plan. He had always been big and strong, in charge, playful. He had taken care of things. Now his legs were useless, his skin no longer resembled skin; his skull looked as though it was covered with an old oilcloth. When she had these thoughts and admitted her own wretchedness, her own boundless cowardice, she fell apart even more. What if he knew how things really were and what she was really thinking? Could he feel it? Could he smell it? Was her betrayal perceptible in the room, did he hear it whispering in the corners? Was that why he'd stopped talking to her, even though he still could speak?

What was going through his mind?

When I'm dead, they'll put me in the freezer, Astrid. I'll have to lie there for several days. Then my cheeks will stiffen and turn cold as ice. Then I'll burn, Astrid, in two-thousand-degree heat. It's so hot the skeleton curls in the casket. I'm so scared, Astrid. Can't you find a solution? Can't you arrange a miracle? Can't you slap my cheek and say, Wake up, Helge, you're having a bad dream!

She pulled another shirt from the pile.

A blue shirt with a white collar and white cuffs, perhaps one of the best he owned. Even though she knew it would never be worn again, she ironed it as best she could; with all the buttons it was difficult. His throat no longer gurgled, and she didn't like the silence either. When she glanced over her shoulder, she saw that his head had fallen to his chest, as if he was sleeping. Maybe he died, she thought, without my noticing. Then she heard him fumbling with something on the table, probably the remote control. No doubt he wanted to change the channel; there were many programs he couldn't watch. He couldn't stand laughter and shouting, or loud music. His life was solemn, his world having narrowed to a dark passage where there was room only for himself: his fear, pain and sorrow.

Just then she looked out the window. She heard something outside, a car, driving unusually slowly. It stopped at the gate for a few seconds, then glided forward, a few meters past the driveway. Letting go of what she had in her hands, she craned her neck. The driver looked as though he was going to reverse into the driveway. What was this? They weren't expecting anybody, and the car itself was rather strange. She remained still, staring. Perhaps I'm dreaming, she thought, this can't be right. A large black car with a cross on its roof backed into the drive. She was about to faint. She held on to the ironing board, and glanced at her husband, who had also heard the car. The low, even hum from the motor, the tires crunching gravel. A door slammed. Astrid Landmark panicked. She didn't know what was going on. There was only one thing on her mind: Helge mustn't see the car, not under any circumstances. He was unsettled. He put his hands on the wheels of his chair; he didn't like people coming to the house, couldn't bear anyone seeing him in this miserable state. Astrid went to the window. Perhaps she'd been mistaken? Maybe the car had some form of advertising on the roof, something she'd misunderstood. But it was a cross. The car was a hearse. A man in a dark suit had opened the rear door, and now stood looking up at the house. He seemed collected and composed. This was his profession. This was what he did every day to earn his wages.

"Is someone coming?" Helge asked anxiously. "Will they have to come inside?" His voice had no strength.

Astrid held on to the windowsill. "No," she said quickly, "they're not coming in."

She was so confused that she could barely speak. As she saw Helge trying to maneuver the wheelchair toward the window, even though it cost him more energy than he possessed, she was seized by desperation.

"Must be a mistake," she said. "I'll go and talk to him."

She trotted to the door, keeping her eyes on her husband. The chair was moving, its gray rubber wheels rolling slowly across the parquet floor.

"No," she shouted. "Just sit!"

As if he could do anything else. But he could sense her panic, could sense that she was keeping something from him, and he didn't want that. He wanted to look out the window. He wanted to see what she saw. When she opened the door, he was halfway across the floor.

The man outside was about her age. He was immaculately dressed in a dark suit, and exceedingly polite. He extended a hand, bowing deeply and respectfully. "My condolences," he said.

"What is this?" she gasped.

He maintained his imperturbable calm. Perhaps he'd seen this before, this confusion. With the next of kin. When death had come to the house.

"Arnesen," he said. "From Memento."

"Arnesen?"

"I'm from Memento," he repeated. "The funeral home. Ingemar Arnesen."

Astrid began to tremble. She stared at the road, wondering whether the neighbors could see the car. What about Helge? Had he reached the window—could he see everything that was happening? She leaned against the door frame for support.

"But what are you doing here?" she whispered, her mouth dry.

Ingemar Arnesen raised an eyebrow. For the first time, he suspected that something might be different this time, though nothing he couldn't handle with dignity. He remained calm.

"I was called," he explained, "to pick up Helge Landmark." He looked directly into her eyes. His irises were large and green.

Then it struck Astrid. She grasped the door frame and stared at him wide-eyed. "Helge Landmark isn't dead. He's sitting by the window watching us as we speak."

Arnesen closed his eyes. The whirling thoughts in his head became visible as twitches to his mouth, and Astrid felt sympathy for him.

"Who called you?" she said.

He straightened up, and his eyes darted toward the window, then back to the black car. "The doctor."

"The doctor?"

"Dr. Mikkelsen from Sandberg Medical Center. Helge Landmark's doctor. He reported the death two hours ago."

She shook her head uncomprehendingly. "We don't know a Dr. Mikkelsen. Helge's doctor's called Dr. Onstad. Martin Onstad. At the Central Hospital." She stared into the open car, and was terrified. "Somebody's playing a trick on us."

"It looks that way," Arnesen said.

"But who is Dr. Mikkelsen? Is it a doctor you know?"

Arnesen seemed lost. She noticed the crease of his trousers, sharp as a knife. Newly polished black shoes. Snow-white shirt. "Many doctors call us," he said miserably. "There are always new doctors, and then the locums—it's impossible to know every name. But he sent me here. To this address." He shrugged. "Helge Landmark. Is he your husband?"

"He's sick," Astrid whispered.

She flinched, because the door to the passenger side of the black car suddenly opened, and a younger man—also in a black suit—stepped onto the gravel. Of course there are two of them, she thought, for carrying the body. She looked nervously at the window, but the reflection in the glass made it impossible to see anything.

The younger man neared the steps. He too greeted Astrid with a respectful bow. "Is this the wrong address?" he asked, a hint of dread in his young face.

"That would be safe to say," Arnesen said gravely. "This is a mistake on every conceivable level."

"But what did he say?" Astrid asked. "The man who called himself Dr. Mikkelsen."

Arnesen tried to recall. "He was rather curt, and maybe a little animated. He sounded quite young, so I thought maybe he'd just qualified. He didn't say that much, just gave me the address. And the name, of course. He said Landmark had been sick for a long time, and that his death was expected. I asked him for the certificate. If he could send it to us by post, and he said, 'Yes, I'll send it by post.'"

"The certificate?"

"Death certificate. Naturally, we've got to have it before we can start doing our job. The doctors often send it by post."

Astrid summoned her courage to return to the house.

"We've got to report this," Arnesen said. "Without delay."

"Do that for me," she pleaded. "I must return to Helge."

Helge sat at the window. His face was bathed in evening light, paler than ever.

The car from the funeral home had started its engine, but it remained parked in the driveway. The motor was barely audible, just a weak hum.

"What are they driving?" Helge asked.

Astrid looked at him sadly. "Someone called them here," she said. "But it was just a prank. We're going to report it. You know, there's been a lot of that going on recently—with fake obituaries in the newspaper and such. And that episode with the baby out in Bjerketun, remember? It's probably the same people. Some boys, maybe, having a laugh."

She turned away. Without knowing why, she imagined that he blamed her. As if she was the one who'd played this cruel trick. Now we'll cross the line, she thought, now death has entered the house. This guest we've never dared talk about.

Helge gathered himself to speak. She saw how he struggled.

"I suppose I could've gone with them," he said. "What difference would it make?"

He sniffed and laughed. The laughter was so bitter that Astrid was utterly racked with anguish. She knew instantly what he needed, and what she ought to do: run to him with assurances that she still needed him. Which was true. She needed Helge Landmark, the airplane mechanic, the tall, broad-shouldered man she'd met at the age of nineteen and whom she later married. But she didn't need this sad man in the wheelchair. Illness had sneaked in everywhere; it was in the walls and in every room. A commode chair in the bathroom. A bedpan in the bedroom. A pill organizer in the kitchen. The last thing she saw before going to bed at night was his wheelchair. The big wheel and its gray rubber filled her field of vision, reminded her of a turbine sucking her in and throwing her around at great speed, until she didn't know which way was up and which was down. Then she awoke to the same wheel in the morning.

The car was still there.

"Why don't they drive off?" she said anxiously.

"He's talking on his mobile," Helge said. "He's probably calling the police." He pressed his face to the glass to see. "Look at that car. It's a limousine."

They stared at the driveway.

"Go and get them," Helge said suddenly.

Astrid was taken aback. "What?"

"Get them. There's something I want to say."

"But Helge," she pleaded, "they couldn't help it. Someone called them."

He looked at her imploringly, and grabbed her arm with a clumsy hand. Rarely did she see this type of engagement in him; it was as though he had been brought to life for the first time in months. "Please do what I say. You have good legs, after all. Hurry before they leave."

Astrid ran to the steps. She reached the car just as it was about to drive off. The men looked at her curiously through the glass, the window slowly sliding down. "He wants to talk to you," she said in despair. "Can you come in? I'm sorry to disturb you, but this is very difficult."

The men from Memento hesitated. The thought of seeing Helge Landmark face to face made them highly uncomfortable. He had something to say, and they didn't feel they had the courage to hear it. But they did as Astrid requested, stepping out of the car and following her inside. They stood in the middle of the lounge and saw Helge Landmark in his wheelchair.

"Good evening."

Helge nodded, and they nodded in return. He pointed at the window with a pale hand. "Sorry for delaying you," he said. "But I'm interested in the car."

The men looked at him uncertainly while they waited for him to continue.

"I mean," Helge said, "that's one hell of a car."

Now they couldn't help but smile.

"It is," said Ingemar Arnesen.

Helge continued to study the limousine through the window. He put a hand in his matted hair. "Have you had it long?"

"Since May."

Helge looked at the other man. He was quite young, and this situation he'd landed in had flushed his cheeks red. "What is your name?" he asked gruffly.

"Knoop," he blurted out. "Karl Kristian Knoop." He bowed for good measure.

"You're an apprentice?"

The young man nodded. Wanting to do everything by the book, he made quick glances at his boss.

"Have you been allowed to drive it?"

Knoop shook his head modestly.

Helge turned to his employer, now with a gleam in his eye.

"You should let him drive. Give the young ones a chance. They have so much more energy than we do."

A pause. Not knowing what to expect, Astrid rubbed her hands together. Helge had made a decision—she recognized the determination in his eyes.

"Tell me about the car," he asked. "What kind of car is it?"

Instantly the men livened up, and Arnesen spoke.

"It's a Daimler. An Eagle Daimler, 87 model."

"Not bad," Helge said. "I imagine it's a pleasure to drive?"

"Indeed it is."

"Not bought here in Norway, was it?"

"We got it from Wilcox Limousines," Arnesen said. "Used. It came from a funeral home called Morning Glory."

"Right." Helge laughed. "Morning Glory. You could see it that way."

"One hundred and sixty-four horsepower."

"Hm."

"Princess Diana rode in a similar car," Arnesen said. "That is, it picked her up at the airport when she came home from Paris."

"It wasn't cheap, that car," Helge said.

"Four hundred thousand," Arnesen said. "But it's full of leather and walnut, and other elegant details. You should smell the cabin. It has a scent of luxury and finesse."

"No passengers complain in the back seat?" Helge winked.

"No." Arnesen cleared his throat. "No one complains. The car's like a ship sailing the ocean. Just a gentle swaying. The engine makes almost no sound."

Helge Landmark looked out at the car again, then back at the men. "Is it possible to make a reservation?"

"A reservation?"

Arnesen gave him a quizzical look. Knoop had fastened his gaze at a point on the floor where there was a knot in one of the oak boards.

"I would like to be driven in that car," Helge said and nodded at the window. "When my time comes. Or when my time is up, if you will."

It was silent in the Landmarks' lounge. But the silence didn't last long. For now the men walked across the room and took his hand.

"It would be an honor and a pleasure," Arnesen said.

"An honor and a pleasure," Knoop repeated.

"That's good," Helge said. "So everything will be easy for Astrid. When you two stand at our door and are old acquaintances. Are we in agreement, Astrid?"

She nodded, her eyes filling with tears.

The short séance was over. Astrid followed them to the door and said goodbye. When the Daimler from Memento drove out onto the road, Helge Landmark asked his wife for a good dram of cognac.

She looked at him apprehensively. It had been a long time since he'd had a nip, and she was afraid all the medicine he was taking would make for an explosive mix.

"Is that a good idea?" she asked carefully. "Mixing it with your medicine?"

With what remained of his strength, Helge banged his clenched fist on the armrest of the chair. "Does that matter now, Astrid? Can you tell me that?"

She did as he demanded. Like an obedient child, she retrieved the bottle from the cupboard, her hands trembling when she poured. She felt strange. Afraid and elated at the same time.

Then she escaped into the kitchen to make bread dough, kneading it forcefully—there was no mercy in her clenched fists. While she was busy with the dough, the doorbell rang. She thought it might be the police and hurried to open the door.

But it was only a young man she didn't know asking for directions to Sandberg Center.

Sejer was outraged on behalf of the couple, and what they'd been through. He asked if anyone had harassed them before. If they had any idea of who could have sent the car. Helge Landmark was unable to respond. When he had asked his wife for a cognac, he'd felt terrific. After meeting the men from the funeral home, he'd felt almost like a man again. He had caught them off-guard, and it had lifted his spirits. But he had come down again. The drink knocked him out. His eyelids were heavy as lead, and his head was spinning. The French cognac had given him a moment's pleasure, a strong, uplifting buzz, another taste of life and all that was good about it. But he couldn't handle it. With a crash he was back in his wheelchair, with the catheter, with the oxygen tank and no strength. There was also something about the inspector which embarrassed him. The man was his age, tall, strong and fit, with broad shoulders and the best of his life ahead of him. With the chance to grow old with style and dignity, not gurgling and sniffling like himself.

"Who knows you're ill?" Sejer asked.

Helge was silent. Astrid leaned forward to answer.

"Many people know," she said. "Family. Neighbors."

"Does anyone visit you regularly?"

"No. We manage on our own. At least, we have up till now." She didn't look at the man as she said these last words. She sat with her hands folded in her lap, and she seemed completely perplexed. "But we sit outside. When the weather's nice. Everyone can see us. See how things are."

Sejer stood by the window looking out at the lawn. There were old apple trees, flowers and bushes with berries. Near the house was a wooden patio set, with a large, white parasol. He asked Astrid to think carefully through the last few days. Telephone calls. Post. People at the door. She provided a description of their routine life as it played out from morning to night. She could recall no irregularities or surprises.

"Not many people come by here," she said. "Other than to sell something or ask directions. We have a son, but he lives in Dubai, and he's not married. He's only home at Christmas, and he stays for a couple of weeks."

Sejer looked at each of them. Helge Landmark seemed immensely tired. For long stretches of time he sat with his eyes closed.

"Who asked directions?" Sejer said, looking at Astrid Landmark. "Has anyone been here, I mean recently?"

She remembered how the doorbell had rung while she prepared the bread dough. "There was a boy I didn't know. He wanted to find the town center."

Sejer nodded. "A boy you didn't know. What did he look like, can you tell me?"

Astrid replayed the moment in her mind. She trawled her memory for images, but couldn't find anything, only a voice. A quiet, modest voice with a polite question. Who had stood on her steps? How had he been dressed? Why couldn't she remember anything—no details or clear recollections—when he had actually stood on the top step and looked directly into her eyes?

"You say it was a boy?" Sejer said.

She shrugged helplessly. She wasn't sure of anything. The black car from Memento had upset her to such a degree that everything else had been erased from her memory. "He seemed young. But it's so difficult to judge a person's age. I mean, whether he was seventeen or twenty-five."

"Try." Sejer encouraged her. "You can probably think of something."

"I don't even think I looked at him," she admitted. "It was like

128

he was a shadow. I didn't see anything else either. I just pointed. The town center is right up the road."

"Was he driving a car?"

Again she shrugged. "I don't know. Suddenly he was there. And when I closed the door, I didn't think anything more about it. I was waiting for you to come."

Helge Landmark raised his heavy head. "I didn't see anything, but I have ears. The person who rang the doorbell—he took off on a moped."

18

EVERYONE WAS TALKING about what happened to
Helge Landmark. Could anyone really just pick up a
telephone, people wondered, and do that? Scare the living daylights out of them and humiliate them simply by making
a phone call? Apparently, yes. The man they now sought, the
man—or boy—had called. And Arnesen from Memento Funeral
Home, who'd answered, had no reason to doubt the polite voice.
That's how society functions; it is based on trust. But now the
question arose over whether a number of procedures should be
changed, especially those concerning death. Even though Helge
Landmark had refused to talk to the newspapers, people of course
learned that he was dying. What was heartbreaking in all this was
that death had made a preparatory visit, had literally entered his
house. This was what most astonished people.

Sejer sat by a lamp reading about ALS. Helge Landmark had
come down with it just six months earlier. Developing very
quickly, in the course of a short time it would lead to his death.
"Amyotrophic lateral sclerosis is a disease of the central nervous
system that attacks nerve cells in the spinal cord and brain. The
disease is incurable and treatment is exclusively symptomatic.
Because they lose strength in their breathing apparatus, ALS patients die of weakened lungs. For some, the first symptoms are

difficulties with speech and swallowing. Or the disease begins asymmetrically, frequently with a weakness or clumsiness in one hand."

Finally he noted the name of some famous ALS patients: Mao Zedong. Stephen Hawking. Axel Jensen.

He was suddenly filled with fear—it leapt on him from behind. Could he describe his passing dizzy spells and his subsequent loss of balance as asymmetric symptoms? The thought was so overwhelming that he gasped for air. To shove the ridiculous idea away, he picked up a sheet of paper that was lying next to the telephone. He'd made a few notes on it. He had called Gunilla Mørk, and they had talked about everything—the most important being the Polish student who had stood on her steps asking for work. She had tried, as best she could, to remember how he'd looked. But she admitted that she hadn't been herself, that she hadn't been able to retain any significant details on account of the obituary, which she had just read and which had shaken her to the core. After that Sejer had talked with Sverre Skarning's young wife. From her he'd obtained a very good description of the man who had come to buy a tray of eggs. Or rather a boy. He had also ridden a moped, or a small motorcycle, she couldn't tell the difference. They had conversed for a while. He had a friendly voice, she said, rather light and pleasant, and seemed sympathetic. Finally he had spoken with Lily Sundelin. She had remembered something from the hospital. A young man with his arm in a cast had walked up and down the hallway, and he had stared at them without inhibition. Putting it all together, he now had a picture of the person he thought was terrorizing people: a young, slender man or boy between the ages of eighteen and twenty-five, with longish hair and dark eyes. Dressed in jeans and trainers. And he zoomed off on a moped, or perhaps a small motorcycle, which in all probability was red. The same color as the helmet. He had a friendly, thoughtful demeanor that won people over. That's why they trusted him. Asymmetric symptoms, he thought, and put his head in his hands. The damn dizziness. As if someone rapped his knees so that his legs would buckle. No, it had nothing to do with paralysis, he thought, it's in my head—if that's any better. He tried to find a kind of peace as he sat in the waning light, but it was taken from him. He leaned his head against the back of his chair and closed his eyes. Hell begins now. It's probably old age coming to claim me, making me think about death. It's what the person who's playing this awful game wants. My heart has pumped hard for many years, and now it's starting to count down.

I have a certain number of beats left. That's just the way it is.

And God knows what he'll do next time.

19

THE CENTRAL HOSPITAL was a square, thirteen-story building. It had been constructed in '64, and two wings had since been added on. If you walked through the main entrance, you came first to an information desk, a wide, curving counter made of light wood. Next to the information desk were several small couches, upholstered in blue fabric. Here you could sit and wait if you had accompanied someone for an examination or a treatment. There was also a large cafeteria, and a kiosk with a little florist's shop which sold ready-made bouquets. There was a pharmacy in one corner. The high ceiling had a dazzling array of tiny light bulbs which made everything gleam. There were always people milling around by the information desk. A thrum of voices, the clinking of coffee cups and glasses, and the endless sound of lifts coming and going. Now and then a telephone would ring. There was also the sound of the double glass doors, which swooshed as they opened and closed. Altogether, four people staffed the information desk, and they worked in shifts. Today it was one of the oldest of the crew, Solveig Grøner, helping people find their way. For a long time she had sat absorbed in a stack of papers, until something caught her attention and forced her to look up—the swoosh of the double glass doors. A woman rushed in. She seemed exhausted, as if she'd run the whole way from the car park. Solveig Grøner let go of the stack of papers. The woman was perhaps forty. Her thick, dark hair gathered at the neck. Even wearing high heels, she reached the desk in record time.

"Evelyn Mold," she said, gasping for breath.

She pronounced the name "Evelyn Mold" with a kind of expectation. As if a number of things would instantly occur, and Solveig Grøner would immediately understand. People would come rushing, bells would ring. But nothing happened. She plonked her hands on the desk, pale against the light wood, and tipped over a box of paper clips. But she seemed to take no notice. She just stood there waiting.

"Evelyn Mold," she repeated, a little louder now.

Solveig Grøner remained calm. During her many years at the hospital she had seen just about everything; besides, it was vital that she make no mistakes. Not here, in this building full of sickness and death. "Mold?" she asked pleasantly. "Is that someone you'd like to visit?"

The woman nodded. She put a hand to her throat. Her cheeks were no longer red; she was beginning to turn pale. "It's me," she panted. "I'm Evelyn Mold."

Solveig Grøner didn't understand what the woman wanted. Because she noticed someone on the blue couches in the waiting area watching them, she leaned forward and lowered her voice. Discretion was important. She was never careless about it.

"How may I help you?"

"You called. You rang and asked me to come! Now here I am. So help me! Help me!"

Solveig Grøner could feel the woman's nervousness beginning to rub off on her. One thing at a time, she thought. Be careful. Do this right. Name. Procedures. "Is there someone you wish to visit?"

The woman was trying not to become hysterical, but she was

losing her patience and growing bellicose. She didn't understand why no one was here to meet her. They should have rushed to her. They should have been in the doorway. "Frances," she said. "My daughter. Frances Mold. She rides a scooter."

Solveig Grøner nodded. Scooter, she thought. "Who told you to report to the hospital?"

"The hospital."

"Here? The hospital?"

Evelyn Mold was now so distraught that she lost her voice.

"Was she in a traffic accident?"

Evelyn Mold began to cry. Her hair, held loosely together, spilled over her cheeks. "They said it was serious," she managed. "I drove as fast as I could. Can you get somebody? Can you tell me where to go? You've got to hurry. They said it was serious!"

Solveig Grøner lifted the handset and dialed a number. She felt very uncertain. This wasn't the hospital's routine.

Evelyn Mold waited. She saw everything as if through a weak shaft of light. She also heard the rising and falling hum of voices, the clinks of cups and glasses from the cafeteria and the sudden, sharp snapping of a newspaper. Exactly the sound you make when you want to emphasize something important you've just said. Then she heard Solveig Grøner's voice.

"Frances Mold . . . Yes . . . Traffic accident . . . Her mother has arrived . . . No, it's a teenager . . . What? What did you say?"

Silence again. Evelyn waited until she felt it in her legs, until tears began to flow. Soon someone would come running to take her arm, lead her to her daughter's bed. Or maybe she was already on the operating table. What had she injured in the accident? Was it her legs? Maybe her head? Would she be the same girl? Was she no longer fifteen? Had she regressed to the level of a toddler? Or worse, was she gone? Was she just something that lay there breathing, with tubes and needles everywhere? Nervously shifting her weight from one foot to the other, she put her hand to her mouth, on the verge of vomiting all over the information desk.

Solveig Grøner started whispering. "Evelyn," she said carefully, extending a hand, "I don't know quite what this means. But we have no patient with that name, nor do we have a patient we aren't able to identify. Do you understand?"

Evelyn trembled so forcefully that her teeth clacked in her mouth. "But they called me. They said I had to come."

Solveig Grøner searched feverishly for an explanation. The woman's panic was in danger of taking over. It occurred to her that there was another explanation, and she clutched at it immediately, like a straw. "Could it have been the University Hospital that called? Could you have misheard?"

Evelyn considered. From where they lived the University Hospital was an hour's drive. Could Frances have driven so far on that little scooter of hers? Of course she could have, because the scooter was brand-new and she was eager to ride it. But that wasn't what they'd said on the phone, was it? Could they have said the University Hospital? She tried to recall. Was it a man or a woman who had called? What had she been told? Why was it all so cloudy? Why couldn't she recall anything, something concrete? All she remembered was that they had said something about the hospital. Something about Frances. Whether it was her daughter, when she was born, and something about an accident. That she should come immediately. After that she had asked for details. About Frances's condition. But she had been told that they couldn't give out details over the phone.

Is it serious? she had asked. Yes, the voice said. It's serious. It's important you get here quickly.

She stood there swaying like an invalid while clutching the counter.

"I'll call them," Solveig Grøner said. "What is her full name?"

"Frances Emilie Mold. She was born in 1994. She is fifteen years old."

As soon as she finished her last sentence, she broke down. She waited for the verdict. Felt as though someone had hung her on a hook and she no longer had any contact with the floor.

Solveig Grøner called the University Hospital, introduced herself and asked for Accident and Emergency. She grabbed her pen, squeezed it. There was something odd about this entire situation. Normally she could deal with tragedy, but here, something was completely wrong. When they answered, her suspicions were confirmed. She thanked them and replaced the handset. Looked over the counter at Evelyn Mold. Summoned all her courage. She felt herself teetering on an edge, staring into the abyss. "Does your daughter have a mobile phone?"

Evelyn was close to breaking point. "They said it was serious," she stammered. "I don't understand what you mean?"

Solveig Grøner knew this was risky, but she had no choice. "I suggest you try to call her right now."

"But what would that do?"

"If she has been admitted neither here nor at the University Hospital, we've got to try another avenue." She leaned forward. Looked Evelyn straight in the eyes. "So many strange things have happened recently. If you know what I mean."

Evelyn Mold needed a little time to understand what the other woman meant. It was as if her brain's compartments had been sealed off; only the chamber for fear was open. She found a mobile telephone in a pocket. Staring spontaneously at the ceiling, she discovered hundreds of bright dots. They were recessed lights, she knew, but they shone like stars. Once again she heard the snapping of a newspaper behind her, a confirmation.

"So many strange things?" she whispered, her eyes now on Solveig Grøner.

"You know, the one who has been playing pranks on people," Solveig said. "The one everyone's talking about, the one calling in fake obituaries and messages."

Evelyn punched in her daughter's number. While she waited for an answer, she stared once more at the stars in the ceiling.

Evelyn and Frances arrived home at about the same time.

Evelyn saw the scooter as she drove into the driveway.

They didn't say much. It was as if they'd been forced into a strange room, and now sought a way out, back to what was near and dear: the familiar routine, with sunlight in the windows and birds twittering in the trees behind their house. The sound of the television in the corner. And the conversations between them, which always flowed easily and without restraint, conversations with much tenderness, love and laughter. Now that had come to an end, and they felt awkward; they didn't know how to handle what they had gone through. Evelyn Mold had always viewed herself as strong and determined. As down-to-earth and realistic. She could handle a setback—had thought so at least. She had rafted down the Sjoa River—admittedly it had been some years ago, but she'd liked the thrill of it. She had run the Oslo Marathon twice, and was definitely not the type to take life for granted. When Frances got her scooter, it had awakened a distant fear in her that, possibly, she could be hit by a car. She'd had that thought but swept it away. She was rational. She didn't look ahead for trouble. But this incident had done something to her. When they entered the house and Evelyn locked the door behind them, she walked a few steps into the lounge and then lost it. She planted her hands on a table and leaned forward, gasping for air. Frances followed her, a little awkwardly. Mama, please. I'm here. We won't think about it anymore.

But Evelyn had trouble breathing. She had never stared into the abysses within herself, and the sensation was so overwhelming it felt like a thrashing. She stood by the table, breathing heavily. It occurred to her that she had been in exactly this position once before, fifteen years earlier when Frances was born and the painful birth pangs were about to get the better of her.

"I suppose we should think about what to eat for dinner," she said helplessly. She had nothing else to say.

Frances protested. She pulled at her mother's arm. "No, let's just sit on the sofa. We'll watch television. We don't need to do anything."

They sat huddled together on the sofa, choosing silence. Finally, in a small voice, Evelyn said it was over, that she had to calm herself and just forget the whole episode. "But it's as though everything has changed," she said, hurt. "I don't quite know what will happen when you leave the house on your scooter. Do you understand that, Frances?"

Frances bowed her head, jutting out her lower lip. "Would you like me to sell it?"

"You can drive a car in two years. You'll be much safer in a car."

Later, Sejer asked if there'd been anything about Frances in the local paper. What had been written? Any personal details given? Had there been, in addition to the article, a photograph of her?

Frances was wearing a pink tracksuit. Like a little kitten, she had coiled up in the corner of the sofa. "Why do you ask that?"

"We believe it's how he selects his victims," Sejer said. "At least some of them. He scans the local newspaper, finds a story and records the name and place of residence. Then he does some investigative work, perhaps through the operator service. It's easy to find people in this country."

Frances went to pick up the newspaper she'd saved. She pointed at the photograph. Then she glanced at her mother. "It's been fourteen days. We were at a dealership to pick out my scooter, and a guy from the Council for Road Safety talked to us. He was writing about traffic safety, so I answered a few questions. At the end he took my photo. It's a bad photo. I look so fat."

Sejer read the short article. She had just turned fifteen, and the scooter was a gift from her father, who lived abroad. When he finished the article, he read the caption under the photo.

"Frances Mold of Kirkeby looks forward to driving. But she is also concerned about safety, and buys the most expensive helmet. She won't, she pledges, be a reckless driver."

"Look," Sejer said. "Your name and address are here, so it wasn't difficult to find you. But he must have also kept this house under surveillance. He needed to be certain you were out on your scooter when he called. More than likely he called from a kiosk." He observed the two women sitting close to each other on the sofa. "When you were at the hospital reception," he said to Evelyn, "do you recall whether you felt as if you were being watched?"

Evelyn seemed perplexed. "There were a lot of people in the café," she said, "and a lot of coming and going through the main entrance. But whether any of them looked at me, I wasn't in any state to notice. I was completely out of it. Do you know what? If a snowman had stood behind the information desk I wouldn't have noticed. Why do you ask anyway?"

"Because he typically shows up to watch his prank play out. Did anyone visit you today?"

"No one. Just you."

"Then I'm guessing he was at the hospital," Sejer said. "He watched this house. He saw Frances start the scooter and ride through the gate. He called you and then went straight to the hospital. He knew you would show up.

"It's quite possible he observed the entire scene at close range."

"I'm speechless," Evelyn said.

"He must have a screw loose," Frances said.

20

H ENRY WAS ASLEEP when he entered the room.
In the frayed chair, with his legs on the footstool. He
slept soundlessly and with an open mouth. A few worn
teeth were visible in his pale gums. Johnny sat down. Proud of
what he'd done, he sincerely believed he was remarkable. Not that
he thought he was worth much — no more than a louse, or a cen-
tipede, or some other nasty creature that crawled around in the
damp dark under a rock: he had no more goals or reasons to live,
had no more answers, no greater right to life. He didn't feel significant or vital, and there was nothing meaningful in his life. He felt
disconnected, like when you pull up a weed that can never again
take root. Indifferent to life and death, to what happened, to what
people might think, he could do as he pleased. What it would
lead to didn't concern him, and it didn't bother him to think of
the consequences. But he felt a bond to the old man asleep in the
chair.

Where will I go when you are gone? he thought. Who will I
visit? Who will I help? This is the only place where I can think
clearly. Here, in this hot, stuffy lounge, on the old footstool. I'll
make a sandwich for you, and then I'll swat a fly. I'll fetch the
post, and then we'll chat for a while.

"Grandpa?" he whispered.

Henry blinked. "I knew you were here," he mumbled. "You come as silently as a cat, but I notice at once."

Johnny moved closer. "Has your carer been here?" he wanted to know. "The woman from Thailand?"

The old man raised a claw-like hand and wiped a droplet of snot from his nose. The hand, with its crooked fingers, resembled those primitive weapons Johnny had seen in films, a wooden club with spikes hammered into it.

"Mai Sinok. Her name is Mai Sinok, and she was here at eight this morning. She brought a pot of cabbage soup, and four nectarines. I've eaten it all up, Johnny, there's nothing left for you." He opened his pale, watery eyes.

"Grandpa, how are you feeling today? You're not getting worse, are you?"

The old man considered this question. He regarded his frail body from head to toe. "I'm not getting worse," he said. "But I'm not getting better, either. I have water in my lungs, you know, and arthritis in every body part and a failing heart. What do you know, it rhymes. Did you catch that, Johnny?"

Johnny put a hand on his grandfather's arm. "You'll live until you're ninety," he assured him. "In twenty years I'll be sitting here, and you'll be like a gnarled tree that I can hang my helmet on."

The old man grunted, apparently a laugh.

"Tell me what it's like," Johnny said. "To be old. I mean, when the body is as worn out as yours. You hardly ever eat. Just sit here sleeping. Hardly ever talk to anyone, just me and Mai Sinok."

"You mean I'm near the edge of my grave." He stroked his hair away from his forehead. The room's heat made him sluggish and drowsy. "You too are on the edge of the grave. Perhaps we're all on the edge of the grave."

"I'm just seventeen," Johnny said. "I've got a full life ahead of me."

"That's what we like to believe. Otherwise life would be impossible."

"Tell me what it's like," Johnny repeated. "Can you feel death getting closer? Can you feel your heart and everything else work more slowly? What's it like to live in slow motion?"

"Oh, it's all right. It's like bobbing in the surf, against the shore and out, against the shore and out. From morning to evening. You've just got to let yourself go."

"You're lying," Johnny said. "Bobbing in the surf, you say."

Again the old man grunted a laugh. With his spiked club-hands he made a slight wave, gave Johnny a clumsy caress. "I'm feeling quite well, lad."

"But I want to know what it feels like," Johnny insisted. "Is the light different? Or the sound?"

Henry sighed. "I see the same things as you. Every person lives his life on the edge. The view is the same. To say anything else would be a lie." Then he added: "Where have you been today? What have you been up to?"

Johnny made himself comfortable on the footstool. In spite of his modest weight, the plastic cover and the nails holding it together cracked.

"Not much. I went to a café. I ate a vanilla pastry and perused the newspaper."

Clearly they'll get me, he thought.

Sooner or later. That's all right. While I wait for them to get me, I'll have fun. I like this game, I always win. But if I were to meet my match, then that would be all right. I won't sulk and complain. It was fun while it lasted, and I've made my presence known.

He stayed with Henry for several hours. They read the newspaper and discussed this and that, but for long stretches of time they just sat in comfortable silence. Close to each other in the hot room.

143

When he finally got up to leave, he caught sight of Else Meiner through the window, and when he was in the garden, she also caught sight of him. She straddled her blue Nakamura bicycle, and it appeared to be fixed. The tires were brand-new. He started the moped and put on his helmet, then slipped onto the road. She waited. Her face was one big grin. He thought about something his grandfather had once said. That a person who teases you was often a person who, deep down, was attracted to you, possibly even in love. So he studied Else Meiner extra carefully. The little girl's pointy face with the large front teeth. Was she in love with him? Deep down? He continued on the road slowly. This time he didn't look away, down at the handlebars or up at the sky. He stared directly at her. She didn't flinch. He had never really looked at that smile, he realized, and it was actually a bright and cheery smile. She knows I was the one who slashed her tires, he thought, that's what she's trying to say. That's why she's not shouting at me like she normally does, because we're even now. We're finally even! He gunned the throttle and raced ahead, across the road. As he passed her, she raised her middle finger.

"Frogface," she called out.

Her laughter crackled like ice cubes rolling across a table.

He was so furious that the heat rose in his cheeks.

"Stupid little girl," he shouted. "You'll get it! Tonight!"

He remembered it was Thursday. That meant the band would practice at the Hauger School gymnasium, and Else Meiner would blow her trumpet until her cheeks puffed out. I'll use the army knife, he thought.

I'll puncture both your lungs.

Then there will be no more sounds from your trumpet.

Later he got to thinking about the Hauger School Band. That Else Meiner would leave on her bicycle, her instrument stowed in a little case over the back wheel. With others she would sit in the gymnasium for two hours, blowing her trumpet. Or an hour and a half. He didn't know how long band practice would last, but he planned to watch through the window. Before he left, he scavenged in his chest of drawers—looking for a little surprise for Else Meiner. He didn't want to be unprepared. Then he slipped his hand into Butch's cage and patted him gently on the back.

"No country for old men," he whispered.

He went outside.

It was late summer, and all the vegetation had begun to dry up. There was no color or freshness, none of nature's optimism, none of its strength. It was as if someone, a spirit or a giant, had swept through the entire Askeland housing estate and left its considerable mark. Don't you rise again. It's getting cold now, and dark. Johnny Beskow looked at each house as he passed, as was his routine. You could buy heroin at Askeland; twice he'd been stopped and offered some. No thanks, he'd said with a superior smile. He put enormous stock in being clearheaded, and he was agile and fast and sharp. The addicts who hung around Askeland reminded him of sleepwalkers.

He stopped when he neared Hauger School, hitting the brakes and quickly surveying the area. The bike shed was crammed with bicycles. A few cars sat in the car park. A rope slapped against the flagpole like a whip. He heard a drum, drumsticks pounding steadily against the tight skin, in an even, definite rhythm. He knew that it was the bass drum, the heartbeat of the march. The band had already started, with percussion and horns. A piccolo whined shrilly above all else. Because he didn't want Else Meiner to hear him, he pushed the moped the final stretch toward the bike shed; you never knew with her, she was awfully sharp. When the moped was parked, he plodded about in the playground, glancing around. Hopscotch patterns, both flyer and niner variations, were painted directly on the black asphalt. Though he didn't have a marker, he couldn't resist the urge to hop through the patterns. I don't weigh much, he thought, as he hopped, and I'm limber. I'm one hell of a jumping troll. His light gymnastics made his heart race; blood raced through his thin body.

He sized up the playground. Straight ahead, behind a red-and-white metal barrier, he saw a bike path; he'd walked that way many times before he'd got his moped. Narrow and paved, it was called the Love Trail. Else Meiner had also come that way, he was quite certain, for she lived at Bjørnstad. And when she went home to Rolandsgata, after band practice, she would again ride that trail. On the blue Nakamura bicycle. At any rate, this is what he was counting on to carry out his vengeance, which he'd plotted so carefully over the past few hateful hours of the afternoon. Energized by these thoughts, he began walking with urgent steps toward the barrier. It would be easy to push the moped past it. He could wait for her there on the trail, hidden behind some bushes — because he noticed they were thick, good hiding places. Now his heart was beating even faster. He was filled with this honey-sweet thing called revenge. For a while he stood near the barrier and considered, glanced right to left, studied the dry, dense vegetation. Then he walked back to the school building. Sneaked down to the basement window and peeked into the gymnasium. The conductor was standing in the middle of the room energetically waving the white baton, his entire body pushing the band forward in the march: pointed elbows, a bend in the knees, eager jerks with his bearded chin. On the left side of the gym were the woodwind players. One of the clarinets had a squeak to it. The percussionists were in the back. And there, in the front right, sat the brass players, Else Meiner and her trumpet among them. Her cheeks were puffed out, exactly as he'd imagined. But she could really play; she was the only one who played pure notes, the only one who kept the rhythm.

Johnny sank to the asphalt, his back against the brick wall by the window, while the band worked its way through a number of marches. Mostly it was the bass drum that interested him. The drumsticks beat with precision and tenacity, keeping the others in rhythm, getting them back on track, so to speak, because it was undeniable they were playing too fast. With regular intervals they stopped, and there followed a sharp rapping sound—the conductor smacking his baton against his music stand. It meant that he wanted to make a change. When the band had played for an hour, it suddenly grew quiet in the gym. Johnny peered cautiously through the window, and he realized it was break time. They had put their instruments aside, and they were on the way up. The boys would probably smoke on the sly, and the girls would probably hop through the flyer and niner, maybe chew some gum while they had the chance. He scrambled from the asphalt and rushed behind the corner of the school building, where he watched them pile out. Else Meiner was wearing jeans and a light blue jacket, and she was wearing it backward—the buttons, he noticed, were on her back. Miss Contrary, then. But he already knew that—that she was bold and different. She ganged up with two other girls; it looked as though they shared some sweets. The girls' voices rose through the air, clear as a bell. He squeezed against the wall and kept them under surveillance, made a note of their gestures, the interaction between them. The Meiner girl was the leader, the one the others listened to.

The break lasted fifteen minutes. At once they ran back into the building, and the playground was empty. When he saw they had returned to their seats in the gymnasium, among the wall bars and gym mats, he slipped into the ground-floor corridor. He continued to hear Else Meiner's trumpet. On the wall to the right was a noticeboard, and he walked over to see what it said. One notice told him, as he'd long known, that Hauger School Band practiced every Thursday at six. But there were other activities during the week in the old, dilapidated school building. Aerobics for beginners and advanced, children's playtime on Tuesdays, chess club each Wednesday at seven, football on Mondays, and a course on cooking and needlecraft. What a crazy lot of things people do, Johnny Beskow thought. For a few minutes he wandered the corridor. Slurped a little water from the fountain against the wall, looked at some pictures. Searched for Else Meiner, and finally found her in a photo from some kind of theater production, *The Living Forest*. Dressed like a pine, she wore green flannel, but the pointy chin gave her away.

Suddenly a man in a green nylon jacket walked through a door. "Are you looking for someone?"

It was the caretaker. Johnny ran off without responding, shoved the doors open and scurried across the playground as fast as lightning. He got his moped from the bike shed, pushed it past the metal barrier and continued on to the paved path. He stopped to recover and catch his breath. The band would be practicing until eight. They would chat for a bit when it was over, putting their instruments in their cases, walking upstairs and out of the building, getting on their bikes and riding away. A quarter past, he thought, that's when she'll come this way. On the blue bicycle. As he looked around for a good hiding place, he walked slowly along the Love Trail. There would have to be enough bushes to hide both him and his moped. And when the deed was carried out, he would have to find cover until she had gone. As he walked he was struck by a stupid thought which flushed his cheeks up to his hairline and down to his throat, made him so despondent he had to pause. He leaned over his moped, blushing from the heat and his embarrassment.

What were the chances that Else Meiner would actually take this path at all? She could easily choose the main road. There was more traffic, but it was shorter. And besides, what was the chance that she would be cycling all alone? Weren't there at least thirty people in this bloody band? Maybe four or five of them would ride together. His doubts lasted more than a minute. He couldn't move. What if people saw how miserable he was? Then he forced himself to snap out of it, straightened his shoulders and raised his head. I'm fast, he thought, they'll probably be too surprised to move, the whole lot of them. They don't know me, either. He pushed the moped farther. After a while the path forked in two. An offshoot veered left and, he thought, south toward Kirkeby. Some of them will split off here, and only two or three will cycle on. And maybe there's another fork. There was, a few minutes ahead. This offshoot went to the right, toward Sandberg. Here another will probably split off. So he imagined only two girls left. I can handle two girls. Soon he saw, to the left, a dense thicket. He pulled the moped off the path, hid it in the undergrowth and squatted down to wait for Else Meiner.

The undergrowth was full of nettles and bracken.

In his hand he held the army knife.

She chose the Love Trail.

She was alone.

She hummed and sang one of the songs playing constantly on the radio. He could never remember what it was called, but it irritated him. The blue bicycle sparkled. Her father had probably bought it, Johnny thought, and made sure she had new tires. Someone who has a father has a place to go when things fall apart. Crawling slowly from the undergrowth, he slid on his belly along the hill, like a reptile. The plan was to rush forward, leap up and jump her from behind. Making use of the element of surprise was important, as was the shock he was sure would paralyze her with fear. And he was lucky. She rode slowly, rolling calmly on her soft rubber tires. Singing and humming. He unsheathed his army knife and pulled out the longest blade, then began counting down. In his excitement he had also begun to tremble; the trembling made him angry, and his anger made him calm again.

Unable to wait any longer, he rose and, with great force,

plunged forward. Leapt for the bicycle and clawed until he got hold of the bike rack and the trumpet case fell to the path with a crash. Confused, she set her feet on the ground, her small body twitching. Just as she tried to turn, startled, he wrapped an arm around her throat and yanked. Her neck was as slender as the stem of a cherry, the blue-green veins like fine threads. Then she sank backward, and the bicycle fell to the ground. Johnny lost his balance and went down; blood pulsed through his body in hard spurts. They lay writhing on the hill, and in the heat of battle he was struck with wonder. She didn't scream, and wasn't paralyzed with fear. She began to thrash around, and with such force that it sapped his strength. Only his left arm was free, for in his right he held the knife. She kicked like a donkey. She wriggled, twisting like a worm. Then, with powerful jaws, she sunk her teeth into his forearm. The pain brought tears to his eyes, and for a few seconds he nearly lost his grip. She took this moment to turn her head and look him in the eye. Through the holes in the gorilla mask he saw the little face and its scattered freckles. He couldn't turn back now, couldn't hesitate, because now, finally, he had to get Else Meiner, this nemesis who poisoned his existence, this troll who always crept from her cave when he rode past. Humiliate her once and for all.

So he clenched his teeth, pressed her down on the path, straddled her narrow back, grabbed hold of the fiery red hair and raised his knife. With one swift movement he sliced off her plait. Just as you cut a rope. He put the plait in his pocket and gasped for breath, but he maintained his grip—to make it known that, if he wanted to, he could also cut her throat if she didn't behave. Finally she lay completely still. He drove his knee into her lower back, clutched her hair, tugged it forcefully more than once, and gave her a final warning shove before running back into the undergrowth. Ran in a zigzag into the woods and squatted down, hid in the bracken watching as she collected herself. She seemed a little off-kilter, stumbling a few steps to the side, her cheeks pale. But she managed to get her bicycle upright and her trumpet in place on the rack. Then she ran her hand across the back of her head, feeling for the plait. Lying in the bushes, Johnny hardly dared breathe. He had stung himself on some nettles, been scratched by some thistles and been bitten on his arm by Else Meiner. But he held his breath. This was just a warning, he thought. Next time, I'll cut off your ears.

21

T HE MEINER FAMILY lived on Rolandsgata in a large, yellow house, which for some time Sejer and Skarre observed at a distance. In the driveway they saw several old broken-down Mercedes.

"Now people have found a scapegoat," Sejer said. "If a house burns down in Kirkeby tonight, he'll also be blamed for that. Even though his actual talent is terrorizing people from afar. So I don't know what I'm supposed to believe about this incident. Come on." He began walking toward the house. "Let's have a chat with Else Meiner."

It was the father, Asbjørn, who opened the door. A big, heavyset man, Meiner slammed doors angrily, clearly upset over what had happened. "Else," he called. "They're here."

When she didn't come immediately, he called again: "Else! The police!"

They had expected a frightened girl, huddled up perhaps in the corner of a sofa, her knees tucked under her chin. A girl with nervous hands and a thin voice, who spoke in short, barely audible sentences. But Else Meiner wasn't that kind of girl. She came through a door down the hall, wearing faded jeans and a vest top. The short red hair—no longer forced into a plait—poked out in all directions. Most of all, she resembled a scruffy troll.

Asbjørn Meiner comported himself like the captain of a ship: broad-legged, hips thrust forward. "Yes, that's how she looks now," he said resignedly.

Else Meiner leaned against the wall.

"She looks great," Sejer said.

This made Else smile. Her red hair was like a flame. She had small, pointy ears, like the elves in fairy stories.

"She had hair all the way down her back," Meiner said melodramatically. He motioned with his long arms.

Sejer and Skarre nodded.

"Growing your hair long takes time, of course," Skarre said.

Meiner ushered them into the living room, but Else remained standing in the doorway looking at the men. She was barefoot, and she had varnish on her nails.

"Else," her father said, "don't just stand there. You're going to have to help out!"

She shrugged, then strode quietly across the carpet and sat down. Sejer watched her small figure. Though she did as her father told her, she did not respect him. Asbjørn Meiner didn't realize that.

"Are you doing all right?" Skarre said affably. She looked up.

"Oh, yes. It's just hair."

"Did he use scissors?"

"No, it was a knife."

"Did you see the knife?"

She nodded. "It was a small knife with a short blade and a red handle. A kind of pocket knife."

"Swiss army?" Sejer asked. "Do you know what that is?"

"Yes. We have one in the drawer."

Asbjørn Meiner closed his eyes. He sensed that the two policemen had a direct line to his daughter which he'd never had.

"Were you scared?" Sejer asked.

"I fell," she said simply.

"Did you see anything?"

"One of his arms. I bit it. He almost lost his grip."

"Did you see anything else?"

"Just his legs when he ran. He was fast." She sank her hands into her jeans pockets.

"What was he wearing on his feet?" Sejer asked.

"Trainers. With black stripes. Old and worn."

"Did you get anything else?"

"The gorilla mask had a strong odor," she said. "It smelled like sweets. It must've come straight from the shop."

Sejer nodded. There was something about this girl, something refreshing and forthright. With her wild, tousled hair and jeans, she reminded him of a disheveled boy. She couldn't be very strong, but she was self-confident. She was moody, but not shy. She had varnished nails, but she didn't seem girlie.

"Did you hear anything?" Skarre wanted to know. "Before or after the attack? Did he say anything? Did you hear a moped, or something? An engine? How did he get away?"

"He disappeared into the bushes," she replied. "I didn't hear anything. Just his heavy breathing."

"Yes, I can certainly imagine that," Asbjørn Meiner broke in.

"Did you have any sense of how old he could have been? Was it a man? Or a boy?"

"You try to guess the age of a gorilla," she said.

Asbjørn Meiner, who felt relegated to the sideline, broke in again. "It's great that you want to be tough, Else. I'm amazed you didn't crap yourself in fright. But you'll have to help out so we can catch this gypsy once and for all."

"He's probably not a gypsy," she said softly.

"Did he say anything?" Sejer asked. "Did he threaten you?"

"He just wanted my plait."

Sejer observed Else Meiner with increasing admiration. Her skin was white as milk, her eyelashes shiny as silk and her large eyes were unusually dark against the light skin, her mouth tiny. She resembles a doll from a puppet theater, he thought, but there certainly wasn't anyone controlling Else Meiner's strings. You'll make a name for yourself someday, he thought. One way or another.

He stood and walked to the window, looked out at Rolandsgata. Then he turned back to the girl. "Has anyone harassed you lately? Has anyone badgered you or teased you? Or threatened you?"

"No," she said firmly.

"Who lives in the other houses?" Sejer asked.

Asbjørn Meiner came up beside him. "Good people," he said. "You won't find anything on this street. The Nomes live on the right side, in the brown Swiss chalet. Beside them live Reinertsen and Green. They're actually cousins, and as you can see, they used the same architect. Their houses are a little silly, I think. Then there are the Rasmussens, the Lies and Medinas. On our side, the Håkonsens, the Juels and the Glasers. The Krantzes live in the brick house."

"What about the old house farthest away?" Sejer said and pointed. "That one stands out."

Asbjørn Meiner nodded, and the motion rode his bulky body like a wave. "Yes," he said, "it's not very nice. But the house was here first, long before the rest. So he's got every right to it. The house was built back when they used asbestos tiles. An old man lives there, his name is Beskow. Henry Beskow. But we don't see him much, because he never leaves the house. A carer visits him, gets him out of bed in the morning. There's also a teenager on a moped who stops by. Must be his grandson. He comes and goes constantly, always in and out. Who is the boy, Else?" he said.

"No idea," Else Meiner said curtly.

She left the room and Sejer turned. She disappeared suddenly down the hallway, slipping inside her room and leaving the door open. Because he had the feeling that she wanted him to, Sejer followed; the open door was like an invitation. He went to the door and looked in. He noticed a golden instrument lying on her bed.

She sat at her desk with a book.

"Was it anyone you know?" he asked gently.

She shook her head. Put her hand in her short hair. "I don't have any gorillas in my circle of friends," she said.

He laughed to himself. He liked her more and more. This boldness, and her unique sense of humor.

"Do you play the trumpet well?" he asked, and nodded at the instrument on the bed.

"Yeah, pretty well."

On the walls she had pictures and posters. He recognized some of them, Orlando Bloom and Leonardo DiCaprio among others. And she had a poster of the Joker. The white face with the red mouth. A few pictures of herself in her band uniform, dark blue with a short white shirt and a sailor cap with a silken tassel. On her bed lay a pile of cushions. One of them was a red, heart-shaped cushion with an elegantly embroidered message: *I love Johnny.*

"Why do you think he wanted your plait?"

She threw her head back. "He probably has a collection, and now it's stuffed in a drawer, with black and brown and blonde plaits. Maybe he sniffs them at night."

Her response confused him. Was it some kind of girlish prank? Had she made it all up to get noticed? Girls did that sometimes. Girls who wanted drama and attention. But he didn't believe this was the case with Else.

She rose, moved to the wall and removed a photo of herself with the plait still attached.

"He's got himself quite a trophy," Sejer said.

He thanked her and left the room, went back to Skarre and Meiner.

"Someone slashed her bicycle tires," Meiner said. "A few days ago. Up near the Sparbo Dam. What's going on? How many pranksters are there? It's one thing after another."

"What do you think?" Skarre asked.

"Someone has made it his mission to terrorize our lives. Some rotten little shit. Make sure you nail him, and make sure he gets a good whipping."

"Watch Else," Sejer encouraged him.

On the way back to the car, Sejer got a call from Frances Mold.

She spoke rapidly and feverishly. She was very concerned for her mother.

"What happened?" Sejer asked calmly.

"It's just been too much for her," Frances said. "She had some kind of reaction, and her heart began beating really fast and irregularly. Now she's been admitted to the hospital. They've got to run tests."

22

WHILE GUNILLA MØRK went around and philosophized about life and death.

While Evelyn Mold attempted to recover.

While Astrid and Helge Landmark slowly reconciled themselves to how things stood.

Karsten Sundelin considered his life.

He thought about the choices he'd made and his motives.

Why did I fall in love with Lily? he thought. Why did we marry? I was smitten because she had French roots, and because her French attracted me. When she whispered to me in that exotic language—words I only suspected the meaning of—it made my blood run faster. Warmed me and filled me with anticipation.

My French lily.

We married, he thought, because we had been together for a long time, because we were adults, and because marriage seemed a natural consequence. I was alone, and I needed someone. People around me began to talk, my parents and friends who saw I was in need; they couldn't bear to see my sorrow. I fell in love because she was petite and beautiful, because she moved through space with the elegance of a goldfish gliding through water. Why did we have Margrete? Did we think it through properly? Was it a matter of course? And what will she do with her life? Is it my responsibility? Fifteen-year-old Margrete? Thirty-year-old Margrete? Forty-year-old Margrete? If she doesn't succeed in life, is it my fault? And how, Karsten Sundelin thought, how can I get out of all this?

The time that had lapsed since the incident with Margrete had left its mark on him in many ways. Cracks had appeared in the foundation, small fractures which continued to expand, and which meant his life was about to collapse. He had a more fiery temperament, which was manifested in his gait and other gestures—something testy and jagged—and he slammed doors more forcefully. Sometimes, when he was completely honest with himself—for example in the evening, after a few beers—he knew he wasn't in love with Lily anymore. No, it was worse than that: he had begun to dislike her. He couldn't handle her femininity, her fear and vulnerability. Whenever he had these thoughts, despair filled him instantly, because maybe he was the one who had failed them.

He hadn't been able to protect them.

A stranger had come from outside and blasted their relationship to smithereens.

Each time he reached this point in his flow of thoughts he tensed up, and immediately had to occupy himself with some project, something that would absorb his energy. He secured loose boards in the picket fence around their garden. Pounded nails with a hammer to use up all his strength. He got the ax and chopped until chips of wood flew. Lily watched him through the window. Just a flicker of her consciousness understood what was actually happening; she was, after all, absorbed by the child. Margrete had gained a lot of weight. The nurse had pointed this out when she visited. When this assertion was made, Lily Sundelin surprised both herself and the nurse by standing up so quickly that her chair crashed to the floor. Then she pounded on the table.

Karsten Sundelin had begun going out for drinks after work.

He happily stopped off at a friend's place, and sometimes they got a beer at the little bar next to the Shell station in Bjerkås. Then he would come home late, by taxi. Even though he was late, and quite drunk, he saw no sign of irritation in Lily.

She was busy with the child, after all.

Nights were the worst.

When they lay side by side with Margrete in the middle of the bed, now and then he would extend his hand and carefully touch Lily's shoulder, or her hair, as had once been his habit. In return he got nothing. Just an involuntary shudder, as if the touch irritated her.

She had drafted a new set of rules.

And he struggled to understand them.

Sometimes he lay awake with his hands behind his head and imagined another woman and another life, a strong and independent woman, a brash woman who could fight for herself. Someone who laughed easily, who was able to push aside trivial matters, and get back on her feet if anyone knocked her down. Who moved on. Who ranted and roared instead of suffering in silence. Of course he could leave. Of course he could find such a woman. He was an attractive, broad-shouldered man with a deep voice, slender hips and long legs. But he was also a decent man. Moral scruples held him in their grip. They closed off the good life, the kind of life where there was room for his whole personality. He had been reduced to a caretaker for two fragile people. He had to tiptoe, always be ready, rush to them whenever one whimpered. Horrible thoughts whirled in his head, keeping him awake. They exhausted him. They led to a mix of self-loathing and anger, and he vacillated constantly between these feelings, tossing and turning while the mattress and bed frame squeaked under the weight of his heavy body.

"Please lie still," Lily would say. "You'll wake Margrete."

23

JACOB SKARRE HAD come home from his shift, and it was afternoon when he opened the door to his flat. He had gone shopping on the way home. His bags stood on the kitchen worktop, jam-packed with food. There wasn't much space. Against the wall sat all sorts of electrical appliances: a food processor from Braun, a coffeemaker, a coffee grinder, a sandwich maker and a toaster, along with a plastic salad spinner which didn't fit in the cupboards. Just as he was about to put the food away, his mobile rang.

He didn't recognize the number.

"Hi, Jacob," he heard. "It's Britt."

It was a bright and excited girl's voice, but he didn't know anyone called Britt. Still, Skarre had been raised in a vicarage, and had been taught to greet people in a mild, friendly manner.

Always, and in every situation.

Be open and accommodating.

"Hello, Britt," he replied. "How can I help you?"

Britt twittered like a lark, and even though he couldn't see her, he imagined her as small and sweet, with a lot of plumage. He pulled a cucumber from the bag. At the same time he trawled his memory. Could this Britt have been a part of his life? Maybe late one evening, after a few beers? With his blond curls and good manners he undeniably attracted a lot of attention from the opposite sex.

"He's been here again," Britt said. "We think he'll be coming back. He forgot his gloves."

The woman relayed this information with a dramatic flourish. Between words she made lip-smacking sounds, as if she had sweets in her mouth. But Skarre still did not quite understand. He had just done an eight-hour shift at the police station and talked to so many people about so many things that his head was swirling with thoughts. He took a box of eggs from the bag and pushed it against the wall. He continued digging around in his memory.

"Be coming back?" he said.

He removed a triangle of French Brie and a bar of dark, bitter chocolate while listening to the little lark on the other end of the line.

"They're motorcycle gloves," Britt explained. "They're black with red skulls. I've never seen gloves like that. They're either completely naff, or totally cool. I can't decide. I mean, skulls!"

Skarre pulled a case of beer from the bag and set it on the worktop. Now it dawned on him, slowly, like the first ray of morning light. "Britt?" he said. "From the Spar?"

He ignored his groceries, grabbing a chair and plopping into it.

"From the Spar in Lake Skarve," she said. "You were here, I'm sure you remember. You gave me your card. I've talked to the other girls, like you asked me to. The other girls on the till, I mean. And you asked me to call you. Ella Marit's been off sick—there's always something with her—but now she's back. She remembers a boy who bought one of those blocks of frozen ox blood. She didn't look at him carefully that day, and anyway, he had his helmet on. But she remembered his gloves, the ones with the skulls, because they're not something you see every day. When he was last here, he left them behind on the conveyor belt. They're in the staff room now. We reckon he'll come back to get them because they look expensive."

Skarre stood up slowly. He returned to the worktop and put his hand on the case of ice-cold beer. He felt an almost irresistible urge to crack it open and gulp down a bottle. Instead he grabbed his keys and headed for the door.

Britt and Ella Marit waited on a bench in front of the shop.

The two friends sat close together, and arched toward the sun like flowers. Ella Marit, who was older, had lit a cigarette, while Britt licked an ice lolly. They wore green Spar uniforms, and had put on whatever makeup they could—they were at the age when such things were important. When Skarre walked across the car park, the two exchanged whispered words, then leapt up from the bench and accompanied him into the shop and the back room where they took breaks. It was a very unpleasant room, with a narrow window high up near the ceiling and bare brick walls pocked with cracks. Like a basement. There was a coffee machine and a small fridge, a table with four chairs and a stainless-steel sink where they could do dishes.

Britt retrieved the gloves and held them out to him.

They were made of soft, black leather.

"They're small," Skarre said. He tried to pull on one of the gloves, but it was pointless.

"He's not that big," Ella Marit said. She stood in front of Skarre with her hands on her hips. "Just a teenager, I think. Skinny as a blade of grass."

Skarre examined the gloves closely. They could be fastened at the wrist with a large button. On the inside was a silk-like flap: *Made in China*. A red skull was embossed in the leather at the top of the glove.

"What did he look like?" he asked.

"Like an angel," Ella Marit said. "Dark and handsome, with really long hair."

"What was he wearing?"

"Jeans and a T-shirt. There was some writing on the shirt, but I couldn't read what it said, unfortunately."

"Did you hear his voice? Did he say anything?"

"No."

"I see you have a noticeboard near the entrance," he said. "Put a little note up. Say you've found a pair of gloves. In case he doesn't realize he lost them here. When he shows up, you've got to work together. One of you goes to retrieve the gloves and dawdles as much as possible. The other leaves the shop and looks for his bike. We believe he rides a moped, or a small motorcycle. Jot down the registration number. And call me immediately."

Britt and Ella Marit nodded.

"The first time you saw him he was wearing a helmet," Skarre said. "What color?"

"Red," Ella Marit said. "With small golden wings on the sides. He's a little poser, if you ask me."

"Let me say something important before I go," Skarre said. "A number of unfortunate things have happened here lately, in Bjerkås, in Sandberg, and out toward Kirkeby. But we just want to talk to him. We don't know anything for certain. So don't start any rumors that might harm him."

Now it was Britt who spoke. "A lot of teenagers here in Bjerkås ride a moped. There's such a bad bus connection into the city. They buzz around on the roads all the time, those under eighteen I mean. Everyone over eighteen, they drive cars. I'll be bloody nervous when he turns up," she added. "If he's suddenly standing at my till asking for the gloves."

Ella Marit leaned heavily against the table. Her Spar uniform was tight, and revealed quite a bit of her plumpness. When she talked, it was with an accent which have might hailed from Finnmark. She had bright brown eyes and a few Sami characteristics, and on her left hand she wore a silver ring, a snake that wrapped around her finger.

"God knows how it'll be when they catch him," she said. "When people find out who he is. I think about that a lot. It'll be pandemonium out here in Bjerkås."

"Exactly," Skarre smiled. "Pandemonium."

24

I T WAS THE middle of September.

Falling from the sky was a rain so cool and fine that it resembled mist from a waterfall. The dampness lent a special
sheen to everything, to the city's roofs and façades, to the blue
asphalt, to rubbish containers and to bike racks. After a while the
sun broke through. Bushes and trees also had their own gleam,
like something pure and renewed. Sejer walked the streets with
Frank. Walking softly and effortlessly, he thought about his childhood. In his life he had been fortunate to have all the important
things, including the most essential foundation: security. His
mother had given him this. She had always, whenever something
happened—an accident or an illness—immediately clutched him
and assured him that everything would work out. It'll be all right,
she said that time he fell over the handlebars and broke his wrist.
It'll get better, she said when his dog died and he almost couldn't
bear it. *It'll get better, it'll work out, I'm quite certain of it.*

Words that were accompanied by her arm, which held him tightly,
and by her warm, assured voice: she was an adult and she knew
certain things. Security was part of his innermost core, a base,
and his entire life rested on it.

But some kids didn't have any of that. They had mothers who

buried their faces in their hands to lament, Dear God, what will happen now? Lamenting led to angst, and angst led to the foundation vanishing beneath their feet. So they searched their entire lives for something to latch on to. The world was full of such kids who'd gone astray.

He continued slowly through the shiny streets, stopping now and then so Frank could sniff the gutter. He thought about the white house in Gamle Møllevej outside Roskilde, where he grew up. Hollyhocks climbed the wall, small white hens trotted around the garden. Being a little boy, playing between the trees in the garden, plucking sour currants from the bushes, eating them, and making sour faces with his friend Ole. Laughing at the tiniest things. Then, when the day was over, he would head back to his house without trepidation. Be welcomed like someone unique, someone loved, as if he, the little boy Konrad, was an event in and of himself, returned home finally after a long absence. But that's not how it is for everyone, he thought. There are kids who open the door, afraid, who cower and sneak into their homes, kids who don't know what to expect. Who flee again because what they see is unbearable. Like drunkenness. Words of abuse. Or violence. Or all of it together in one hellish, destructive cocktail. He thought again of his childhood friend Ole. He was just a guest in his mother's house. *No, you can't be here now,* she'd say, *the weather's so nice. No, not today, I'm cleaning. One of my friends is visiting. I have a migraine. You should be outside. Now, out you go!* And Ole would leave. In rain and storm and cold. In the evening he would sneak back in, make himself a sandwich and tiptoe to his bed like a masterless dog. There was no violence in the house, no one drank. But no one loved him either. Sejer bent down and stroked Frank's back. Some people claimed that you couldn't blame parents for the misery that plagued their children. But he disagreed vehemently. You could blame mothers for a lot. The child was at the mercy of her moods, her anger and her doubt, her bitterness and her shortcomings. And they were at the mercy of their father's despair, his absence and lack of attention.

Frank had stopped to sniff at a half-eaten bun. When he was done, he raised his leg and urinated on an old rusty gate. They continued through the city, the tall gray man and the small, wrinkled dog. Admittedly, I'm a little heavier in my steps, Sejer thought, than I was a few years ago. But I'm also older and wiser. At that moment a sudden, brief dizzy spell overcame him once more. The city and the back alleys sailed away in front of his eyes. To be on the safe side he moved closer to a house wall, leaned against it and closed his eyes. Stood and waited for the spell to pass. Frank stopped too. He looked up at his master with his black eyes. I wobbled a few steps to the left, Sejer thought. I always wobble to the left. Maybe this is an asymmetric symptom? No, cut it out, he thought, it's probably just some calcified veins in my neck. Maybe I'm anemic.

He began walking again.

His mobile rang in his pocket.

He recognized the number, and listened to Skarre's account of the forgotten gloves. At the end of the conversation Skarre mentioned something else.

"Helge Landmark's health has taken a turn. He's been admitted to the hospital, and he's on a respirator."

25

SOMETIMES JOHNNY BESKOW dreamed that everyone was out to get him.

That the police had sent a throng of people that now chased him through the forest with German shepherds snapping at his heels. The night was black as pitch and they searched for him with torches. He saw cones of light dance between the trunks of trees, heard threats and shouts and dogs panting, but he was faster than they were, and craftier.

Like a weasel he slipped away.

He found a cave and hid inside, balled up against the wall listening. Lightning quick he clambered up a tree and looked down through the leaves at the crowd. Wading over a brook, he put them off the scent.

He still had this dream. Each time he woke with a feeling of satisfaction, because it wasn't a nightmare—more like play, a game he always won.

They can't even catch me in dreams.

Because I'm faster, he thought.

I'm Johnny Beskow, and I'm invincible.

The moped wouldn't start. It just coughed a few times, and spluttered out. The tank was just about empty of petrol, and he had no money. So he walked. He had good legs and good trainers, and he didn't want to be at home. As he walked, he remembered the gloves he'd lost, and it occurred to him that they might be at the shop in Lake Skarve. Perhaps he had taken them off and put them on the conveyor belt when he was paying, and then left them behind. It could've happened that way, and maybe they'd kept them. He decided he would go to the shop and ask, so he took the path down to the water. He walked fast. The heat filled his body from his feet upward; it rose to his head, and he felt light and good. Before going in he strolled around by the lake for a while, watching the ducks and the neat rings they created in the water. When he crossed the car park and walked to the entrance, he hesitated a moment. Something rang in his head, a warning bell. He felt as though he was being watched. At the same time he caught sight through the window of a notice that said a pair of black-and-red gloves had been found.

Ask Britt, it said.

He opened the door and went in, continued cautiously to the till, to two girls sitting idle and staring at him with large, round eyes.

Afterward, when he considered it, he thought the two girls had acted strangely. The simple question, Could you get the gloves? had led to an incomprehensible commotion. They opened their eyes wide. They exchanged glances. One disappeared immediately into the back room, and she took her time. The other went outside, walked aimlessly around the car park as though searching for something. Now and then she stopped and glanced about, puzzled, as though something was missing. She's looking for the moped, he realized. I'll be damned. Perhaps there was a reason for the empty petrol tank. The other one finally came back, and gave him the gloves. He slipped out the door and bolted as fast as he could, heading toward Bjerkås.

Again he thought about the dream he'd had. The fun might

soon be over, he thought, they're on my trail. Maybe I have to do something spectacular while there's time.

One way or another.

Then he walked all the way to Rolandsgata. In the sunshine and the mild late-summer breeze, surrounded by ditches with wildflowers and green meadows. It took an hour. As he went, he hummed a song, "Hermann Is a Cheery Fellow." When he arrived, he called through the house.

"Didn't you ride your moped?" Henry Beskow asked. "I didn't hear it."

He explained that the tank was empty. He said it in a light, indifferent way, because he wasn't the kind of person to beg, and he had good legs to walk on.

"I'm pretty fit," he said. "And it's good to walk sometimes."

"Out in the shed there's an old plastic canister, Johnny. You can fill it with petrol. Then take some money from the glass jar in the kitchen. You've got to have your moped, it's important that you can get around."

Johnny took care of food and drink. He buttered slices of bread and mixed squash in a jug, carried them into the lounge and set them on the table with the two-handled mug. Then he had a thought. As usual, it was boiling hot in the room. He went to the windows; both were closed. He examined them carefully, traced the sill with a finger. Squinting out at the road, he was blinded by the low sun.

"You need fresh air," he said.

"Can't," the old man protested. "The wasps."

Johnny turned and looked at him. He wanted to be the boss, so he stood tall and crossed his arms. "I'll call a carpenter. We'll get him to put in one of those insect screens. One for each window. Then they can stay open all summer. You'll be fresh and clear-headed, not heavy and sluggish like you are now."

"So that's what you think now, eh?" grumbled Henry.

"Have you got one of those folding rulers? I'll take measurements."

His grandfather told him to look in a kitchen drawer. The folding ruler was old and sturdy. He measured both windows twice, noting the figures on a sheet of paper.

"Ninety-eight by one hundred and ten," he said cheerily. "I'll find a carpenter in the phone book."

"Ask what it costs," Henry said. "Can you bargain?"

"I'll tell them you're retired."

Johnny riffled through the Yellow Pages and found a carpenter who lived in the area. He explained the situation and they agreed on a price and a time for him to come and install the screens.

"If everyone were like you, Johnny," Henry said contentedly, "this world would be a better place."

Johnny patted him on his nearly bald head. "I know. I'm a man of action."

They talked about this and that, as was their routine, and a few afternoon hours passed quickly. Because he had so much care, Henry felt spoiled, and Johnny felt indispensable. "It's us against all the rest of them," he told Henry.

Johnny carried the mugs and plates to the kitchen and put them on the worktop. He found the plastic canister in the shed, walked down to Bjørnstad Center and filled it up. As he walked back across Askeland with the heavy can in his hand, he fantasized. His mother would look up when he entered, perhaps from her knitting, smile and say, There you are, how lovely. I've waited so long. Are you hungry? Can I make you something to eat? What do you feel like eating, Johnnyboy?

He liked this fantasy, so he continued to let his thoughts wander.

I've baked you a kringle, she might say. It's cooling on a rack on the worktop.

With almonds and sugar on top.

Let's have a nice, quiet evening at home together.

When he was finally home after his long walk—the ten-liter canister had made his right arm numb—he filled the moped tank. Draining the can properly was difficult.

He heard it splash at the bottom, probably only a drop left. Thoughts of the sweet kringle were swept away and replaced with bitter ones. If she's lying on the sofa pissed, he thought, I'll pour the rest of the petrol on her head and light it.

My mother in flames, he thought.

The smell of grilled hyena spreading over Askeland.

He went inside the house.

There was nothing on the stove, and no hot, sweet kringle cooling on a rack.

He headed into the lounge and stood stock-still in the door frame, staring. His mother sat on the sofa, the tension between them palpable as humidity in the air.

"What do you want?" she said. "Been with the old man, I imagine. What did you get out of him today?"

He lowered his head. She was right: his grandfather had given him money. But he hadn't begged for it. He had only mentioned the empty tank, had said it without complaint, as an explanation.

"Don't stand there gawking, it makes me nervous. Do you know you have a piercing stare? Go to your room."

Johnny did as his mother told him. In his room he took Butch from his cage, lay down on his bed and closed his eyes, letting the hamster crawl across the duvet on its tiny, fast feet. Low sounds reached him from the kitchen. Maybe she had started dinner. He heard drawers and cupboards opening, and footsteps shuffling back and forth. The clatter of cutlery. Well, he thought, the hyena is scraping a meal together. Another thought slithered through the silence into his room, an evil and shrewd one. The police were right behind him now, so it was important to exploit the time he had left. He listened to all the noises in the kitchen, noticing how she paced from the kitchen to the lounge and back. She kept busy, turning on the taps, slamming cupboard doors. Finally, after twenty minutes, he heard her go into the bathroom. He leapt quickly from the bed and opened a drawer in his chest of drawers. The box of rat poison was hidden behind an old T-shirt. He removed the lid and studied the pink grains. You would think the grains looked tasty, if you didn't know any better—that is, if you didn't know they were deadly. Keeping his ear trained on the bathroom, he listened for his mother. I'll have to act fast, he thought, while I'm at my most vicious. While I don't care what's happening, either about the night ahead or tomorrow—to hell with the consequences. He tiptoed into the kitchen. A saucepan simmered on the hob. On the worktop next to it was a wooden spoon. The meat and vegetables in the pan were mixed in a dark sauce. He drained the entire box of rat poison into the pan and stirred it around, until it was absolutely impossible to see the minuscule grains. This will be interesting, he thought. He stuck the empty box under his pullover and ran back to his room. The entire operation had taken only a few seconds. When he heard his mother leave the bathroom, he slipped into the hallway and opened the front door, his cheeks flushed.

She heard him and immediately stepped into the hallway. "So," she said, "just when I make dinner for us, you leave."

"I'll eat later. Don't wait for me, go ahead and eat."

She returned to the stove, stirring the food in the poisoned pan. The last he saw of her were her blue-veined legs.

Johnny Beskow stayed away from the house for several hours.

Hot, out of breath and excited about what he'd done. Now there was no way back. His fantasies ran wild, imagining dramatic scenes of his mother and the poisonous stew: of her eating from the spoon so that it ran down her chin, of her emptying the pot and scraping the bottom. He had visions of his mother convulsing. He saw her teeth clattering in her mouth, saw her suddenly collapse onto the table, then leap up and stumble around in the throes of death, eyes bloodshot and foam spilling from her mouth. She sounded her death rattle, drooling and falling, then scrambled to her feet and stumbled through each room. When she reached the telephone to call for help, her eyesight was weak, and she couldn't see clearly. She tried to open a window, to call out to someone walking past, but her fingers disobeyed her and she failed to pop the latch. And anyway, she had lost her voice. Now she was poisoned. Her arms and legs were poisoned; her heart and brain were poisoned. Poison pumped through her bloodstream, made its deadly way to every last cell of her body. Finally she went down for good. Maybe she dragged something with her when she fell, made a violent commotion. Because she shouldn't be allowed to die in a peaceful manner. She should leave this world in pain and suffering.

Or so Johnny Beskow thought.

He rode to the Sparbo Dam. Parked the moped against a spruce, put his gloves inside his helmet. He walked ten steps along the dam wall, and sat down. The water roared and foamed on its way through the pipes and down into the valley. He sat there a long time waiting for the poison to take effect. Restlessly he roamed the forest trails, rode here and there and watched the time. After four hours he figured it was over. He set his course for home, rolled into the driveway and parked.

He stood there a while, listening.

The house had never been so quiet.

He imagined her lying in the bathroom.

On the floor, her face flat against the old yellow tiles. Maybe she had fallen next to the sofa, having attempted to reach it. Or maybe she had dragged herself into the bedroom and lain on her bed.

Standing still in the hall, he could not hear a sound. From there he went into the bathroom, and from the bathroom he went into the lounge. Where she stood rummaging in a drawer of her writing desk. She looked up.

"What's wrong with you?" she shouted. "Why are you sneaking about like that? You look like a thief in your own house. For God's sake, you scared me. Why do you stand there gawping like that? Have you seen a ghost or what?"

Alive and kicking, she gesticulated wildly with her hands. She had a pulse, she made sounds. She could think, cobble sentences together into bad thoughts—just as he had done. She could go on pouring her vodka. In his confusion Johnny was mute. She didn't look sick at all. There was even a trace of color in her cheeks.

He went into the kitchen, puzzled. The pan was on the stove, but it was empty. His mother had poured the stew into a large, blue Tupperware container with a lid. She came in.

"Take what you want," she said. "I'll put the rest in the freezer. We'll eat it another time."

Escaping to his room, he felt gloomy and disappointed, because he hadn't been able to create a spectacle and hadn't got rid of her once and for all, as he'd thought. He spent the entire evening on his bed pondering while Butch scampered around on the duvet. Apparently she hadn't eaten enough of the poisonous stew, or hadn't eaten any of it.

Night came, and he went to bed.

He heard his mother bustling about in her room. A logical thought struck him: maybe she had eaten, maybe even a good portion, but the rat poison worked very slowly. That's what he'd read on the package—that the rats need several doses before they breathed their last. So maybe it would take the hyena a while to die. The thought of her pain lasting several days excited him. Poisoning was like a war, and there was a kind of logic to the way the small grains attacked. First they destroyed the liver and kidneys, then the lungs and the heart.

He wrapped the duvet snugly around him, a warm lair of down and cloth.

He tried to make plans for the following day. I'll have to do something creative, he thought, while I wait for the poison to do its work. While I wait for the hyena to fall to her knees.

26

LITTLE THEO BOSCH sat attentively in front of the television, a bag of De-light crisps in his lap. With just 9 percent fat, the crisps were approved by his mother, who was careful about such things. He had put a DVD in the machine and followed closely what happened on the screen. Watching Lars Monsen's green canoe slice through the water, Theo thought he looked like a real mountain man with his tangle of hair and beard: fishing for trout, making up a campfire, sleeping under the open sky. If the wolf howled out there in the dark, Lars Monsen didn't get scared, because it was just Good Old Graylag gathering his flock. A fearless man, Lars Monsen wandered the wilderness with such confidence that Theo dreamed himself far away. After he'd watched two whole episodes, he leapt from the sofa and ran to find his mother. But she wasn't in the kitchen or out in the garden. His father came in while he was searching for her.

"She's resting," he said. "She has a headache. That's women for you. They need a room of their own where they can be in peace."

Theo raced up to his parents' bedroom on the first floor, where he found his mother lying on the queen-size bed, her face toward the wall. It was stifling hot. She had removed all her clothes and had simply pulled the sheet over her. But the sheet had slid down, and her naked white rump glowed in the dark room.

Theo stood there, staring, a finger in his mouth.

Hannes tiptoed in. He leaned against the door. "Look at that," he said. "Her bottom looks like two soft buns."

At that they laughed in the way of boys.

"Can I hike to Snellevann?" Theo asked. "By myself?"

Hannes Bosch furrowed his brow. He glanced down at his wife's tempting behind, and then looked at his son. Theo was an obedient child with a certain intensity which often served him well.

"To Snellevann. By yourself? Now? Do you mean right now?"

Theo nodded. He looked pleadingly at his father. His head was filled with images of the wilderness and so too was his heart. He could hear the song of the forest in the enormous spruces. He wanted to hear the birds sing, see the fish jump. Theo the explorer, that's what he wanted to be.

"I'll take my lunch," he whispered. "You can help me pack my rucksack so I've got everything I need."

Hannes Bosch cast a glance at his watch. It was still early. He put his hand on his son's head. Theo wasn't much more than a tiny tot, but he was a bright boy, and no sissy. To Snellevann, he thought, on his little legs. That would take him an hour. Then he'd probably sit at the water's edge for twenty minutes before coming home; all in all, it'd take two hours and twenty minutes—a long time for a little boy. To Snellevann. All by himself. Hannes walked to the window and looked out. The weather was fine, and nightfall was a long way off. There was also a good deal of pedestrian traffic on the way to Snellevann. Landowners and farmers spent time in their fields seeing to their cows and sheep, putting out salt blocks, checking the fences. Not to mention hikers and cyclists, and maybe people picking berries. But Theo was just eight years old. On the other hand, it's safer in the woods than almost anywhere else. They'd agreed on that long ago.

"Your mum would probably tell you no," he whispered.

"But we won't ask her," Theo said cleverly, with a sideways glance at his father.

They tiptoed out of the bedroom.

Hannes rested a hand on his son's shoulder. "If you're going out hiking, then you've got to plan ahead. Having a plan is important. Lars Monsen never goes off without planning first, right down to the smallest detail. Food. Equipment. Clothing. Everything."

Theo nodded.

"You've got to dress properly," Hannes said. "Don't wear sandals. Find something else."

"Shorts," Theo said. "Because it's hot. And trainers. An extra jumper in my rucksack. Food and water."

"And you've got to have a good knife," Hannes said. "You can't go to the woods without one. I'll let you borrow my hunting knife. But don't tell your mum. You know how women get with knives. They don't understand."

Theo collected everything he needed. He was flushed and eager. When he became a famous explorer, like Lars Monsen, journalists would ask him about his very first expedition. Oh, that, he would say. I was just a boy. I hiked to Snellevann and back, and I was really proud of myself.

Hannes packed Theo's lunch. While he did that, he prepared a few good arguments for when Wilma woke up to find that her little boy had gone off to Snellevann on his own. With a heavy hunting knife in his belt.

But for God's sake, Wilma, he's eight years old. You know how he is, with all his Lars Monsen ideas. He's got it into his head he wants to be an explorer, and you'll never be able to stop him. I think we should be proud and happy. Some kids can't be bothered to get off the sofa. What did you say? He'll get lost? He's going to Snellevann, Wilma. He's following the trail, which he's done a hundred times before. No, the weather is fine, and he will be back in a couple of hours. Or I should say two and a half hours. Think about how proud he'll be. Self-confidence is pretty important, Wilma, don't you agree?

He put salami on a slice of bread.

I made sure he took his mobile phone. He's just a dial away. You can call and check up on him. That is, if you want to ruin the whole experience for him.

So that his son would have some variety, he put Swiss sausage on the second slice and cheese on the third. He mixed black-currant squash and poured it in a Thermos. Theo came into the kitchen. He had retrieved his rucksack, and in it he had put his favorite toy, Optimus Prime.

"Get a belt," Hannes said. "Where you can put the knife. It should always be easily accessible, you know. In case the Indians come," he winked.

Theo fetched a belt. He put on his trainers and tied the shoe-laces in a double knot, and was so excited his cheeks flushed. There was something manly about him, something brave and grown-up.

"I'll walk you to the metal barrier," Hannes suggested.

"Yup."

They closed the door and locked it. Wandered down the main road. It took them a quarter of an hour to reach the barrier near Glenna. They stopped and exchanged a few words.

"Put your jumper on if you get cold."

"I will, Papa," Theo said.

"And don't leave any rubbish behind. Put it in your rucksack after you've eaten."

"I will. I'll clean up after me."

"If you use the knife, do so carefully. It's sharp."

"I'll be careful, Papa. I promise."

Then Theo turned and walked on. He had inherited his father's big feet, and in the enormous trainers, he reminded his father of a little tottering duck.

Hannes watched his small son until he disappeared round a bend. Then the boy was absorbed by the forest.

Wilma Bosch wasn't merciful.

Though they were still attractive, the soft cheeks Hannes had admired had disappeared into a pair of bleached jeans. But he knew better than to put his claws on them, because now she was on the offensive.

"How will he cope if something happens?" she said.

"What do you mean, 'happens'? Nothing will happen in the woods, Wilma. There are only acorns and hares as far as you can see. What are you really afraid of?"

Wilma moved to the window facing the road. She had clogs on her feet, and they clopped against the wooden floor. Even though she couldn't see Theo from there, it was her attempt to get closer to him.

"You ask what could happen," she said. "A lot, Hannes. An eight-year-old boy is so helpless. He could slip on the rocks, then hit his head and fall in the water. There are snakes and they're big this year, at least that's what everyone who knows anything says. There are cows grazing, and moose. Sometimes they attack people," she said. "You know, when they have young."

Hannes tried to digest what she'd said.

"You're afraid he'll be afraid," he said. "Is that what this is all about?"

"Yes. He's just eight!"

"But everyone's afraid now and then. Maybe he'll hear strange sounds in the trees, and maybe his heart will leap.

"But so does my heart, and I'm thirty-eight. I could slip on the rocks too, hit my head and end up on life support. With no contact with the rest of the world. If we were to discuss all the things that *could* happen."

Wilma fell into a chair so heavily that it moved a few centimeters. "Sometimes," she said, "I think all that Lars Monsen stuff is too much."

She pouted. She had folded her hands in her lap, and Hannes noticed the remains of dark red nail varnish. It looked as though tiny drops of blood had trickled from her nails. He patted her arm lightly, then reached into his pocket for his mobile. He punched in Theo's number and waited. He pushed the speaker button so Wilma could hear.

"Howdy, Theo," he said. "How far along are you?"

Wilma sat listening to the short conversation. She imagined, at that instant, her son on his way into the big forest.

"You're past Granfoss?" Hannes said. "OK. Have you run into anyone? . . . No one? What about animals? . . . No, OK. . . . You're not cold? . . . Good, good. Put on your jumper if it gets cloudy. . . . You're out of breath," he added. "Are you going up the hills over toward Myra?"

"About halfway," Theo panted. "I may have to rest a bit."

"You don't need to rush. You have the entire afternoon. Your mum wanted to know that all was well. You know how it is with women."

Theo's voice could be heard clearly through the mobile's speaker. "All's well."

"Can you repeat that?" Hannes asked, smiling at Wilma.

"All's well."

"And you're not afraid or anything? You haven't heard any scary sounds in the woods?"

At that, Theo's laughter rolled through the room. "No scary sounds, and I'm not afraid." His boy's voice was soft and clear as a bell.

"Could you call us when you reach the water?"

"OK, captain."

Hannes ended the conversation and put his mobile on the table.

"I will tell you one thing," Wilma said. "Bears have been spotted as far south as Ravnefjell. It was in the paper."

Hannes Bosch tugged at his hair. "Ravnefjell! He's just going to Snellevann. Honestly, Wilma," he said and took her hands. "Are you afraid that Theo will run into a bear? You're not quite yourself. Did you take too many painkillers?"

He couldn't help but laugh, because now he thought she had completely lost it. She pulled her hands from his.

"I hate it when he leaves the house," she admitted. "When he's out of my control. It drives me crazy."

Hannes touched her cheek. "I know," he whispered.

At that moment Hannes Bosch felt carefree. "It's a dangerous world out there. People drop like flies. Let's sit on the porch and drink a bottle of wine before the bear gets him."

Theo stopped at St. Olav's Spring. The water glinted, and was almost silver fresh.

The spring was marked with a small sign that outlined its brief history. His father had read it to him many times. He stood there for a while paying respect, because the water in the source was holy, and to him the water had its own special shine. St. Olav was a holy man, Theo thought, and his spring was too. So if I drink from it I'll also be holy. He drank big gulps of the fresh water, and he thought it tasted good. Some believed the water had healing powers, and he felt it too—that his energies were renewed.

He pushed on. The holy water had given him new powers, he was certain. He used his eyes and ears, but everything seemed quiet and sleepy. Nature seemed to have settled down, and took no notice of the little boy with big feet who walked the path. Sheep manure and cow dung dotted the trail, and he had to be careful not to step in it. He walked in a zigzag, hummed a song.

Wondered whether he should call his father, but decided against it. There's got to be a limit, he thought. When Lars Monsen's out in the wild he doesn't make calls all the time. Ha! he thought, and quickened his pace. One two, one two, one boot and one shoe. Let the snakes come, I'm wearing good shoes.

When he had found a rhythm, he kept it, marching the trail at a good clip. The rhythm stuck with him and gave him speed and strength, and his thoughts focused on one thing: reaching the water. It's actually quite easy being a man of the wilderness, he thought, once you've made up your mind. And you have to have the right equipment. He felt for the hunting knife to make sure it was still on his belt. When a bird fluttered up from the brush, he started. His heart jumped, but his nerves quickly settled.

The final few meters he walked barefoot.

Over the rocks down to the water. He found a fine place to sit, approaching close enough to the edge that his white toes reached the water.

That water is bloody cold, he thought. That's what his father would have said, if he sat at his side with his toes in the water. His trainers stood neatly beside him with his socks stuffed inside, like two balls of white cotton. He shrugged off his rucksack and opened it, set his lunch with the three slices of bread next to his shoes. On the other side he put his Thermos with blackcurrant squash, and finally Optimus Prime. Because he'd run the last bit, he was out of breath.

I'm in the wilderness, he thought, and I'm really tough.

On his way up he had carried a strong willow branch. Now he snatched the hunting knife from his belt. He struggled slightly getting it out of the sheath. How quiet everything was. Even the tiniest sound was clear, a mosquito humming over the water, rustling leaves and heather. There probably aren't any snakes, he thought, looking around. His toes were a tempting offering, perhaps, round and a little like marzipan such as they were. But nothing disturbed him as he sat at the water's edge. Everything was beautiful and silent. He whittled and whittled on the willow branch. The wood smelled so good.

The whole forest, when it came to it, is edible, he thought, the foliage, the grass, the heather, bark and berries. He heard a sound in the distance and leapt up to peer toward the trail. It grew louder and he thought it was a motor. A tractor, perhaps, or a car. The sound came and went, and his imagination began to run wild. That never happened when he walked along a road, Theo thought, because cars drove past all the time. He sat down again, putting the branch down. He drove the knife back into its sheath and began to eat. Of course there were others in the forest. There was nothing to worry about. Just then, he heard voices—no doubt some men cycling the trail. He stood to have a look and one of them waved. Theo waved back. Wow, he thought cheerfully, it's swarming with people.

He sat. With an enormous appetite he devoured the Swiss sausage and salami. His mother had baked the bread, and what he loved most about it was the crust. Though he was sated after the first two slices, he forced himself to eat the third. A hiker needs his calories. Once again he pulled out the knife and resumed whittling the branch. He fashioned a spear to a point, like an awl. He had to take care not to cut his finger, or accidentally drive the knife into his thigh. If something like that happened, he knew he wouldn't be allowed to go on any more solo hikes. What excited him most was the thought of coming home and reporting to his parents everything that had happened. Well, OK, nothing had happened so far, but there was still a chance that something *could*. And if it didn't, he could easily invent some minor story to make it more interesting. Wasn't there an eagle circling high up in the sky, on the hunt for prey? Wasn't there a big trout jumping out of the water? He saw the rings quite clearly; they spread slowly and prettily over the water. When it came down to it, anything could happen, Theo thought, and waved the sharp stick. With the stick he stirred the water as you stir a pot. The silence at the water's edge and the spreading rings put him in a sleepy trance.

He fell out of reality. Into another, dreamlike landscape that seemed familiar to him. Here, too, there was a little forest lake and a trout leaping from the water. But suddenly a man paddled into view on his right. Theo blinked sleepily, disbelieving what he saw.

Wasn't that Lars Monsen in his green canoe?

Lars pulled his oars into the boat. The canoe continued to glide, soundlessly like a knife, through the water and toward the bank where Theo sat. Lars's curly hair had grown wild, his eyes narrow slits, the irises sharp and black like flint. The boat rammed the rocks with a little thunk.

"Well, well, boy. You're out trekking," Lars Monsen said. "Have you been out long?"

Theo shook his head. He sat with the willow spear across his knees and gazed devoutly at his hero. "I had thought about going to Ravnefjell," he said cheerfully. "But I ran out of provisions." He pointed at the rolled-up wax paper which lay at his side. There were only crumbs left.

"Bad planning," sneered Lars Monsen. His teeth were sharp and white.

Theo nodded. The green canoe had some deep scratches in the bow where it had scraped the rock. His equipment was packed in two leather sacks at the end of the boat. In addition, he had a rifle and a fishing rod.

"Did you catch any trout?" Theo asked.

"Yup. Got two big ones at the tip of the cove early this morning."

They sat in silence for a while. Lars Monsen had a cap on his head. Now he pulled the brim down so that his eyes remained in shadow.

"So you're on your way back?"

"Yes," Theo replied. "I figure I'll be home in an hour. Will take a longer trip tomorrow. I'll take more provisions then."

"Where's your tent anyway?" Lars asked. He narrowed his eyes at Theo.

"Eh, the tent," Theo stammered. "No, this is just a one-day trip," he said, embarrassed. "But I'll get myself a tent, and a canoe," he said quickly. "One like yours."

He put his lunch paper in his rucksack. He wasn't the kind of person who left a mess in the wilderness.

"I met a teddy bear up here," Lars Monsen said and pointed.

Theo opened his mouth in fright. "What? A bear?"

"Yup," Lars said. "Or rather, three bears. A fat mama bear and her two cubs. Damn, she was a giant, you should have seen her. Shaggy as a bumblebee, heavy as a hippo. There's fresh bear scat in the whole area."

Theo's heart transformed from a small hard muscle into something hot and fluid that flowed through his body.

"I shouted some swear words at her." Lars Monsen laughed. "Which was a little too much for Mama Bear. Ladies don't like it when you're rude. It was up near Ravnefjell," he added. "You're not going that way, are you? You're going south, to Saga, down through Glenna?"

Theo raised the branch from his lap. He seemed to be on shaky ground. "I've got a spear," he stuttered, "and a hunting knife."

He pulled the knife from its sheath and brandished it, then saw Lars's rifle lying in the green canoe. That's what he needed. So he could have blown off the head of the mama bear and her cubs.

Lars Monsen smiled. He threw his curly head back and burst into laughter so booming it rang across the water, making the birds flutter up, and sending squirrels scampering through the heather in fright.

"So you'll poke a stick at the mama bear," he sniggered. "Did you make that spear in woodwork at school? That's the funniest thing I've seen all day. Yes, Mama Bear will be scared, I'll bet."

He grasped the oars with both hands and paddled off. The green canoe gained speed. Theo heard his laughter until the canoe was beyond the headland. I've got to get home, he thought, confused, and gathered up his things. He put on his socks and trainers, and stuffed everything in his rucksack. I can't sit here any longer doing nothing. Lars Monsen. How terrific to see him paddling around Snellevann. But still, Theo thought, even if it was one of his silly daydreams, it was lousy of Lars Monsen to frighten him that way. Talking about bears and stuff, when everyone knows there weren't any bears this far south. Theo put on his rucksack and got back to the trail. He tried to walk calmly, but couldn't find a rhythm. Then he began to run, and a cold, sudden wind put the woods in motion. He grew agitated and rushed along, gasping, certain that something was about to catch him. Someone on the edge of the trail was observing him, and something terrible waited farther ahead.

Hannes Bosch was an optician, as his father Pim had been before him, and he had a sense for light and refraction — everything that was the eye's delight. He raised his glass of wine up to the sun and admired the deep, red color through the crystal. Wilma sat with a newspaper on her lap. She glanced at her husband, and noticed that he had put his feet on the table.

"Your feet," she commented, "are heavy as rocks."

"They may be heavy," he said, "but I can stand upright, whether the sea is calm or stormy." The wine had made him lightheaded; he felt good, and happy. "When it comes to you and all your attributes, I keep my mouth shut," he laughed. "I'm not looking for trouble."

They sat in the hammock. Wilma put her newspaper down, leaned her head against his shoulder and sighed. When the sun was low, as it was now, it was warmest. She could smell Hannes, his fine scent, could hear his heart beating calmly and evenly.

"You're never afraid," she said and turned her head to look into his mild, gray eyes.

He rumpled her hair, a thick, strawberry-blonde mane smelling of shampoo. "Not before I need to be," he said. "And right now I don't need to be. I'm sitting here in the sun with you, and I have wine in a crystal glass."

"But why hasn't he called?" Wilma said.

Hannes tugged at a lock of her hair, twining it round his finger. "Maybe he's trying to tell us something. That he's not afraid. It's a demonstration. We shouldn't spoil it for him by fussing."

Wilma maneuvered in under his arm. "You're so confident," she said. "I'm glad. That's why I want to be with you forever. But you're only human, you make mistakes too."

"Not often," Hannes said. He let the mild red-wine buzz lead him far away. Wilma's lock of hair felt like silk string between his fingers.

"What if he's actually afraid," Wilma said, "but too proud to admit it? So he walks the trail alone, his heart in his throat. Being tough for us. Maybe hoping we'll call him so he'll be spared the humiliation. That's another possibility."

Hannes got up from the hammock. Walking a few paces with a mixture of determination and gravity which made the wooden boards creak with each step, he fished his mobile out of his pocket and called Theo. While he waited, he began crooning. "Joy to the World, the Lord is come. Let earth receive her King!"

"Why are you carrying on like that?" Wilma laughed at her singing husband.

"It's his ringtone. I think it's from Handel's *Messiah*. "Joy to the World." You probably know it. He took a few more steps. Wilma followed him with her eyes.

"He's not answering?"

"Calm down now," Hannes said. "His mobile's probably at the bottom of his rucksack, and he's a bit clumsy, as you know. I can just see it."

They waited. Hannes continued to pace, listening to the mobile ring.

"He's not answering?" Wilma repeated. Abruptly she got up from the hammock, which swayed a few times before coming to rest.

"Maybe it's in his back pocket," Hannes suggested. "And he's fumbling with his small hands. Or maybe he's absorbed by something. Stay calm, darling," he teased. "We'll try again."

27

I T WAS SKARRE who called Sejer.

He was so agitated that he could barely speak. Over the years he'd seen so many things: people floating in lakes, or hanging from beams. They had each witnessed tragedies great and small, and they had found methods to help them remain calm. But this was something else, something absolutely hideous.

"You must come at once!"

Sejer pressed his mobile against his ear. "What is it? Where are you?"

Automatically he searched his pockets for his keys, because he knew he would have to get going. He heard Skarre breathing, and other voices farther away. Even this background murmur sounded ominous.

"Where are you?" he repeated.

"We're out in Bjerkås," Skarre said. "Near Saga on the trail they call Glenna. You need to get here quickly. Sverre Skarning has opened the metal barrier, so you can drive all the way in. We're at the first fork in the road, it's called Skillet. There's a big sign made of wood, with a map. You'll see us."

"OK. What's the situation?" Sejer asked.

"W-we don't quite know yet," Skarre stuttered. "We can't tell what's happened. But between you and me, something dreadful has occurred here."

"Can you be a bit more specific? What's the situation?"

"As far as we can see, it's the remains of a little boy."

Thirty minutes later Sejer was at Glenna.

He saw them clustered at the fork in the road, milling about. Some had their hands on their heads. Others, perhaps unable to stand any longer, rested on logs gathered at the side of the track. A woman officer sat sobbing into her hands. A police car and an ambulance were parked farther along. He opened his car door and got out, caught sight of the big wooden sign. Something lay in the road, and it immediately unsettled him. He felt a violent tug in his belly. Without wanting it to, his heart began to thump. He started walking, but very slowly, staring at the group of eight or ten crime scene officers. As they watched him approach, they stepped aside.

A green tarpaulin lay in the road. There was a very modest lump in the center, indicating that it held quite a small body.

"Take a deep breath," Skarre said. "It's not pretty."

The thin, synthetic material swished when they pulled the tarpaulin aside.

Sejer gasped. He couldn't understand what he was looking at. The remains of a little boy, they had said. But what he saw was just a tangle of limbs, a hand, a foot, a blank, staring eye. He noticed a small rucksack with a Kvikklunsj chocolate bar patch sewn onto it. The rucksack was open, and something resembling a toy had fallen out. Shafts of bone stuck out from the flesh like thin, white sticks, the left arm was torn off at the elbow, and parts of the face were gone. A few small, round children's teeth gleamed against red gums. Sejer could also make out a piece of khaki cloth, shorts possibly, and a white trainer. He glanced around for the match, but he couldn't find it. The torn-off arm was nowhere to be seen, either. He had to get away, it occurred to him, a simple reflex. He was ready to bound back to the car. Give me something to drink, he thought, right now.

"Has anyone touched him?" he said.

The assembled shook their heads. The woman officer who had sat sobbing pulled herself together and wiped away her tears. But her face was filled with pain.

"Who found him?"

"Two cyclists out training," Skarre said. "We sent them away. We'll talk to them later."

"Adults?"

"Adult enough," Skarre said.

"Did they hear anything?"

"No. But the boy had clearly been all the way to Snellevann. They saw him on the way up, sitting on one of the rocks eating his lunch."

"Was he alone?"

"Yes," Skarre said, "they believe he was alone. But he did have this with him." He lifted the toy off the ground and gave it to Sejer. "Optimus Prime."

Sejer didn't understand.

"It's a Transformer. You know, one of those toys that changes shape to become something else."

Skarre held the robot. He didn't know what he should say, or what he should do, because it was all incomprehensible. He pawed around the rucksack again and found a Thermos. A crumpled strip of wax sandwich paper. A mobile phone. When he stood with the mobile in his hand, it sent out a small beep: *One missed call.*

"Someone tried to call him."

Standing there with the mobile, Sejer felt they were all waiting for him, perhaps to give them an order. He looked down at the remains of the little boy.

"What the hell happened here?" Skarre asked.

"Dogs," Sejer said. "A pack of them."

A couple walked up the trail.

They came quickly and decisively, as if they were looking for something. When they saw the cluster of people, they stopped, exchanged some words, and began walking again, faster now.

One of the officers panicked and began to shout. "No! You can't be here now. You must turn round at once. Turn round!"

They didn't. Noticing the desperation in the man's voice, they picked up the pace, drawing swiftly nearer, holding hands. The officers placed the tarpaulin over the boy again and took up position, like soldiers on guard duty.

"You must turn round! You can't be here!"

Finally they stopped.

"We have to go through here to get our boy!" the man said.

To get our boy. What had been their son now lay under the green tarpaulin, and he'd been torn to pieces.

One arm was missing.

Sejer went to them. Extended his hand in greeting.

"My name is Bosch," Hannes said. "We live down the road. We're looking for our boy, he's out on a hike. We tried to call him, but we didn't get an answer. So now we're here just to be on the safe side, looking for him. What's going on? Has something happened?"

He craned his neck to see. His eye settled on the green tarpaulin, and an expression of alarm came over his face.

"There was an accident," Sejer said. "We can't let anyone pass."

Hannes took a step forward, pale with worry. "What kind of accident are you talking about? Has something happened to our boy? What's the tarpaulin doing over there? Has he been hit by a car?"

Sejer searched deep inside for composure, for calm. Words entered and exited his head, but he rejected every single one. All the same, when he addressed Wilma his voice was firm. "Tell us about your boy."

"Theo," she said. "His name is Theo Johannes Bosch and he's eight years old. He's on a hike in the woods, he was going to Snellevann. Now he's probably on his way home, and we've come out to meet him. That's all. We can't stand here dilly-dallying. We need to get past. What's happened here? Can't you say?"

"What did he have with him?" Sejer asked.

"A rucksack," she said. "With his lunch and a Thermos."

Hannes broke in. "And he has a knife in his belt. A hunting knife. We tried to call—he has his own mobile—but we got no answer. So we've come out looking just to be sure. It's not a boy over there on the road, I hope. Is it? Is it a boy?"

He waited for an answer.

They'll begin to scream soon, Sejer thought. They will scream so the sky will tear, scream until it cuts the ear.

He felt dizzy and had to take a step to the side. "We found a little boy," he began. He glanced at the group of people, each looking grave as they waited, watching. With the parents standing a few meters away, they looked very uncomfortable. "I think it might be Theo," Sejer said. "But exactly what happened to him we can't be certain."

"B-but the ambulance," Wilma stammered. "There's an ambulance right there. Is he injured, or something? Why is he covered up? Tell me what's going on."

Sejer put a hand on her shoulder. He had never, ever felt this miserable, never seen anything so terrible, never felt so poorly equipped to handle a situation.

"The boy we've found is dead."

Wilma pulled herself loose from Hannes and began crossing the road. Sejer held her back, and she crumbled to the ground, writhing. Trying to get up, her knees kept buckling.

Hannes Bosch held out hope that they were wrong. After all, there were other people in the forest, and they couldn't be certain. He looked at the green tarpaulin. He got his mobile out of his shirt pocket, then punched a button and put the thing to his ear, staring at Jacob Skarre who still held Theo's mobile in his hands.

Instantly its thin melody began.

Joy to the World, the Lord is come. Let earth receive her King.

They were helped into a patrol car and driven away, accompanied by a female detective. The crime scene officers started doing their job, a considerable task. A number of pictures were taken. Skarre paced back and forth along the trail. Now and then he shook his head, as if arguing with an inner voice. Then he walked over to the pathologist, Snorrason. "Did he die quickly?"

Snorrason, who was squatting by the side of the mutilated body, glanced up, his face filled with anguish. "Can't say," he mumbled. "Not yet."

"But they would have gone for his throat, right?" Skarre tried. "It's possible he died quite quickly?"

"It's possible."

"What should we do if the parents ask to see him?"

"We'll have to say a prayer," Snorrason said.

Sejer walked slowly toward them, his legs heavy as lead. "I've never seen anything so awful," he said. "Never in my life. We've got to find out who owns the dogs."

28

BJØRN SCHILLINGER HAD a house at Sagatoppen.
It was a spacious, red house with fifty square meters of outbuildings attached, and it looked rustic and welcoming. Behind the house the forest was dense, and Schillinger knew all the trails. One went to Saga, another to Glassverket, and a third all the way to Snellevann and Svarttjern. He had walked these trails many times, had run them as a little boy, jogged them as a grown man trying to stay in shape. At the front of the house was an expansive garden. Schillinger had fashioned a table and two benches, so he could sit outside on pleasant days. Like today, in the low September sun, when everything was beautiful and hot and golden.

He drove up the steep hillside leading to his house in his yellow Land Cruiser, and as he drove, he hummed a simple melody. Life is quite good, he thought, all things considered. Despite the fact that his wife, Evy, had recently left him, he was optimistic. The bachelor's life was comfortable—even if his finances were tight—and he wasn't downbeat at all. He was the master of his own days, and he could cast hungry glances at other women whenever he wanted. He had a good deal of contact with his daughter, June, whom he loved more than anyone else in the world. He was just returning from her birthday party, from singing games and chocolate cakes and red fizzy drinks. June, who had turned six, wore a red dress with white polka dots; he had teased her, telling her she looked like a poisonous toadstool. There's something about kids, Bjørn Schillinger thought: they are so bold and cheerful and refreshing. They have their entire lives ahead of them, and can take pleasure in every little thing. Like a birthday with gifts. He had given her a pair of Rollerblades, and she had spun around on them for over an hour. Evy was angry, of course, since they scratched up the parquet floor. That's how women think, he thought. They worry about the floors, about furniture and rugs and wallpaper. God knows how they're put together. They don't focus on the important things, only the superficial things—how things appear.

And what others think.

He'd reached the house.

He hit the brakes. The big Land Cruiser stopped so abruptly that gravel spat from the tires.

The dog kennel was empty. The doors were wide open.

Everything skidded to a halt. How was it possible? He sat there desperately clutching the steering wheel. Even though he blinked repeatedly, even though he slapped at his forehead, the picture was the same: the dog kennel was empty, the doors were open. All seven dogs were gone. Someone must have been up here, it occurred to him. It simply wasn't possible for the dogs to get out of the secure kennel by themselves. Not a chance in hell. How could it have happened? The doors were in order; he kept a close eye on such things because he was aware of his responsibility. The dogs were big and strong. What the hell happened? Was someone here? Where have the dogs gone? He got out of the car, and saw Lazy sitting near the house, tenaciously licking its paws. The dog was bloody and soiled around its mouth. Schillinger walked across the grass. The car idled, his heart beat fast, as if he had run up the hill and not driven. Yes, the kennel was empty; all seven of the dogs had gone hunting. They had found prey, and the blood around

Lazy's jaw came from that prey. What had they killed? God forbid it was a house pet. You can't lose your composure, he told himself, there's got to be an explanation. He continued up to the house, carefully distributing his weight as he went, like crossing ice in winter. He felt a little weak. Halfway across the driveway he had to pause, bend over and put his hands on his knees.

The large husky stopped licking its paws and raised its head to look at him, and Schillinger moved toward it slowly. He spread his legs and stood tall, not yielding an inch, even though the dog was in a strange mood. Lazy got up and lowered its head. Definitely blood, Bjørn Schillinger thought. My heart, God, how it's beating, they must've killed a cat. Or a fox. Or a dog. Please, don't let it be a dog. Then he heard the low growl. Lazy bared its teeth. It no longer subjected itself to Schillinger, no longer treated him like the leader of the pack, which both frightened and angered him. He took the risk and rushed forward, throwing himself at Lazy and pressing the dog to the ground, taking hold and forcing its jaw open. He stared directly at the blood and patches of skin clinging to its teeth. They probably got a sheep, he thought. I'll placate Sverre Skarning and pay him for the loss. Pay him damned well. As he knelt there fighting his panic, the dog on its back beneath him, two more dogs came sauntering out of the woods. Ajax and Marathon. Their jaws were also bloody. For one moment he had no energy, and little by little he grew nauseous. He wanted to get up, but his body was so heavy that his arms wouldn't obey.

The dog kennel was open. How had it happened?

In anger he leaned down and growled into Lazy's throat, growled like a madman. Finally the dog gave in. It whimpered weakly, and its strong body relaxed. He went off to collect the other two, steering them across the garden and into the kennel. They slinked about inside and looked at him furtively, embarrassed, pacing from side to side in the cage, with an energy they could no longer direct anywhere. They'd become different dogs now, dogs he had no feelings for, just large beasts with sharp teeth. He tried to bare his own teeth at them, and it brought tears to his eyes. He investigated the kennel's aluminum gate, and found it intact. None of the metal bars had been cut. Everything was in place, the bolt and everything. But I couldn't have forgotten to lock it, he thought.

Then he saw more dogs coming out of the woods. They too were bloody. They too behaved differently. Now his thoughts began to go in circles. There were people in the woods, of course, on these fine late-summer days. Some rode bikes, others hiked to one of the many streams to fish. And if they ran into seven dogs . . . no, he wouldn't even entertain the thought. He had to act now. He got Bonnie and Yazzi into the kennel, then with a stick chased Attila and Goodwill into the enclosure, slammed the gate, pulled the bolt, flipped down the latch and ran to get the garden hose.

The dogs were out.

They were all bloody.

Now he had to think clearly. So much was at stake, his and the dogs' future. His good name and reputation. His entire life. He pulled and yanked at the hose; it just reached the kennel. Then he rushed down to the cellar to turn on the water, ran up again and took hold of the hose, then began spraying the dogs. They pulled back, recoiling to their corners, but weren't able to evade the hard blast of ice-cold water. He kept at it until the dogs were completely clean, at the same time listening for cars and people, in case anyone was on the way. I always close the gate after me, he thought. I feed them, and then I close the gate. Three quick movements: shutting the gate, pushing the bolt and flipping down the latch. Besides, I'm not the only one who owns dogs. Down near Svarttjern is a man with four huskies. What's his name again? Huuse. I might be able to get away with it. OK, so they got a sheep. But there are so many sheep, and only seven of the kind of dog I have. He hosed the dogs again, jets of water showering them in the eyes and jaw. The terrible part, he thought, is that people will be hysterical, will demand that the dogs be put down. No matter what. Whether they nabbed a fox or a deer. He kept the water trained on them a while longer. When finally he rolled up the hose and threw it on the ground, the dogs were dripping wet and quite clean. Then he went into the kennel and headed over to Attila, the alpha dog. He bent down, lifted the dog's head and stared into its yellow eyes.

"Where have you been?" he snarled. "What the hell have you done?"

After the shower of ice-cold water the dog was back in its subordinate position, and it licked its master's chin. Schillinger gave it a powerful shove, cursing low and earnestly. Then he left the kennel and carefully closed the door behind him.

The gate, the bolt and the latch.

Just to be certain, he pulled at the gate twice.

I can't have forgotten the door, he thought. Someone must have been here. They got a sheep, I'm sure. But either way, it'll be pure hell. People don't tolerate much.

He realized the Land Cruiser was still idling and cut the motor. Then it was silent as a grave. With no more sounds now, either from the woods or from the dogs, he carried on into the house. Sitting by the window, he stared out toward the road, waiting for someone to come.

29

WILMA BOSCH WAS out of her mind with grief.
It happened when they explained her son's fate to her. That it had been several dogs, possibly an entire pack. That they had lunged at him. That they had shorn the skin from his muscles, and the muscles from his bones. Immediately she was taken to the Central Hospital and treated for shock. Torment and sorrow tore her to pieces; she felt teeth and claws slice into her bone marrow. And she screamed. As Theo had screamed. They gave her strong, calming medicine so she would fall asleep. When she woke up, she continued screaming.

Theo's remains were laid in a body bag, and taken to the Institute of Forensic Medicine. Hannes and Wilma were strongly advised not to see him. At first Hannes had insisted, but he finally gave up, burning in shame.

It's my fault, he thought. It's my fault, and now I'm a coward. When Sejer and Skarre visited him, he sat in a chair with Optimus Prime on his lap. He tried changing the robot into a truck, as Theo had done in a few simple moves, but he couldn't do it. He had sat like this for a long time. Several times he'd heard a little clicking noise in the hallway, and at once imagined it was Theo returning, that he'd met his grandfather Pim on the other side and had been told to return to Earth. Because Wilma needed him. And because small boys should stay on Earth as long as possible. Again and again he heard the little clicking beyond the door. But no Theo slipped quietly into the room. Now I'll lose my mind, he thought, just like Wilma. Then, himself again, he realized that the police were waiting for him to reply.

"I can't go to the hospital," he mumbled. "She keeps screaming so unbearably. She won't see me, anyway."

"We're compiling a list of everyone in the area with dogs," Sejer said. "Can you help us?"

Hannes thought about it. Sitting with the robot on his lap, he resembled a big, unhappy child. To put thoughts into sentences cost him so much energy.

"God and everyone have dogs out here in the country," he said. "There's a Dalmatian down by the bus stop, and a German shepherd. Two Labrador retrievers in the house next to that. The Labradors are big. Then there's a guy a little farther out with Australian cattle dogs, two of them."

"We believe we're dealing with a pack," Sejer said. "The injuries indicate many dogs."

Hannes considered. "Huuse," he said finally. "And Schillinger. Huuse has huskies. Four or five. He lives near Svartjern. But I think he might be away. Schillinger has another kind of dog, American Eskimos. Some say those types of dogs aren't legal here in Norway. The neighbors have been complaining."

Again he twisted and turned the robot's arms. But it was as if the robot wouldn't obey him as it had Theo.

"Not legal?" Sejer said. "Because of their temperament?"

"I don't know. But there's been some talk about it."

Skarre scribbled in his notebook. "Schillinger?"

"Bjørn Schillinger. He lives at Sagatoppen. In the red house."

"But if he has several of them, they're probably in a kennel, right?"

"Yes," Hannes said, exhausted. "Sometimes we hear them howling in the evening. Half past seven. Before they're fed. They sound like wolves, and that's pretty much what they are."

He was silent for a while. The entire time he kept working at Optimus Prime. It was difficult, because he thought he might collapse.

"Talk to Huuse," he said. "And talk to Bjørn Schillinger."

He put the robot down and set his eyes on Sejer.

"Whoever's responsible for this deserves to rot in prison, and I hope the dogs get a bullet between the eyes."

They sat with Hannes for an hour.

Sejer didn't want him to be alone.

"They'll give you a bed at the hospital," he said. "If you need someone around."

"I don't want anyone around. Don't deserve it. I've squandered all my rights, just ask Wilma."

His voice was hard and raw.

Sejer made his way from the lounge onto the porch. He looked at the hammock and the flowery pillows, and noticed the hammock swaying slightly, as if someone had just left it. He went back inside. "It might sound stupid," he said to Hannes, "but there are medications you can take. Let me know if there's anything you need. Here's my number. Call if there's anything, day or night. Just call."

He gave Hannes his card. Hannes accepted it indifferently.

"We're going to go and have a talk with Schillinger now," Sejer said. "We'll let you know."

They pulled up in front of the red house, parked beside the Land Cruiser and went to the dog kennel, observing the animals through the chain link. The dogs seemed playful and energetic, hopping and leaping enthusiastically, and made a few friendly little barks.

They had returned to their master, and they had nothing in common with wolves.

A man walked across the garden. Clearly he had seen them from the window. There was something hesitant about the way he moved, with short steps and slightly raised shoulders. He wore a green hunting jacket, camouflage trousers and thick black boots which he hadn't bothered to lace up. Schillinger was in his forties, and the wind and weather had marked his face, for he was outside much of the time. He trained with his dogs throughout the year, and in all types of weather. In the outhouse he had two sledges and a wagon which he used on the trails in the summer.

"What's going on?" he asked. "Can I help you with something?" There was a sharp edge to his voice.

"Perhaps," Sejer said and nodded toward the kennel. "Nice-looking dogs."

Schillinger kicked at the ground. His chin was jutted forward, and his back was stooped.

"American Eskimo dogs?" Skarre asked.

Schillinger hesitated. "That's right. They're rare here in Norway," he said quickly.

"Rare," Skarre repeated. "And maybe illegal?"

Schillinger scratched at his neck. "They're legal all right. But people have started strange rumors. Just because there are only a few of them doesn't make them unlawful. I got them in the proper way, I'd like to point out. One hundred percent legit. I have papers," he added. "I'll get them if I need to. I have papers for every one." He spoke faster, sliding his fingers through his hair. His beard was gray.

"And now they've been out on a run?" Sejer asked seriously. "Or am I wrong?"

Schillinger felt a little lurch in his gut. What if they got into a horse pasture? he thought. It's happened before—going after a horse. No, it must be sheep. They would definitely kill a sheep if they had the chance. Bloody hell, they're not poodles. He breathed heavily. Looked toward the trees, then at his seven dogs. Three of them had lain down comfortably. Four were still standing, sniffing through the fence.

"Did someone complain?" he asked nervously.

"Yes," Sejer said softly. "Someone complained."

Schillinger began pacing back and forth. He avoided looking them in the eye, stamping the ground with hard steps and quick turns, like an animal in a cage. "I put a lock on when I'm out," he said. "This time it was only for an hour. The kennel was empty when I got home. It was empty, plain and simple."

He gesticulated helplessly. Sejer and Skarre waited for him to continue.

"Who complained then?" he asked. "People get so worked up when they talk about these dogs. They probably think my place is full of wild animals."

No answer. He didn't understand why the men were so quiet and was unsettled by their stares, so he continued his nervous pacing.

Sejer nodded at the table and the two benches Schillinger had made. "I think we should sit."

"Why?" Schillinger asked suspiciously.

"Sit," Sejer ordered him. "You're going to need to sit."

They sat. Immediately Schillinger began picking at a splinter of wood. He had large, rough hands, with dirt under his nails. On one finger was a narrow band from a ring which had been there a long time, but which was now gone.

"We found a little boy," Sejer said. "Down by Glenna. We found him near Skillet. In all likelihood, he was attacked by dogs."

Schillinger made a sucking noise, growing deathly pale almost instantly. He pulled hard at the splinter, tore at it as if his life depended on it. "Is it serious? Is he badly hurt?" And then, with a glance at the dog cage: "Will I lose the dogs?"

"You'll lose the dogs," Sejer said. "The boy is dead."

Bjørn Schillinger was silent. The gravity of the situation struck him like a blow to the body. "No," he gasped. "It can't be true. Not my dogs. No, you've got to talk to Huuse, he has four huskies. It can't be my dogs."

Sejer and Skarre observed him in silence. It made an impression to see the tough man lose his composure.

"Huuse took his dogs with him to Finnmark," Sejer said calmly. "We've talked to the owners of the cabins down by Svartjern. He's been gone for four weeks."

"No," Schillinger repeated. "It can't be my dogs. Not a little boy. I refuse to believe it." He supported himself on the table. His face was gray with fright.

"Your dogs are wet," Skarre commented. "Did you hose them down?"

"They were hot," Schillinger said quickly. "I just wanted to cool them off. With all their fur, they boil easily. I never forget to close the door behind me when I've fed them!" he shouted. He buried his face in his hands. He couldn't handle what the men had told him. A little boy. And the seven beasts behind the fence. No, he refused to believe it. "I always close the door behind me. I can't be blamed for that!"

He pounded the table with his clenched fist.

"Let's go in," Sejer said. He nodded toward the house.

They went into Schillinger's lounge, a small, silent cluster of serious men. The house was dark, and sparsely furnished. The floorboards were scratched up by dog claws. In one corner was an old wood stove, and next to it an armchair covered with dog hair.

"Whose boy are we talking about?" Schillinger asked, avoiding their gaze. He was leaning over and waiting for the verdict.

"Wilma and Hannes Bosch's boy," Sejer said.

"The Dutch family? The ones who live in the log cabin?"

Sejer nodded. The defiant look left Schillinger. He was pale and trembling, and Sejer couldn't help but feel compassion for him. He studied the dark room. The walls were crowded with photographs, all of dogs. Each dog's name was written under each photograph; he found one wall for females and one for males. There was an Eva Braun and a Grete Waitz, a Volter, a Bajaz and a Bogart.

"I've had dogs for thirty years," Schillinger said. "I know everything there is to know about them. Ask anyone if there's ever been any trouble with my dogs. Ask anyone if I haven't always run a responsible dog team and been considerate of others. When I go in to feed them, when I go to check their paws or trim their claws, I slam the door behind me. I latch the bolt so the iron screeches. I flip the hook down, listen for the click. That's the whole procedure. I never forget to do it—it's ingrained in my mind. At this point it's a reflex. I live for these dogs. They are my life, and you can't prove it was my dogs that killed Hannes's boy, either. Maybe you're wrong. Many people have dogs out here, and sometimes they run off."

"The dogs will be confiscated," Sejer said. "We'll get DNA from all of them. Then we'll see where your dogs have been, and what they've done."

Schillinger closed his eyes. This nightmare pained him to the bone.

"We will investigate the scene of the crime," Sejer said, "so that we can determine how the dogs got out. You might be held in custody during the investigation. We'll come back to that."

Schillinger put his hand to his mouth. He thought he was going to vomit. What was happening seemed all too real. Hannes and Wilma Bosch's boy. Mauled by dogs. *His* dogs. Attila and Marathon, Yazzi and Goodwill. Bonnie, Lazy and Ajax. The dogs that lay at his feet in the evening when he needed company. Who pulled him across the snow-covered expanses and through the abundant forest with remarkable strength. Who breathed hotly on his face, and poked at him with their cold snouts. Who hopped and leapt about each morning when he strolled across the garden.

"I have a little girl," he said. "She turned six today. I was at a birthday party for her when the dogs got out. I don't understand any of this." His voice was about to fail him. "People will drive me out of town. I'm not to blame."

"It's up to the justice system to mete out punishment," Sejer said. "But as a dog owner you're responsible, naturally, for keeping your dogs locked up."

"And I've always done that!" Schillinger shouted. "Now I stand to lose everything. What will people think when word gets out? I'll lose the right to have dogs ever again. Imagine losing your children like that," he groaned. "No, I can't bear it. I can't be held responsible, I don't understand any of this. You can't blame me, I won't survive this. It's sabotage. Someone must have been up here and opened the gate."

"Why would anyone let your dogs out?" Sejer said. "Explain what you mean."

"Someone let all of Skarning's sheep out," Schillinger said. "Probably for a laugh, what do I know? But there've been a number of hoaxes around here this summer. You can start with the person who's made all the prank calls."

Sejer considered this theory. "Have you been in the newspaper? A little piece about you and the dogs? Recently? About how important the dogs are to you, perhaps?"

Schillinger thought this through. "No," he said, "not since last year. When we were in the Finnmark's Run, and we did well. The local newspaper was here and took pictures. Why do you ask?"

"I don't need to go into that," Sejer said. "But it might have supported your case."

When the long, black day was over and Sejer was at home, he went into the bathroom. He stared at the mirror, at his careworn face. He leaned over the sink and splashed water on his cheeks, but nothing helped. Frank was at his feet, craving attention. Sejer pushed him away, irritated, kicked at him angrily. He was just a dog. Really, you couldn't trust them, not one of them. So he continued his business with the ice-cold water. It still didn't help. Snorrason, the pathologist, called, and they talked at length. In detail he accounted for the injuries that Theo had suffered. "I could have done without this," he said. "Don't tell anyone, but I think this is the worst I've ever seen. Even his knuckles were mauled."

Sejer went to bed and lay there wide awake. Frank, his pet—the Chinese fighting dog—lay on a mat beside his bed, an animal with impressive premolars and a potential for brutality he would hopefully never see. The image of tiny Theo, as they had found him, wouldn't leave his mind. He tried to fill his head with something else. Like images from *Swan Lake*, young girls in tutus, feathers in their hair. And to a certain degree, it worked. In his thoughts he spanned his career, and the cases he had investigated. How they had affected him. What he had felt and thought.

There was nothing like this.

He thought of the wolverine postcard he'd found on his doormat. If you're involved in this, it occurred to him, then you're right.

This is no longer a game.

Hell begins now.

And for Hannes and Wilma Bosch it would last until they died.

He leaned over the edge of the bed, looked at Frank asleep on his mat. The peaceful sight of the little wrinkled dog shifted his imagination to thoughts of life and death and the power of nature. To what was raw and brutal at the heart of every living creature.

If we took a walk, the two of us, and something or other happened. If we had an accident or were locked up in a cellar, or a cave, and nobody found us. If it was just you and me, Frank, in the cave, without food or water. Imagine if I had a heart attack, and you were alone with my dead body. You would eat me. You would gnaw and tear the flesh from my bones; and everything that stood between us, all the good things, you would forget. Do you hear what I'm saying, Frank? You would eat me. When you got hungry enough. It's your nature, and you follow your survival instincts. We humans do that too; it's our fate, and our presumption—we cling to life. But it comes at a price. His head dropped back to his pillow. He felt heavy and tired. On the bedside table his mobile gave off a little beep, and Sejer recognized Chief Holthemann's number.

"I know it's late," he began.

"Yes," Sejer said. "It's late."

"But I've thought about something. The dogs. Schillinger's. Should we let our people put them down? Give them a bullet? Make a strong statement—out of consideration to the Bosches?"

Sejer looked at Frank curled up on his mat. "Taking them to the vet is enough of a statement," he said. "Besides, it would be a strain on the man who would have to do the deed. Who did you actually think would do it? Jacob Skarre? He's religious. And anyway, there are seven of them. It would almost resemble a slaughter. I have a dog myself," he added. "No, it's bad enough as it is."

"Are you getting a little soft?" Holthemann asked.

"Maybe. There's something about this case. I'm not getting any younger, either."

"What about Schillinger? Can he be trusted?"

"He's going through a crisis. Of course not."

"What about the kennel? Is it up to standard?"

"Absolutely. And it would be impossible for the dogs to get out on their own. If, that is, the door was shut."

"What about the dogs? Some people have said they aren't legal here in Norway."

"It's a little unclear," Sejer said. "But either way, it's a fierce breed. They have tremendous energy and a very independent nature, and require regular and strict discipline. They also have a strong pack instinct, and often fight for a higher position. Plus they eat anything that's edible, wherever they can find it. Other animals are seen as food. If that's not enough, they get to be seventy centimeters tall and weigh fifty kilos. Theo didn't stand a chance."

Holthemann was silent on the other end of the line. Finally he regained his voice. "We'll do as you say. We'll take them to the vet. It's probably enough of a strain to stick the syringes in, I would imagine."

They ended the conversation. Sejer settled in for sleep, his mind full of grave thoughts. What life has in store for some of us. Imagine if we knew.

30

THE DAY, A SUNDAY, began like any other, with his mother shuffling about in her bedroom. She was searching for something to wear, more than likely. In the sea of dirty laundry she would find something random. Utterly fresh the hyena was, not poisoned at all. She was on the move and more alive than ever. Listening to the noises she made, someone might think there was a powerful storm raging in the house. In her wanderings around the room she brushed against furniture and other objects. Like a whirlwind out of control, she had no order; she plucked something up only to throw it down again somewhere else, continuing her crazy roaming. Things were spread everywhere, across bedposts and the backs of chairs, in piles on the floor. She rarely did any washing. But then again, she never went out with other people. Never went to work, never went out in public—unless she had to leave home to scrape together some money.

In the spotted coat.

Johnny Beskow decided to remain in bed until she had dressed. He lay listening to the water pipes in the bath, which whooshed when she turned on the taps. Afterward she would go into the kitchen to boil some water, stir instant into a cup and drink her coffee standing by the kitchen window. Her cheeks were sunken,

her nails were unkempt. She was visibly marked by the affliction—as though it had spread into all her joints like a chronic
inflammation. She had probably made some rudimentary plans for
the day. But because she always had to drink a shot of vodka first,
and because this always led to a second, the plans never amounted
to much. Instead she would plop down in a chair to ponder her
own unhappiness and, at the same time, reflect that she was in
fact pretty and resourceful and badly misunderstood. Fate had
been cruel and unjust to her; it had pushed her into a wasteland
of misery.

Who could demand that she get up?

And anyway, she was comfortable in her familiar misery.

It was so easy.

Johnny lay quite still, waiting. He heard Butch running around
in his little red-and-yellow maze, his tiny feet scratching at the
plastic. After about a quarter of an hour he sneaked into the bathroom, put on his jeans and T-shirt, drank cold water from the tap
and left. She didn't notice he'd gone, didn't get to ask any questions. In a flash he was on his moped, accelerating and zooming
down the road.

No doubt she saw him from the window.

He could feel her eyes on the back of his neck, like a knife.

Rolandsgata was deserted.

He didn't see the Meiner girl.

But maybe she saw him from the window. Maybe she sat with
her forehead pressed against the glass, cursing him. He figured
that she suspected him of being behind her new hairdo. He didn't
mind being the subject of someone's anger. Wasn't that the meaning of his life? Wasn't that the very objective of his little game? To
make people talk about him and say, That bastard, who the hell
does he think he is?

I am Johnny Beskow, he thought, and I am invincible.

"Is it you, lad?" Henry called out when Johnny walked into the house.

"Yes, Grandpa, it's me." He paused to breathe in the aroma of the house. There was a lemon scent in the hallway and in the kitchen, and another scent in the living room, possibly furniture polish. "Has someone been here?"

"Mai Sinok was here. She gave me a bath. I'll smell like pine needles all evening."

"But today's Sunday."

Henry Beskow had to clear his throat and hawk. Slowly he raised an arthritic hand to his mouth. "Didn't I tell you?" he coughed. "She comes on Sundays, too. But no one down at social services knows she's here every day. I pay her a little under the table, so don't tell anyone or she might lose her job. But come over here, I want to show you something. A miracle has happened since you were here last. By God, it's never too late for an old bag of bones."

Johnny went into the lounge. He stood looking at his grandfather.

"They were here Friday," Henry said. "Two fellows from the council, both were black as coal. I think they were Tamils. But you know what, Johnny? Black muscles are as good as white muscles. If not better. They brought a big box. Come here now, chop-chop. You're young and spry! Has someone nailed your feet to the floor?"

Johnny did as his grandfather asked. As always, Henry sat, wearing his green cardigan and his coarse, checked slippers. Some kind of pillow lay on the seat of his chair. Fifteen centimeters thick, it was soft and gelatinous and the color of blue clay. When Johnny drove his fist into it, his fist sunk in and left behind a depression, which slowly filled. It was so fascinating that he tried it several times. The pillow, it seemed, had a life of its own.

"Isn't it wonderful?" Henry said. "Mai ordered it, and I didn't have to pay a penny."

"You've paid taxes all your life," Johnny remarked.

To demonstrate the pillow's elasticity, Henry twisted and turned his old arthritic body. "They say astronauts sit on pillows like this when they're launched into space," he said. "The gel is perfect because it doesn't press on the bones. You know, because the force, Johnny—what is it called again?"

"G-force."

"Exactly. The G-force is really something else entirely. Social services is paying," he added. "It costs several thousand kroner, you see. But it was Mai's idea. Mai, my good Mai, my little Thai." He laughed. "Sit down. Do I smell like pine needles? Eh, Johnny?"

Johnny sat on the footstool. It sank under his weight and the plastic cover creaked; obviously it didn't compare with the designer gel pillow.

"May I try it?"

Henry chuckled contentedly. "I thought you'd ask. Yes, of course. Even though you're young and your body is soft like rubber. Just help me up."

With some difficulty he leaned forward and pushed against the seat, rising slowly. He held on to the armrest the whole time, but finally was up, bent like a troll woman.

"That's it. Try it now, you rascal."

Johnny sat. At first he felt nothing and thought he might not weigh enough. But just as he was about to express his disappointment, he began to sink. The gel grew warm, and the warmth filled his entire body, until it felt as though he was being held by a thousand chubby hands.

"Wow," he said excitedly.

"You see what I mean?" Henry said. "Isn't it just sheer luxury?"

Johnny gave the chair back to its rightful owner, then returned to the footstool.

Something caught his eye.

The Sunday paper lay on the table—Mai had brought it in—and he saw the front-page headline: TORN TO DEATH BY DOGS.

He read these vivid words and looked at the photograph of a little boy with his coarse blond tufts of hair. Farther down the article was a subhead: *Suspicion of sabotage.*

"What happened?" he asked. "Was he killed by dogs?"

Henry looked at the newspaper. "Yes, something terrible happened to him. At Glenna, up near Saga. Mai read the article to me. A little boy on a hike, and out comes a pack of dogs."

Johnny read the article. And while he read, his mouth dried up completely.

"But did they just attack him? For no reason?"

"Dogs do that sometimes when they're in a pack," Henry said.

"But why? The dogs were pets, weren't they? Someone owned them?"

He continued reading, rushing through the sentences. The boy was attacked, it said, by seven dogs and died of substantial injuries. He hadn't stood a chance.

Henry shook his head. "The laws of humanity no longer apply when they run off like that," he said. "The hunting instinct takes over. They grow wild again. People would too, I tell you. In extreme situations. The dog owner—what was his name again?"

"Schillinger," Johnny said.

"Right. Schillinger. He says it's sabotage. He says someone must have opened his dog kennel as a lark. Just to see the dogs run off."

"And who would that be?"

The old man rested his eyes on him. They were filled with a surprising intensity. "You need to ask? We have enough riffraff around here. They're everywhere with their horrible pranks. The man who's calling people, they haven't caught him, have they? And he's been at it for weeks."

Johnny set the newspaper down. He could no longer sit still. He had to get up and pace. After a few moments he returned to the footstool.

"The dogs can't open the gate on their own," Henry said, "and their owner swears he's always mindful to close it. When something like this happens, it's no surprise the prankster gets blamed. After so many weeks of terrorizing people, he's going to have to put up with it." He tapped his gel pillow. "He'll probably have some sleepless nights. Whether he's guilty or not. Because this is negligent homicide. They're out searching for leads. And he'll have to pay for it!"

"But," Johnny said weakly, "the guy who's calling and placing announcements and all that, he's just playing. They're just innocent jokes."

"Innocent jokes?" Henry got worked up. "Did you hear about the little girl displaying her two angora rabbits at an exhibition? She got her photograph in the paper and all of that. Two days later someone crucified a stuffed bunny on her door. Do you think that's a joke?"

Johnny stared at the newspaper on the table, then turned it over so the front page was face-down. Sitting motionless, he let his arms dangle at his sides. "How convenient for Schillinger to have someone to blame," he mumbled.

Irritated, Henry gesticulated with his hands. "Are you defending the joker now or what? You know what he's been up to? I've thought about it often; one day he'll go too far, and he'll get a taste of his own medicine. It's no longer a joke. But you're a caring lad, Johnny, and you don't understand such mischief."

Johnny didn't have anything to say.

"Did you read the entire article?" Henry asked. "It's awful

about that boy. One arm was torn off. They found it in the woods, several meters from the body. Think about his mother and father. I mean, think about them!" Henry's eyes began to run, and he had to wipe away some tears. "When I was a boy," he went on, "I grew up near a mink farm. We would gather there, a group of us boys, and look at them through the fence. They certainly smelled. You could smell it for miles around. None of the neighbors were especially happy about them, that's for sure. To be honest, Johnny—because we're always honest with each other, are we not?—we let them out of their cages a few times. Just for the fun of it. We weren't against the fur trade or anything like that. We hadn't a clue about those things. If old ladies wanted to wear fur, it was OK with us. But it was awfully funny to watch them dash off in every direction. So they put up an electric fence and the fun was over. But as you know, these are the things boys do." He coughed. "When I buy strawberries at the shop—" He paused and started over. "Well, I never go to the shop anymore. But before, when my legs held up, I would sometimes go to the shop to buy strawberries, and in some of the baskets I would find a rotten berry on top. So I would immediately think the entire basket was rotten. Isn't that right? That's how we humans function. No," he added, "perhaps that's a bad comparison. But you know what I mean.

"You look a little pale, Johnny. Why don't you go to the kitchen and get yourself a drink from the fridge."

Johnny got up, disappeared into the kitchen and found a Coke. He uncapped it and stood bent over the worktop drinking.

"The scoundrel ought to go from door to door in the whole area," Henry Beskow shouted. "Kneel on every single doorstep and beg for forgiveness. What do you think of that, Johnny?"

Johnny clutched at the worktop. It was as if the room spun wildly and he stared down into an abyss so deep and so black that he grew dizzy.

"Johnny!" Henry shouted from the living room. "Don't you think he should kneel on every doorstep?"

"It's too late," Johnny mumbled. "People will think what they want to think. And anyway, you can't beg forgiveness for everything."

31

GUNILLA MØRK DIDN'T believe Schillinger and his claims of sabotage. She didn't care for his bitter tone, or his hostility and aggressiveness. He lacked humility in the face of the terrible thing that had happened, and she suspected him of exploiting the situation. The prankster who'd made fun of them for weeks had a touch of sophistication, she thought—there was no escaping that. He was creative and imaginative, and he had style. She had cut her own obituary out of the newspaper and hung it on the wall in a little silver frame. Each morning when she entered the kitchen, she read it and thought, Oh no, not yet. I'm still here. It gave her a certain satisfaction.

Sverre Skarning discussed the incident with his Syrian wife, Nihmet. "He's been everywhere," Nihmet said, "our terrorist. Done all sorts of strange things. No wonder he's being blamed for this, that and the other. It's the price he's got to pay. He should turn himself in. If he doesn't, we'll have our own theories."

"Bjørn Schillinger grew up here," Skarning said. "He's had dogs for thirty years. When he trains with the wagon in the summer, he brakes when people walk on Glenna. In the winter he lets skiers pass. He's considerate, and he's meticulous in everything he does. The dogs are his life, and he cares for them in every way. He would never allow something like this to happen. Forget to close the gate? Never!"

No, it was impossible to comprehend. It didn't make any sense.

"I don't like him," Nihmet said. "He drives like a maniac in his Land Cruiser. He's a crude person, Sverre. And he has a wild look in his eyes. Haven't you noticed?"

Frances and Evelyn Mold still carried a grudge against the person who had put them through hell. But even they had their doubts about the dog kennel. That someone would go up there to open the gate—no, that didn't sound right.

Astrid Landmark no longer had anyone to discuss the matter with: her husband had been disconnected from the respirator. And he had been driven in style in the Daimler from Memento, surrounded by leather and mahogany and walnut, to his final resting place.

Little red-haired Else Meiner, she had her own ideas on the subject.

"Didn't I tell you?" her father roared. "Didn't I say one day he would go too far? Now everyone's feeling the pain. He'll lug this around for the rest of his life. A little boy. I'm speechless. Do you know what he'll do now, Else? He'll hunker down, and he'll never be caught."

Else didn't respond. She sat in her room, at her desk, and painted her toenails. Now and then she glanced out of the window to look for the red moped which zipped so frequently down Rolandsgata, to Henry Beskow's house.

But a few people did believe Bjørn Schillinger's version. There was enough riffraff in Bjerkås—everyone knew that by now—and not everyone was happy about the brutes that howled so wretchedly in the evening. With the big beasts on the loose, they could get rid of both the dogs and their owner once and for all. One of those who believed Schillinger's story was Karsten Sundelin.

One day the two fell into conversation.

They ran into each other at a petrol station down by Bjerkås, a chance meeting, and instantly found common ground: they were bitter men craving revenge.

"I can't believe that son of a bitch is playing with people's lives like that," Schillinger said. "Kept it up so long and no one can manage to catch him. I'm going to lose everything."

"My wife's moved out," Sundelin said. "She's taken Margrete and gone to live with her parents. I feel completely exhausted. Our lives have fallen apart, and there's nothing I can do about it. What about you? Do you have a good lawyer?"

Schillinger filled the tank, banged the nozzle back on the pump and screwed the cap back on.

"Yes, I've got a lawyer. But when it comes to justice, I don't have much faith in the authorities. They have too many rules to follow, and there's so much red tape."

There was a pause. In the silence they found an understanding, as if they had gathered around something that couldn't be named. But each knew what this mutual understanding meant.

"Let's grab a beer sometime," Schillinger said.

"Yes," Sundelin said.

In the days and weeks that followed they were regularly seen together, conversing intensely in a nook at the local bar.

Deep, muzzled voices.

Huddled together.

32

THE FALSE ANNOUNCEMENTS and devilish telephone calls ceased.

Some said it was an admission of guilt—that the unknown tormentor had pulled back in horror and shame. Others said he had grown tired of his macabre game, and didn't care one way or another what had happened to little Theo Bosch.

How were they going to catch him now? He had terrorized people at a distance and had left no traces, no fingerprints, no clues. Just fear and shock.

One day, in the middle of September, Sejer and Skarre drove out to Bjørnstad after getting a call about a suspicious death.

A patrol car was already there. It was parked, its doors open, along the fence near the last house on Rolandsgata. A couple of crime scene officers were investigating the perimeter of the house.

"It's not pretty," one said. "At first we thought someone had attacked him with a bat. But everything in the house is in order. There are no signs of vandalism or theft."

Sejer and Skarre went in. They noted the name under the doorbell: Henry Beskow. Sejer glanced toward Meiner's place down the street. *The house was here first,* Meiner had said, *so he's got every right to it.*

They passed through the small hallway and into the kitchen. There, a small dark-skinned woman sat. She had wrapped herself in a shawl, and though it was far from cold in Henry Beskow's house, she looked as though she was freezing. The heat was the oppressive kind you often encounter in old people's homes. The woman introduced herself as Mai Sinok. With a quivering hand she pointed at the lounge where the old man sat in his chair with one foot on the footstool. The other foot rested on the floor, while his torso was slumped over the armrest. Possibly, they thought, he'd attempted to stand, or escape, but he hadn't had the strength. There was blood around his mouth and chest, and some had dripped onto the floor. He wore an old green knitted cardigan. His trousers, which were much too large for him — presumably because he'd lost weight — were held up by a narrow belt into which someone had punched an extra hole. One of the crime scene officers had brought a box of latex gloves. Sejer pulled one out and slipped it on, leaned over the old man and opened his mouth carefully with two fingers.

He had a full set of teeth.

"I think he threw up," Sejer said.

"What was that?" Skarre said.

"I think he threw up blood."

Mai Sinok moved closer. She stopped a few steps away. She looked at Henry Beskow, her face filled with fright.

"He started bleeding from his nose a few days ago," she explained. "He wouldn't go to a doctor for it. For a nosebleed. He wouldn't go to a doctor for anything, Henry wouldn't. He was stubborn as a mule. He claimed that it was just nature running its course. Then he began to bleed in his gums too, which was a little alarming. May I go now?" She came forward and put a hand on Sejer's arm. "Please, may I go? I've been here for a long time, and I don't feel well. I would like to go home and lie down for a while."

Sejer went to the kitchen. He found a glass in the cupboard, poured cold water from the tap and gave her the glass. She clutched it with both hands, drank, spilling like a child.

"Who comes to this house?" Sejer asked. "Apart from you?"

"Almost no one. Just his grandson, and he comes often."

"I see. We have to let him know. Where does he live?" Sejer wanted to know.

"In Askeland. He lives with his mother."

"How long have you been helping Mr. Beskow?"

"A year," she said. "I come every day. He's a fine old man." She drank the cold water. "All the care Henry got, he got from that boy. They are best of chumps."

"You mean best of chums," Sejer corrected her.

Mai Sinok smiled, but immediately became sad again. "May I go now?" she pleaded. "I feel very weak."

"You may go," Sejer said. "But we will need to speak to you again. I'm sure you understand. One of our officers can drive you home."

She rejected the offer. She wanted to take the bus as she always did. It stopped at the bottom of Rolandsgata, and it came regularly.

Sejer walked around Beskow's small living room.

"Can you imagine?" Mai Sinok said. "Suddenly he bleeds everywhere. Something inside him must've broken."

Sejer examined some photographs hanging on the wall, of a little boy. "Is that his grandson? The little boy on the tricycle?"

"Yes, it's the boy. He's so blond there. His hair is completely dark now."

"And also the one with the backpack over here?"

"Yes, and there he is on the moped. With his gloves and helmet and gear. He got the moped from Henry. Henry's very generous."

"It looks like a Suzuki," Sejer said. "What's his name?"

"Johnny. Johnny Beskow."

I love Johnny, Sejer thought, and stared out the window at Asbjørn Meiner's yellow house.

"What if there's a connection?" he mumbled.

"How? What connection?" Skarre said.

"Between all these events."

"That never happens," Skarre said, glancing at the inspector. "At least, not in real life. What exactly is on your mind?"

"We've looked for a boy on a red moped," Sejer said. "And here's one on the wall. Find out if Johnny Beskow has a mobile phone."

Skarre called directory inquiries, and jotted down the number.

Sejer addressed Mai Sinok.

"I need you to call Johnny Beskow. Tell him he must come to Rolandsgata, and that it's rather important. But don't say anything about us, and don't tell him what's happened."

Mai Sinok borrowed Skarre's mobile, and she completed the simple task without asking questions or protesting. Sejer took her arm and escorted her out.

Then Sejer caught sight of a girl. She sat on a small knoll up the road, watching everything. Perhaps she had been there for quite some time, and knew everything that was going on at Beskow's house. He raised his hand and waved, and Else Meiner waved back. Mai Sinok walked off down the road to wait for her bus.

Sejer strolled over to the knoll and looked up at the girl. "Else Meiner," he said. "How are you?"

The response was short and direct. "I'm well. Hair grows back."

He nodded. "Yes, it does. Have you seen anything suspicious on this street?"

She smiled broadly. "Johnny swings by often. Several times a week. But he's not suspicious."

"Right," Sejer said. "Johnny Beskow."

"Henry's grandson."

"Right. The one with the red moped. We're waiting for him now, he's on his way. Anyone else come here?"

"The little lady from Thailand, who just went past. I don't know her name. But she cleans for him, I think. She comes every day on the eight o'clock bus. She comes on Sundays, too. Maybe she doesn't know that Sunday's a day off."

She nodded at the patrol car, and the two crime scene officers near the house. "Is Henry dead?"

"Yes," Sejer said. "Old Henry Beskow is dead. Have you seen other people come and go? Strangers?"

Else Meiner nodded. "A man was here recently with some window frames, the kind with screens to keep out the flies. And there was a lady three or four days ago. But she isn't exactly a stranger. I've seen her a few times. She was wearing one of those spotty fur coats, and she was really wobbly on her feet. So that was a bit of a sight."

"Do you know who she was?"

"Henry Beskow's daughter."

Sejer wrote down this information and bowed deeply to Else Meiner. Then he returned to the house. Through the kitchen, into the living room and to the chair. He stood there looking at the old man, puzzled that such a skinny body could bleed so much. For reasons he couldn't understand, the blood had gushed from him onto the floor. It had poured from his mouth and nose, and seeped into his clothes.

"It looks as though he died while eating," Skarre said and nodded at the blue plastic Tupperware on the table. The remains of food were left in the bottom of the container, and the lid lay to the side, together with a spoon. "What the hell happened?"

"Don't know," Sejer said. "We'll have to see what Snorrason comes up with. He's on his way. He'll work it out." He pulled out a chair, sat and glanced around. "It must be some kind of medical phenomenon," he said. "I've heard of internal bleeding. But this seems like something else. He had blood coming from his gums too, his home carer said. What on earth does that mean?"

They sat deep in thought for a while. They heard the crime scene officers rustling outside the window, searching in the grass for leads. Sometimes death is beautiful, Sejer thought, and observed the old man, who sat in his chair, mouth open, glassy-eyed and bloody. Sometimes. But not often.

A half-hour ticked away. Then a moped droned into Rolandsgata. Sejer went to the window. He saw a boy riding into the driveway. The boy stared nervously at the patrol car, and hesitated for a few moments before removing his red helmet. He hung it on the handlebar. Then just stood there, a little confused, sizing up the scene.

"Here comes Johnny Beskow," Sejer said. "Red helmet. With little wings on either side."

They went out to greet him.

Sejer noticed several things. The moped was a Suzuki Estilete. The boy before him was small and thin, with dark, shoulder-length hair. He had pale, almost paper-like skin and large dark eyes, which looked very sad.

"So," Sejer said. "You're Johnny Beskow. Is Henry your grandfather?"

The boy didn't answer. Wanting to get inside, he headed immediately for the steps.

"Don't go in there if you get nauseous easily," Sejer said. "Do you hear what I'm saying? It was his carer who found him. Do you know if he was ill?"

Johnny Beskow continued into the house. He went quickly through the kitchen and straight to the old man's chair. He put a hand over his mouth.

"He died while eating," Sejer said. "Anyone else visit besides you and the carer?"

Johnny Beskow looked at him with a strange spark in his eyes. "Someone brought food," he said. "I recognize the blue container."

"Where do you recognize it from?"

"It's my mum's container," he whispered. "It's her stew, and he ate most of it."

"Why shouldn't he?" Sejer asked.

Johnny Beskow walked to the window. Stood there looking out, supporting himself on the sill. "She was after his money," he said. "Mum was always after his money. And now she brought him food."

"Johnny," Sejer said. "We have to talk, you and I. We have a lot to discuss. Do you know what I mean?"

Johnny turned. He plopped onto the little footstool beside the old man. "It's Mum you need to talk to," he whispered. "She's the one who brought him food." He pulled his gloves out of his pocket and set them on his lap.

"Nice gloves," Sejer said. "With skulls. You slipped between our fingers, Johnny."

"You can ask me whatever you like," Johnny said. "You can put me in handcuffs, and we can talk until tomorrow. We can talk as much as you like, and I'll admit to everything. But I wasn't at Schillinger's place. I didn't let those dogs out."

33

S NORRASON CALLED FROM the Institute of Forensic
Medicine.

The food in the blue Tupperware container was laced
with large amounts of a chemical called bromadiolone, he reported.

"That means nothing to me," Sejer said. "Put that in layman's
terms."

"It's the same active ingredient that's found in rat poison. It
prevents the blood from coagulating, so you bleed everywhere.
Easy to get your hands on too—they sell it at the supermarket.
And it doesn't cost much."

If you wanted to get rid of somebody.

Trude Beskow was arrested at her house in Askeland, and taken
into custody, suspected of poisoning her father, Henry Beskow.

She had never been sober for so many consecutive days, and
with her sobriety came a rage she was unable to rein in. Her body
broke down; like a motor without oil, it stopped. There was nothing to assist her through the day, and she was trapped, powerless,
in each and every shrill second. The officers at the jail called her
"The Cyclone." She liked to throw the furniture in her cell, and
sometimes she screamed for long stretches at a time. Stubbornly

she proclaimed her innocence, asserting that it was the carer, Mai Sinok, who had poisoned her father's food.

"No doubt he promised her money," she declared. "Or he promised her the house. That's the kind of thing old people do when someone takes pity on them."

"We have no reason to believe that," Sejer said. "She is not a beneficiary in his will. But you are."

Johnny Beskow was appointed a defense lawyer. Sejer was pleased it was a woman, and he knew she had a son Johnny's age. Because he was a minor, he could not be held in custody. But he had to report to the police station three times a week, and he was always right on time. After he'd reported to the front desk, he would go straight to Sejer's office. There they would talk over a glass of mineral water. Johnny Beskow put all his cards on the table, and admitted it had been fun to scare people senseless. But it was a game, he said. "I just wanted to stir things up a bit. I never meant to hurt anyone."

"But you did hurt people," Sejer said sternly. "You hurt them badly, perhaps for life. And even if you don't understand it today, you may understand it later, when you're older." He looked directly into the young man's eyes. "What has your life been like? Your life with your mother at Askeland?"

Johnny grew morose, and his face assumed a bitter expression. "She's never sober. And she takes it out on me. It's really unfair."

"Yes," Sejer said, "it is unfair. What about you? Have you been fair? I mean, have you been fair to Gunilla? To Astrid and Helge Landmark? To Frances and Evelyn Mold? Have you been fair to Karsten and Lily Sundelin?"

Johnny leapt from his chair and paced the room. Threw angry glances at Sejer over his shoulder. "Why should I be fair when nobody else is fair?"

"Do you know this for a fact?"

Johnny didn't respond. He continued his irritable pacing.

"I've always been fair," Sejer said. "Throughout my entire life. It was never difficult."

"Aren't you a saint," Johnny said.

"Let's talk about Theo," Sejer said, "and what happened to him. You say you've never been up to Bjørn Schillinger's house. But you know his house is on the top of a hill. How do you know that?"

Johnny stopped pacing. He leaned over the table, grasped Sejer's burgundy-colored tie and tugged at it. "He lives at Sagatoppen. It's obvious he lives on *top* of a hill. You can blame me for everything except the dogs! I will tell you one thing: either way, my life isn't worth much. If what happened with the dogs was my fault, I would've drowned myself."

He stuck to his story. As if the truth had given him a special power.

He stared into Sejer's eyes without wavering; he held his hands out as if to demonstrate how clean they were.

His voice was strong and firm.

Don't blame me for what happened to Theo.

They came to like each other in a quiet sort of way. Sejer had nothing against being a father figure to the delinquent boy, and Johnny had lost the only person who had ever meant anything to him. Because Johnny had to report so often, they met regularly. Occasionally Sejer bought simple food, which he heated in the microwave.

"You'll have to be satisfied with frozen dinners," Sejer said apologetically. "I'm a terrible cook."

"OK, Grandpa," Johnny said. "But you're pretty good at warming up meals." He shoveled mouthfuls of food and looked at Sejer. "All this attention you give me, is it part of your plan? So that I'll make more confessions? You're mistaken if you think it will lead to something. I'm not walking into that trap." He put his index finger to his temple. "I'm not stupid."

"You're too skinny," Sejer said. "That's the only reason."

One day, after they'd talked for a while, Johnny leaned eagerly across the table. "What's going to happen to my mother?"

"It's too early to say," Sejer said. "But it's not looking good for her."

"She's never going to admit to anything. She'll deny it until her dying day. But she can't be trusted, not one damn bit. Will she get life?" he asked hopefully. "Will they give her only bread and water? Will they keep the lights on all night? Cell inspection every hour?"

"Would you like to see that happen?"

"I would've liked to see her in the electric chair. Or in the gallows. Or in the garrote."

"Such medieval methods are no longer used, thank God," Sejer said.

"Everyone complains about the Middle Ages," Johnny said. "They say everything was so much worse then. But the garrote was used right up until 1974."

"And where would that be?"

"In Spain."

"How do you know these things?"

"I know everything about that kind of thing," Johnny said. "It's the way I think."

Sejer sized him up. "I want to talk about what happened to your grandfather. We have to get to the bottom of it. Be prepared to have many long conversations. We'll need to do it right."

"If my mother is convicted, she'll be disinherited, right?"

"I would imagine so," Sejer said. "Would that make you happy?"

"Yes. It would've made Grandpa happy too."

34

SOMETIMES JOHNNY BESKOW seemed indifferent and detached, sometimes childish and playful—only in the next second to appear very mature. No one had taught him how to interact with others. He understood neither written nor unwritten laws. But other times he grew sentimental, like when he talked about old Henry. Time and again, Mai Sinok confirmed his concern for the old man. Regularly and faithfully he had visited the house on Rolandsgata, both eager and attentive. Sejer thought the justice system would let him off easy, because he was young and had no prior convictions, and because his upbringing had been of the unfortunate variety.

Justice for Theo was another matter.

Schillinger was interrogated on multiple occasions. But regardless of how hard they pressed him, he stuck to *his* story with the same intensity Johnny Beskow stuck to his.

No, I have never forgotten to close the gate, not once. I'm not trying to wriggle out of my responsibility, but there should be some justice here. I refuse to shoulder blame for another's crime. Should some young brat be allowed to destroy my entire life?

The rumor spread quickly: a teenage boy from Askeland was

behind the acts of terror which had beset the community for weeks.

October arrived, and Matteus auditioned for the part of Siegfried in *Swan Lake*, a unique opportunity to get noticed by important people in the world of ballet. Late that same afternoon, he stood at Sejer's door with his Puma bag slung over his shoulder. Something in his smile and in his eyes seemed promising.

"How'd it go?" Sejer asked. "Come on. Did you get the part? I need to know this minute. Don't make me wait."

Matteus entered his flat. He dropped his bag on the floor with a little thump.

"The part went to Robert Riegel," he said.

Sejer looked at him in exasperation. "Robert who? What did you say?"

"Riegel," Matteus repeated.

He squatted down to stroke Frank's head. He seemed oddly unmoved by it all. When he petted the dog his brown hands had a special sensitivity.

"And who is that?"

"Well, he's a phenomenal dancer," Matteus said simply, without looking at his grandfather's eyes.

"Hm. Is he better than you? Are you telling me he's better than you?"

"Clearly," Matteus said, getting to his feet. "In any case, Robert Riegel is the one who gets to throw himself in the lake with Odette in the fourth act."

"So that's how it ends?" Sejer said, slightly perplexed.

"Yep. They throw themselves in the lake."

He moved into the living room and did so with the self-assurance of someone with a strong, athletic body. Sejer followed. When it came down to it, he felt old and a little stiff in the knees.

"Can't you be a bit more indignant? You seem so indifferent. I mean, can't you at least swear?"

"I'm not indifferent. But self-control is a virtue." He sat down. Searched his pockets for a packet of mints, plucked one out and put it on his tongue like a communion wafer. It melted instantly. "I've learned from you. You're always so calm. I can't waste energy, I have to go on. To new heights, if you will."

Sejer plopped down in a chair. Frank lay at his feet. "I thought Riegel was a chocolate bar," he mumbled. "When I was a boy, it cost no more than thirty øre."

"You've got to stop pouting now," Matteus said. "How's it going with Johnny Beskow?"

"His mother's in custody, but he's at home until his trial. His only company is a hamster. He has to report to the station three times a week. He's a smart kid. A little twisted, of course, but I like him well enough. Others could learn to like him too, if they just gave him the chance—if anyone bothered to teach him some basic rules."

"What about the dogs?" Matteus said. "Did you find out about that?"

Sejer shook his head. His disappointment—at Matteus's not being considered good enough to land the role of prince—festered in him, and he had to strain to change the topic.

"He denies it."

"Do you believe him?

"Actually, I do."

"Why do you believe him?" Matteus's brown eyes were almost black in the lounge light.

"Well, it's mostly a feeling."

"You trust this feeling? He tricked everyone for a long time. Why should you trust him now?"

Sejer shrugged. "Intuition is important. And I believe that mine is especially well developed. After many years on the police force, after meeting so many people from all walks of life. I believe people use their gut feelings more than they realize. That's what carries us through life."

"But the police have to assess facts and clues and things like that?"

"Of course. And we haven't found anything at the crime scene which would indicate sabotage. So it's word against word."

Matteus looked hard at his grandfather.

"I think he's trying to pull one over on you."

"Is that so? Why do you think that?"

"Because it's his biggest talent. It's what he's done the whole time. It's what he's good at."

"Come on, I'm not clueless," Sejer protested. "I think I know a lie when I hear one. It sort of has its own tone."

"You think so? Its own tone?"

"Like a rusty nail in an empty tin can," Sejer said. "That's just an image, but you know what I mean."

"Right," Matteus said. "Now you're beginning to sound really unprofessional. Listen to this. The part in *Swan Lake*—of course it's mine. I'm just pulling your leg."

"What are you saying? Is that true?" Still seated, Sejer gawped in surprise.

"If you like someone, you'll believe anything they say," Matteus said. "Think about that for a while. When you sit in your office talking to Johnny Beskow."

35

ONE AFTERNOON SEJER received a message from the duty officer.

Johnny Beskow hadn't reported to the front desk, and he wasn't answering his mobile. An officer out on patrol had driven to the house at Askeland. The Suzuki was gone. But the door was open. The officer had found only the small, champagne-colored hamster in its red-and-yellow plastic maze.

"I'm worried," Sejer said.

"Why?" Skarre said.

"Up until now he's been so punctual, and he has a lot on his conscience. Maybe it's a pity we couldn't hold him in custody after all—we could've kept an eye on him."

He kept waiting for the telephone to ring, perhaps with the message that Johnny had simply blown it off. But he never got that call. He tried to finish his tasks, but couldn't concentrate. As though I'm responsible, he thought, and of course I'm not. But he called me Grandpa. That made an impression.

When his workday was through, and they still had heard nothing from Johnny Beskow, Sejer drove to the medical center where he'd finally made an appointment. For his dizziness, which came and went, and which continued to worry him.

He went in and sat among others in the waiting room, picked

up a magazine, began to read. But he just sat there, his head buzzing with thoughts about what could be wrong with him. Some clogged arteries in his neck, maybe, so the blood flow to his brain was inhibited. What would they do if that were the case? he wondered. Can they be unclogged? He pulled himself together, reprimanded himself with his inner voice, a very austere voice. We'll find out at least, he thought. Now that I'm sitting here, I'll hear the verdict soon. Ingrid will be satisfied.

He tried to read again, but the letters crawled like ants on the page. How long has this actually been going on? he wondered. This sudden dizziness. The feeling that everything is moving, that the floor slopes. The doctor will ask, he realized, and I should be able to answer; and he'll ask which illnesses run in my family. It occurred to him that no illnesses ran in his family. They had all been big, strong people in good health, and everyone had lived to a ripe old age. But they'll do their tests, he thought, and I'll have to wait for the results. For fourteen days, or for three weeks — these kinds of tests are sent to the laboratory, after all. So I'll have to walk around in a vacuum while my fantasies run wild. And how they run wild! Could it be a brain tumor?

A name was called, and a woman got up and walked across the floor. Right, Sejer thought, glancing at his watch. I'll be sitting here for an hour, no doubt. He got up and drank some cold, fresh water from a cooler. When he sat down again, his mobile rang in his pocket. He made his way out of the room. Heard Skarre's slightly out-of-breath voice.

"We've found Johnny," he said. "Up at Sparbo Dam."

Sejer pushed the main door open. The sharp air made his eyes water.

"OK, what's he doing up there? Has something happened?"

"He was floating face-down."

"He drowned himself? Is that what you're saying?"

"We don't know yet. But we believe it happened very recently.

His moped is parked against a tree. A man from the city found him. He was here to inspect the dam. Where are you, anyway? Are you busy? Can you come?"

Sejer turned and glanced back at the medical center. The wide double doors with the frosted glass meant to impede looking in. What had his son-in-law, Erik, a doctor, said about his dizziness? He had rattled off some possible diagnoses, and now Sejer tried to remember them. His dizziness could be a side effect of medications. But he didn't take any medications. It could be a sudden drop in blood pressure, like when he sat still for too long and then got up quickly. And there was something called labyrinthitis, which was apparently some infection of the inner ear. Not to mention Ménière's disease, which was a chronic illness with terrible bouts of dizziness, followed by loss of hearing and ringing in the ear.

But it's probably just a virus, Sejer thought, infecting the balance nerve.

Which comes and goes. I'll tackle it another time.

Then he began walking to his car.

Johnny Beskow was a sad sight.

His lean, bluish body had long, wet tufts of hair covering his forehead and face. Bony hands with bitten nails. Underdressed. Sejer walked around the edge of the dam searching for clues. Had anyone been here? Had there been any kind of confrontation?

"Maybe he was balancing on the wall of the dam," Skarre said. "Then fell. Maybe he couldn't swim."

Sejer stared at the sluice, where the water gushed through the black pipe. "Why would he do that?"

"I've heard it's a tradition out here. For graduating students. In the middle of May."

"Johnny wasn't graduating," Sejer said. "And it's mid-October."

Skarre noticed the inspector's gloomy face. "What are you thinking about?"

"This is where Johnny Beskow's story ends."

"And not a soul in the world will miss him," Skarre noted.

"Don't say that."

"Perhaps his remorse got the better of him," Skarre said.

Sejer's mobile rang just then, a cheerful tone. He let it ring. "I don't believe so," he said. "I mean, he didn't repent. But there's another possibility."

"That someone helped him over the edge," Skarre said. "Aren't you going to take that call?"

"Yes. Don't pester me. When is Schillinger's trial?"

"In January. He's banking on reasonable doubt. If he gets reasonable doubt, he'll be able to take home new dogs. You've got to take that call. Maybe it's important."

Sejer walked over to a tree and leaned against the trunk. He stood there for a moment, his gaze on the dead body on the stretcher, while the mobile continued its cheerful melody.

"He's taking some secrets to the grave," he said. "Don't you think?"

Skarre nodded. "Where they won't be disturbed."

"It's very possible someone helped him over the edge," Sejer said, pulling out his mobile. He held it to his ear and stared at Skarre. "I can think of a few people with a good motive. But you know what? We'll never be able to prove it."

36

FROM A DISTANCE *she resembled a little boy, with her short red hair. She didn't know the two men, but she made note of what they looked like and how they were dressed. When they walked back from the water, she skittered quickly away and sank down against the trunk of a tree. She squatted until her thighs hurt, and she hardly dared breathe; she made note of the car. A Toyota Land Cruiser. The paint gleamed golden in the sun. The men didn't talk to one another, but they glanced vigilantly around before climbing into the car. Luckily for her, they didn't notice her bicycle a little way off in the heather. She curled herself into a tiny ball. She thought her heart would burst, thought her blood pumped so forcefully inside her they would hear it through the roar of the water thundering against the dam wall.*

But they didn't hear a thing.

They drove away, and everything grew silent.

And Else Meiner got on her blue Nakamura bicycle.